"What do y...   ...id.

"I see a hu... ...ger than any I've ever
seen. The size of a tiger—no, larger. It has silver
fur. It has long, long claws. Its teeth are like
spikes. And its eyes, God, its eyes are big and
round and fiery. I've got to run. I've got to get
away. It wants to kill me, too."

"Before you go, tell me what you know about
the cat. Where is it from? Who does it belong to?
Tell me anything you can."

"It's from hell, I think. And it belongs
to . . . to . . ." Kris paused, as if she was too
terrified to continue, then said, "It belongs to
Eliza. No. Behind the eyes is another creature,
another being."

"What is it? Concentrate."

"I can't," Kris said desperately. "I have to
escape before it traps me."

"Please tell me what is behind the eyes," Alan
said. "I have to know. Then you can run. Who is
it?"

"It's . . . it's Eliza Noman."

MAUREEN S. PUSTI

NEIGHBORS

LEISURE BOOKS ⬛ NEW YORK CITY

A LEISURE BOOK ®

March 1991

Published by

Dorchester Publishing Co., Inc.
276 Fifth Avenue
New York, NY 10001

PROLOGUE

UNDER A DARKENING SKY A LONE FIGURE STRUG-gled to the top of the steep incline. Heavy breathing and the slow, steady grind of rubber against asphalt broke the rural stillness. Above, the purple hues of twilight descended, and on the horizon violet clouds reflected a setting sun.

He pedalled faster.

Scott Benson was late and most assuredly would be grounded for the next two weeks, a fate worse than death for a 14-year-old on summer vacation.

He moved on swiftly and steadily, wishing his parents would learn to relax but also knowing that wasn't about to happen.

Since Jason Woods had vanished in March, they had gradually turned into tyrants. Then to make matters worse, as if things weren't bad enough, Claire Etters had disappeared in April, followed by Louise Hartman in May.

As a result, Margaret and Roger Benson seemed to lose all capacity for rational thought. They were convinced something dreadful had happened to all four kids and if he, their one and only, wasn't careful, the same would happen to him. A typical adult overreaction, he thought.

The curfew started—home before dark, no matter what.

He told his parents that Clair Etters had been in his ninth grade English class, and rumor had it that she ran away from home because her father beat her. Hell, once he had even seen the bruises. One Monday morning she came to school with a black eye. She also had ugly red welts that looked like belt marks all over her legs.

When he explained this case of obvious abuse, his father said, "Fine. But how do you account for the others? They can't all be runaways."

Scott could only shrug. He didn't know about the others, but he did suspect they were runaways, too. It didn't matter. His parents weren't convinced.

Home before dark, no matter what! That was the edict. Parents could always get away with such bullshit.

Scott pushed the impending showdown with his mom and dad from his mind. He would deal with them later. The way he had it figured, he'd be grounded for the next two weeks, so he may as well enjoy himself now, a final wild ride.

He grinned as his bike descended the hill at a speed that would be considered dangerous by anyone over the age of 40, namely his parents. He felt the skin on his face pull back tight, and his lips stretched taut over his silver braces. He felt the cool, moist, heavy June air rake through his smoky blonde hair and tug like long slender fingers.

The bike continued to accelerate, racing downward at nearly 40 miles an hour. His open red plaid shirt billowed out behind him like a parachute, the kind used on Air Force jets or dragsters to help slow them down.

Eventually the road began to level off, reminding him of a winding black snake. Both sides of it were flanked by a thick band of trees that went as far as the eye could see.

Before the end of summer he and Billy Wilcox, his best friend, planned to go exploring in those woods. They would take a back pack filled with ham and cheese sandwiches, chips and cartons of apple juice. They would spend an entire day out there, alone, away from parents and the ever present hassle.

Every summer, five so far, they had hiked through the woods, but this year they suspected it wouldn't be allowed because of all the missing kids. They planned to go anyway.

Scott looked up at the sky. The purple streaks that rose from the horizon were almost black. The sun had already set, and the landscape was both compelling and frightening. Automatically, his legs pumped harder like two giant pistons, pumping, pumping, pumping the cherry red Schwinn.

That was when he first saw it as he negotiated a wicked curve. Barely 50 feet in front of him, something, huge and silvery, emerged from the dense trees on the right and leapt across the road. It disappeared into the gully on his left.

Instinctively, he hit the brakes. The bike shuddered and trembled and shimmied. The rear tire began to skid. His heart pounded wildly as he attempted to bring the bike under control.

Shifting his weight, pumping the brakes, and maneuvering the handlebars, he finally steadied the bike and immediately began to pick up speed. He raced forward, glancing over his shoulder.

He was scared.

It had to be an illusion, he thought, a trick of the eye caused by the fading light and the shadows. It could have been a deer. He was almost convinced of that when suddenly the cry rang out. A shrill, high pitched scream of some enormous animal came from behind. It resembled a wildcat, but louder and angrier.

Scott sucked in his breath, tucked his head between his shoulders and pushed on.

Something was out there and very, very close. It wasn't his imagination. It was real, and it made him shiver.

He pedaled faster.

On his right, the trees blurred, then gave way to rolling fields. He could see a string of development homes in the distance, looming up against a blue-black sky like giant boxes. The warm glow from their windows helped him to relax. He was almost home; he had passed the halfway mark.

But the inhuman scream came again, this time much closer.

He felt another wave of panic. His breath hitched inside his chest. Forcing himself to glance over his shoulder, he saw nothing.

Up ahead he could see the last hill, the last obstacle reaching up and melting with the sky. His legs pumped harder until he reached the top. Then he descended over the bumpy, uneven road with his skinny arms fighting to control the handlebars that threatened to break free.

Never before had he gone this fast, and he never would again.

In the distance, about a mile up the road, he got a glimpse of his house, surrounded by five wooded acres. The porch light was on, cutting through the darkness like a beacon of safety.

They were waiting. Thank God, they were waiting.

His parents would ground him for sure, but it didn't matter. He just wanted to be home and away from whatever was out there.

Why had he stayed so late at Billy's? If only he hadn't played that last game of pool . . .

Once again, the scream shattered the night, this time even closer than before.

The peripheral vision of his left eye picked up movement, but he was too scared to turn his head to look. He concentrated on the road and prayed—God, how he prayed—but his eye was picking up something. Finally he forced himself to look.

It was massive. It was keeping pace with him, moving swiftly among the pines, stirring and ruffling their boughs, angling toward the road. He saw the huge silvery beast, the same animal that had crossed before him minutes earlier.

The fear twisted inside him, as his heart pushed and throbbed against his bony chest as if trying to escape. Tears blurred his vision.

What was it? Why was it following him?

From behind, getting closer and closer, came the clicking sound—*tick, tick, tick* against the macadam. He heard the panting and felt the steamy hot breath on his back. He smelled the rotting meat odor that hung heavy in the air, working its way up his nose.

He hunched over and pulled his shoulders up past his ears. He tried to pedal faster, but by this time his aching legs could go no faster.

Then it hit him. It rammed him from behind and forced the air from his lungs in one great *whoosh*. It knocked him from the bike like a rag doll, and he flew through the air and dropped like a thud to the asphalt.

He tumbled and skidded toward the ditch beside the road, his arms and legs on fire as loose gravel ripped through layer after layer of tender skin.

The sky was pitch black when young Scott Benson opened his eyes. The moon illuminated the scene with stars dotting the sky.

The coppery taste of blood filled his mouth. A

trickle of salty tears escaped from the corner of each eye, causing the raw flesh on both cheeks to burn. He wanted to scream for his mother, but instead he let out a small whimper and clamped his teeth together hard. He forced the scream back into his lungs.

He lay motionless in a ditch four feet wide and three feet deep, reminding him of an open grave. He shuddered and smothered another scream.

He needed to compose himself, to gain control. But how? He was just a boy, a boy in need of his mother, but he was alone and somehow had to help himself. Margaret and Roger Benson would never make it to his side in time.

He listened for movement but heard nothing. Not even the chirp of a cricket broke the stillness. That alone terrified him. Rural areas always reverberated with the sounds of nature.

Slowly, he pushed up onto one torn and bleeding elbow then fell back down as shards of pain coursed through his arm and up into his shoulder.

This time the tears flowed freely, the scream came easily.

Taking deep, uneven breaths, preparing for the pain he knew would come, he pushed up again and gasped.

Sitting on its haunches barely three feet away, with huge almond-shaped eyes and irises the size of golf balls that glowed a fiery red, was the beast—waiting.

Never had he seen anything so terrifying, and never would he see anything quite like it again.

He froze as the creature threw back its head and howled. He saw the long, curved, serrated fangs and the jagged claws. He caught a glimpse of hell.

Stealthily, with the grace of a tiger, it approached and forced him back into the blackness of the pit.

With one huge front paw, it pinned him down at the chest; with the other, it extended the three inch fangs and tore open his throat.

ONE

AT THE CORNER OF MAIN AND ELM, IN FRONT OF the ice cream parlor, Tom Roberts braked for a red light. He turned to his wife, took her hand and squeezed it gently. "Feeling better?" he asked.

Smiling weakly, she nodded.

Kristen thought about the wave of nausea that had flattened her early this morning before leaving their apartment. The bout had lasted for over an hour, and when it passed she had felt exhausted and drained. She had no idea what had caused it. She wasn't pregnant and didn't think she had a virus, but it had been more violent than anything she had ever experienced. Her stomach still ached from the dry heaves that had come every five minutes.

Now, sitting next to Tom, surveying the area

they were about to make their home, she didn't even want to think about it for fear it would come again.

She turned her attention to the 1950's style ice cream parlor. Shielding her eyes from the slanting rays of the sun, she read the large neon sign above the door: The Dove. Through the rectangular, plate glass window, she got a glimpse of wrought-iron tables and chairs, and a crescent counter behind which a red-haired teenaged boy whipped up some sort of frozen confection. The place overflowed with young people, some of whom spilled out onto the sidewalk. They were giggling and dancing to the loud music that came from inside.

The town seemed nice enough, but something about living here bothered her.

Since late May, when Tom accepted the position of Assistant Professor of Experimental Psychology, she had an uneasy feeling about the move to Burnwell. Come to think of it, that was when she first started to feel sick. She had pleaded with Tom to wait for another offer, but he insisted that for the present this was all that was available anywhere.

He was excited about the job and the move, since the Randolf Sebastion Burnwell college was one of the most prestigious private colleges in Pennsylvania. She, on the other hand, was not.

Tired of watching the antics of the teenaged population, she turned her attention to the other side of the street to Brandies Coffee House. It had a small, quaint, brick storefront that had been painted the color of cinnamon. The solitary bay window was rimmed with patterned lace curtains, and on each windowpane stood a lighted candle. At the very bottom of the window there appeared to be another shelf lined with plants and ceramic figurines that she couldn't really identify due to their distance.

The place gave her a warm, cozy feeling, and even though the temperature was near 80, she still found herself thinking about what it would be like drinking coffee inside on a cold, blustery winter day. The thought made her smile and gave her a feeling of contentment.

Brandies was also brimming with people, but those of a different generation. An elderly woman with bright red rouge on her cheeks sat beside an elderly gentleman near the bowed window. The woman's mouth moved continuously like a battery-operated robot's that someone had forgotten to turn off. Kristen shook her head. Suddenly, she felt disappointed about the clientele. In her mind she renamed the restaurant to The Gossip House, because she was sure that's what went on inside.

The light turned green, and they continued down Main Street.

Maybe that was what bothered her, she thought. The gossip. The one big happy family syndrome where everyone minded everyone else's business.

She had grown up in the city and become accustomed to its impersonal indifferences. She had learned to treasure her privacy. Now here she was, suddenly transplanted into rural, small-town America. Living here was going to drive her mad.

It would start slowly. Then after getting to know the neighbors, it would be a matter of time before they knew the type of toilet tissue she used, or the type and color of her underwear, or how many times a week she and her husband made love. Soon the entire town would be privy to that information. Maybe she was exaggerating, she hoped, but somehow she doubted it.

It wasn't as if she really had anything against small towns or the people who lived in them. She didn't even blame them for the way they snooped. They had little else to occupy their time—no theater, no cultural events, no concerts—and regardless of what Tom thought, she wasn't being finicky. She had experience.

When she was 18, the summer before she started college, she had spent three months at her Aunt Millie's home in a farming community in West Virginia, so she knew about small towns. Life had been boring, gossipy and unbearable.

Her aunt was always leaning over the back fence, talking about one neighbor or the other —who had remodeled their home, who had money, who didn't, whose unmarried daughter was in a family way.

Maybe it was normal for people to behave like that. She certainly didn't want to judge them, but she also didn't want to be forced to be like them.

Maybe that's what she feared most— becoming like them. The thought made her shiver, and she wished she could turn the car around and go home right now before it happened.

She sighed, then concentrated on the scenery.

Downtown Burnwell was unique. She couldn't help but admire the restored 200 year-old residences that lined both sides of the street. Their old bricks had been painted glossy shades of yellow, green, pink and blue, and under each of their long narrow windows were shiny black flower boxes that overflowed with a blur of colors.

Since it was lunchtime, she couldn't help but enjoy the students who milled through the streets, some of them wearing backpacks, others carrying books in their arms. Most of them were dressed in shorts and tank tops or jeans and tee shirts. They bustled in and out of Burnwell's unusual shops.

There was the International Deli, where ropes of sausages and balls of cheese hung in the windows; The Donut Hole with fresh baked goods every day; The Green Thumb, its huge windows jammed with lush foliage; Hoagies Plus and Grace's Gifts.

The first smile of the day tugged at the corners of her mouth. She liked downtown Burnwell. Unfortunately, it wasn't where she'd be living. She liked the activity brought by the college and liked the students who seemed to keep the town alive. Once the fall semester arrived, there would be thousands more. The college catalogue claimed the population of Burnwell swelled from September through May to 16,000 people, 6000 of whom were students.

She smiled and leaned over to kiss Tom's cheek.

"What was that for?" he asked, flashing her a look of surprise.

"I guess I love you," she teased.

"You guess?"

Giggling, she moved closer to him and put her head on his shoulder. "I know," she said and raised her eyes to see a wide grin break out on his face. When he smiled, he was the most handsome man on earth. He had dark hair and crystal blue eyes, and sometimes, when he looked at her a certain way, he reminded her a little bit of Tom Selleck. He even had the same bushy mustache. When he teased, he automatically raised his eyebrows up and down.

"Tired?" he asked.

"Yes," she whispered.

"We're almost home."

The word "home" sent a jolt up her spine. She slid back into her seat and looked at him. "Please don't call this home. I'm sure I'll never be able to think of this area as home."

Tom took a deep breath and then let it out very, very slowly. "Come on, Kris, you promised to give it a chance. It'll be great here. No noise, no pollution, and no crime. Just think, we can go out at night without worrying about getting mugged."

"I said I would try and I will, but stop trying to brainwash me!" She really was in no mood to argue, not again, but she was tired of listening to him. "For you I'll give it a chance. Now why don't you give me a chance to get used to it?" He didn't answer right away, and she thought he was going to start another argument.

She was stunned when he said, "I'm sorry." He looked dejected. "I guess I just want you to be happy."

"I will be. As long as we're together I'll be happy."

He smiled and nodded, then continued to the end of Main Street in silence.

When he made a left turn onto Willow Road where their new home was located, Kristen settled back into the seat to watch the scenery. On her left was a group of newly built brick townhouses and the West End Fire Company. A Presbyterian church was on the right, its slender white steeple reaching up and almost touching the cloudless azure sky. The church was painted white and had black shutters framing each window. Most of the homes surrounding it were also white with black shutters, screen porches and immense manicured lawns. It was almost like looking at a calendar picture, the ones that celebrate America's splendor.

Farther down the road, they passed a Wendy's, a Hardee's and a pizza place called Pietro's. Then, except for the occasional farmhouse which was surrounded by mile after mile of fields that resembled a patchwork quilt and the wooden telephone poles where birds perched like tiny ebony sculptures, most traces of civilization disappeared.

The quaint charm of downtown Burnwell faded quickly in her mind as they traveled the winding black ribbon of Willow Road. A feeling of doom set in once again as the farmland gave way to an area of thick, dense forest. The trees—pines, maples, oaks and birches—were huge, full and towering. Some of the upper branches reached across the road and formed a natural canopy, making the area dark and ominous.

Kristen felt uneasy. They were entering a land best left to the hearty pioneer wife of long ago. It was definitely not for a city girl like herself. She closed her eyes and tried to block out the scene, but images of wild, rabid animals and spiders the size of softballs flooded her mind. She shuddered.

The forest continued on for what seemed like forever, even though it was actually only a couple of miles. When she felt the warmth of the sun on her closed lids, she opened her eyes.

To her left was a row of identical box-shaped development homes that were packed together. She found herself wishing one of them was hers instead of the isolated older home her husband had insisted upon.

Once past the last house, the multicolored blanket of farmland resumed. Fields of tiny cabbages, acres of sprouting two foot corn and mounds of clover lined the road.

Soon they approached an area where a single row of tall pines were planted against the shoulder of the road. Tom made a sharp right turn, squeezing between two enormous trees onto a partially hidden macadam drive. At the top of the drive stood a two-story, white frame house, situated on three flat acres. To the left of the house was a corn field. Behind the house, at the end of their property, was a tangle of thick, dense forest. To the right was a huge, pale blue Victorian that stood in the middle of five acres.

The three-story Victorian had tremendous wooden lattice-work porches and long, old fashioned windows bordered by white shutters. It had a gabled roof with towering spires that rose up to the sky. The house looked well-kept, with a manicured lawn and sculpted shrubbery. Ivy trailed upward along its side, and a macadam drive led to a small garage.

Tom parked the car in front of the adjoining two-stall garage, then got out and stretched. He opened the garage door and headed for the white New Yorker that his father had given him as a graduation present. She watched him run his hand over the smooth finish.

Kristen stepped out of the car, her eyes focused on the dark, shadowy woods. She wondered what kinds of creatures lived inside such darkness. She wondered if they would soon come bounding out to greet them, or worse, tear them apart. Perhaps they would wait until nightfall.

At this point, she knew she had little choice but to learn to live in harmony with whatever resided in the area.

She quickly shifted her eyes to the Victorian and felt a strange chill. Suddenly, her nausea returned. She swallowed hard, forcing the bile back down to her stomach as she hurried up the front steps of her new home.

For some reason, the house bothered her even more than the woods, but she didn't know why.

Unfortunately, she would find out soon.

TWO

KRISTEN LEANED INTO THE OPEN HATCH OF THE blue Honda, digging into Tom's toolbox for a screwdriver he needed for a jammed upstairs window. The nausea had subsided, but she still felt tired and irritable. The tremendous amount of work that lay ahead wasn't helping. Moving was a bitch.

"Did you buy the house?"

Startled, Kristen jumped and whacked the back of her head on the open hatch.

She wondered how the frail, old woman sneaked up behind her so quietly. The woman appeared near 80 years-old. Her eyes were a translucent shade of green, her short permed hair a shimmering silver. Her face, deeply furrowed and leathery, bore traces of too many years in the sun. The woman wore a dark blue shirtwaist dress covered with tiny lemon-colored flowers, and to Kristen's surprise, she had on a pair of red leather Reeboks, hightops.

"Oh, I hope you didn't hurt yourself, dear," the woman said, grinning. Her face expressed concern, but her voice lacked sincerity. "I just wanted to know if you bought the house," she said again, locking her eyes with Kristen's.

"Yes," she answered, still rubbing her head. A lump formed beneath her fingertips, and she had the beginning of a massive headache.

The old woman nodded, turned from her and pranced toward the front porch. Kristen couldn't help but notice she moved like a cat, smooth and graceful. No wonder she hadn't heard her sneaking around.

Kristen never had any great love for cats. She hated their eyes and the way they were always underfoot. She most definitely hated their cunning.

"I'm glad you'll be my new neighbor," the woman said, turning back to her and eyeing her up and down. "You're such a pretty little thing." Her voice was so high-pitched it reminded Kristen of a whistle.

Kristen lowered her eyes, and her cheeks began to flush. Dressed in a torn Eagles tee shirt and her oldest, most tattered jeans, she certainly didn't feel pretty.

But Kristen Roberts *was* pretty, no matter how she was dressed. She had large, expressive brown eyes that shimmered with tiny flecks of gold; her auburn hair was short and had a natural curl and framed her delicate face with tiny ringlets. She had a small upturned nose with a splattering of freckles that trailed off onto each cheek. She stood five-foot-two and weighed about 100 pounds. Pretty was definitely an understatement.

"I'm Eliza Noman," she said and pointed to the Victorian home on the slope to her left. "I live in that house over there. Now who are you?"

"My name's Kristen. Kristen Roberts."

"Are you here alone?"

"No, my husband's inside." She held up the screwdriver and waved it back and forth. "I have to go. He's waiting for this."

The woman's eyes clouded and turned a muddy shade of green.

"Look, I'm sorry. I don't mean to be rude, but we have a lot to do. Maybe you can come back another day. It was nice meeting you." Kristen smiled sweetly.

"I guess you do have a lot to do." There was a twinge of regret in her voice—or was it hurt?

"Yes, I really do."

The Noman woman grunted and turned to leave in such a huff that Kristen wanted to burst out laughing. Instead, she forced the laugh back and covered her mouth with her hand. But before the old lady had gone ten steps, Tom opened the front door and came out onto the porch.

"Kris, what's the holdup? I don't want to spend the entire day up there." He descended the wooden porch steps and glanced at Eliza Noman who had stopped dead in her tracks. "I'm sorry. I didn't know you had company."

Eliza Noman whirled in his direction, her eyes sparkling like lights on a Christmas tree. Their eyes met, and for a moment that seemed like hours not a word was spoken.

Immediately, Kristen felt the magnetism between them. It seemed as if a strong current of electricity hung in the air. At that instant, a pang of jealousy coursed through her, similar to what a wife would feel if some gorgeous, voluptuous woman was seducing her husband and succeeding. This woman was ancient, and there was no reason for jealousy, she told herself.

"I just stopped by to say how thrilled I am to have neighbors again," Eliza Noman said as she slinked over to Tom's side and linked her arm through his. "My last neighbor wasn't all that nice. He had such little time for an old woman." Her voice dripped with syrup, and her eyes twinkled like diamonds as she looked at him. She winked. "Already I can tell that you'll be much better." She let out a schoolgirl giggle.

Tom smiled and patted the hand that had wrapped around his forearm. In a way it was funny. They acted like a pair of lost lovers.

From behind came a low rumble and the deafening blare of an air horn. When she turned, she saw the orange and blue moving van swaying up the drive. She turned back to Tom and Eliza Noman. "It was so nice of you to stop by." Her voice sounded insincere and rehearsed. "And I do hope you can come back soon, but . . ."

Eliza Noman appeared to ignore her, craning her neck to see the truck. Once it came to a complete stop, she looked at Kristen and said, "Don't worry, dear, I won't get in the way. I'll help."

Kristen looked to Tom for support. She hoped he would help get rid of her, but to her surprise, he said, "Great! Maybe Kris can make some coffee."

She gave him a sharp look. Great? I don't have enough to do without having to entertain her?

"The coffee will have to wait. My coffee maker's in the truck," she said to both of them sarcastically.

Let him entertain her, she thought as she walked toward the movers. I don't know what she's got, but you can have her.

Soon she'd wish she had never had such a thought.

Eliza Noman stood at the top of the steps watching as Tom Roberts talked to the movers. The sight of him sent shivers through her old decrepit body. His resemblance to her beloved Louis was uncanny. Both had the same dark hair and the same intense blue eyes. Tom was taller and more muscular than her Louis had been, but it made him even more appealing.

She felt a flutter inside her stomach. Her breathing quickened, and her excitement grew. She giggled, then covered her mouth with her hand. She hadn't felt such attraction to a man since Louis.

Even though she had known she was getting new neighbors, this was totally unexpected. She couldn't be more pleased. It couldn't be more perfect.

THREE

BY 5:30 THE MOVERS HAD LEFT, BUT ELIZA NOMAN
had not. Kristen had spent the entire afternoon
chasing after her like one would chase after a
two-year-old. She was exhausted. The woman
had gotten into everything—poking and probing each piece of furniture, peeking into each
box and inspecting its contents. She had been a
nuisance and had irritated everyone except, for
some reason, Tom. He didn't seem to mind her
at all.

During the course of the day, one of the
movers, a huge, muscular man who reminded
Kristen of a linebacker, had lost his temper with
the old woman. He had been carrying the brass
headboard through the front door when Eliza
Noman scurried up behind him. She had looked
like a child, her eyes wide and full of wonder, as

if she had just been given the key to the candy store.

The man hadn't seen or heard her coming up behind him, and he backed into her and rammed her with one massive arm. She yelled "Oooooh!" loudly and stumbled backward and landed on the floor. First the mover bent over her to make sure she was okay, then he stood up and grimaced. Red-faced, he bellowed, "Lady, why don't you stay out of my way? You're gonna get hurt."

Eliza Noman winced, and as soon as he turned his back, she made a snooty face at him, curling up her lip and sticking out her tongue. She sat in the very spot she had fallen, pouting, until Tom rushed to help her get up. Kristen, unable to control her giggles, ran from the room, her hand clapped over her mouth.

An hour later she found herself counting to ten when she saw Eliza Noman going through the box containing her good china.

"Lennox! Oh, my," she said as she carelessly turned the rose-patterned dinner plate over and over in her hands.

"Please don't," Kristen said, reaching for the plate. "This set was a wedding gift from my parents. I would appreciate you not handling it."

Eliza Noman recoiled. "I'm sorry, I'm sorry," she said. "I didn't mean to upset you. I was just admiring your dishes." Her eyes filled with tears, and her voice cracked. "You have such pretty things. I adore your crystal animal collection. They sparkle soooooo much. And the piano is marvelous too. Do you think Tom will play me a tune?"

"I don't know," Kristen answered, still irritated. "You'll have to ask him." She glared at the woman, but as she started to walk away, Eliza Noman's arm shot out and her long slender fingers grabbed her.

"Please forgive me."

The fingers on Kristen's bare arm felt like ice. She quickly pulled away and rubbed vigorously at the numbness left by the old woman's touch.

"I usually don't behave this poorly," she continued, "but it's been such a long time since anyone's been near. I guess I got carried away. I really am sorry."

This time, unlike earlier when Kristen had banged her head, the apology seemed sincere, and as warmth returned to Kristen's arm, it also returned to her heart. She felt herself melt inside. Maybe the old woman *was* lonely living out here alone. Maybe she just needed companionship. And maybe she, herself, was irritated because she was tired.

Kristen wondered if she had been taking out her own frustrations on the woman. No, she didn't do things like that. The truth of it was the woman was nosy and got on her nerves. Still, she felt horrible for being so terse with her. It wasn't like her to have such little patience.

Against her better judgement, she said, "Okay. You're forgiven. Just stay out of the way. Please. I'd hate to see you get hurt."

Eliza Noman behaved herself as the movers were finishing up and even apologized to them.

Mostly she walked around with a pout, as if her candy had been taken away. She was so like a child, Kristen concluded, that one must deal with her as one dealt with a child.

Later, as the last vestiges of sunlight streaked through the back door and the toasty smell of coffee filled the room, they sat in the newly remodeled kitchen with its polished maple cabinets and burnt orange appliances and countertop.

"So, you're a psychologist, too?" Eliza Noman asked.

Kristen nodded. She traced her finger around the rim of her coffee mug. "Yes, I am. I have a Master's degree in counseling."

"Who do you counsel?"

"Mostly children. Teenagers. Abused children. Delinquents."

"Hmmm." She studied Kristen closely. "Did you meet Tom in college?"

"Ah huh. When we were undergrads at Temple. Of course we didn't marry until later when I finished graduate school. He was up at Penn State then, working on his doctorate, and I joined him there."

"Don't tell me you supported the two of you."

"Yes."

"That must have been hard."

"Not really." She smiled shyly. "His father helped out."

"I bet his father helped buy this house, too."

Kristen felt her spine tingle. The woman was too much. She never ceased to amaze. She opened her mouth to tell her it was none of her business, but instead, to her own surprise, she said, "He loaned us the downpayment."

"What a nice man."

Although stunned by her own words, she agreed. It was as if she had lost control of her mouth. But her in-laws were nice, and there was no reason why she couldn't give them credit. At least she hadn't told her the amount of the downpayment—$35,000, half the price of the house. She had been embarrassed to tell anyone about it.

"How about *your* family? Are they as nice as Tom's?"

"My father died five years ago, and my mom has been ill ever since. But we get along fine."

"What's wrong with your mother? Is it serious?"

Kristen wasn't certain, but she thought she detected a lack of true concern in the old woman's voice. It sounded almost as if she felt pleasure at another's misfortune, but that simply couldn't be the case. No one ever feels pleasure at someone's misfortune, at least no one she knew. She hesitated before answering then brushed her suspicions off as imagination.

"It's really not serious. She just had trouble accepting my father's death."

That, of course, was an understatement. A week after her father's funeral, her mother had insisted that he came to visit her every night before bed. Another week passed, and she insisted that he lived in the bedroom with her. But that wasn't the worst of it. The worst came when her mother wouldn't leave the room. She spent each day sitting and talking to an empty chair, refusing to eat or to take a bath. Dr. Hager, the family physician, hospitalized her.

But she was getting better. She still took a great deal of medication and still spent most of her time in her bedroom, but she no longer claimed her husband was with her. Mostly she sat quietly, a rosary in her hands, staring out the window at her rose garden.

"Is she all better now?"

"Yes, she's fine." She didn't want to talk about it anymore. She didn't want to reveal that her mother was just pretending to recover because she knew she'd be back in the hospital if she didn't. That was the truth Kristen never told anyone. She had seen it in her mother's eyes, in her blank stare.

Kristen picked up her head and looked at Eliza Noman who was covering her mouth with her hand. A smile? But why? Certainly not because of her mother's illness.

She looked again. This time the woman's face appeared sympathetic. How odd!

Maybe it was about time she learned a few things about her neighbor.

"So tell me about yourself. Where are you from?"

The old lady frowned as she said, "Burnwell, of course. Spent my entire life here."

"Are you married? Were you married?" she asked, noticing the absence of a wedding band. "Do you have any children?" Kristen watched the old woman's expression turn to one of grief.

"No," she replied, dropping her eyes and staring into the coffee. "I never married." When a mask of sadness came over her face, Kristen wished she hadn't asked, but the old woman intrigued her and she had to probe deeper.

"Why not?"

"I almost did, once upon a time, but it didn't work out." Her eyes moved past Kristen. Dreamily, she stared outside.

Kristen followed her gaze. She seemed to be looking into the woods as if the whole scenario of her lost love was being replayed beneath the trees.

"Oh, he was a fine man," Eliza continued, "so much like your Tom." A tear trickled from the corner of her eye, and she brushed it away with the back of her hand. "But it was such a very long time ago." She sighed, took a lace handkerchief from her pocket and dabbed at her red-rimmed eyes.

So much like Tom! Was that why she was so attracted to him? Did he remind her of her lost love? She had to know more.

Reaching over she touched the woman's hand but then quickly withdrew. A prickly sensation ran through her fingers and up into her shoulder. The woman's flesh felt as if it had been immersed in ice water for hours. It was as cold as her father's had been the day he was buried. It frightened her and made her want to get up and run away from Eliza Noman, away from Burnwell. But that would be silly. She couldn't run away.

Sighing, she continued, "Maybe talking about

it would help," Kristen said, massaging the numbed fingertips of her right hand. The awful cold from the woman's flesh still lingered. It was the worst case of poor circulation she had ever encountered.

Eliza Noman turned to her. "I really don't want to talk about it. I don't like to dwell on the past." She flashed Kristen an angry look. "You of all people should know how destructive that can be."

Of course, the woman was right. Dwelling on past hurts could be destructive. It was better to forget, but how could one forget if one never faced the hurt? Maybe Eliza Noman never faced it, and maybe, Kristen thought, she could help. If she knew more, she would be better able to understand her, and if she understood her, she'd find it easier to like her. Liking her was important. After all, they were going to be neighbors, probably for a long time.

"I am sorry, but I do think that . . ." Kristen stopped and looked out the door.

Standing on the porch just outside the screen door was Tom. He struggled with the latch, and balanced two enormous pizza boxes from Pietros Pizzeria in one hand and held a grocery bag in the other. She jumped from her chair and hurried to his aid.

Tom waltzed past her and placed the pizza on the kitchen table before dumping the grocery bag on the countertop. He pulled out a folded newspaper and threw it on the counter, then reached into the bag for the two-liter bottle of Pepsi and dangled it in front of her face. "How about some cups," he said, "and don't forget the paper plates. Better hurry. I'm not sure I can control myself much longer."

She laughed and walked into the hallway that connected the kitchen to the dining room. Somewhere amidst the mess was the box containing the paper plates and cups. She rummaged through two huge cardboard boxes before she finally found them, tucked a stack of plates under her arm and picked out half a dozen cups. Then she headed back to the kitchen feeling a little disappointed that Tom had returned when he did. A few more minutes with Eliza Noman and . . .

She still couldn't decide if she liked the woman or not. Eliza Noman baffled her. One minute she was kind and sympathetic; the next she seemed to be laughing at her. Maybe it was the smile she had noticed when she had spoken of her mother. Why smile at another's misfortune?

As she stepped into the kitchen, she saw them both huddled over an open box of pizza, their mouths full, their eyes locked as if in silent conversation. Instinctively, she took one step back and watched them from the doorway. The sight of them like that unnerved her, even frightened her. She wanted to interrupt, to walk up to them and ask what the attraction was, but her feet felt cemented to the floor.

Suddenly, Eliza Noman shifted her gaze and looked directly at her. The old woman's eyes were cold, hard and horrifying.

The terror came in waves, a terror so primal, so evil and so deadly that she felt faint. Her stomach rumbled and felt as if it were pushing up into her throat, and the pulse in her neck throbbed out of control. She tried to turn away. She wanted to run, but some unseen force was holding her. As her eyes fused with Eliza Noman's, she felt her knees weaken, then buckle.

She was falling forward, and it was impossible to stop. She hit the tile floor hard, her right shoulder absorbing the brunt of the fall. The pain of impact was immediate and intense.

She was barely aware of Tom at her side, his powerful hands turning her onto her back. Her eyelids fluttered, and she fought to remain conscious.

There was a blur of white paper plates around her. The cups rolled past her and came to a stop at Eliza Noman's feet. Behind Tom she saw the old woman, smiling.

Some people do laugh at another's misfortune, she thought, then blacked out.

FOUR

ON THE SCREEN PORCH, THE NIGHT AIR FELT cool. A damp, musty smell enveloped the house. From the distance she could hear the croak of a solitary frog and the high-pitched chirp of the crickets.

Kristen stepped closer to the screen. Tiny gray moths, drawn by the light from the kitchen, clung to the netting. She lifted her hand and gently tapped the supporting wood frame, then watched as they fluttered in all directions. Somehow they reminded her of souls, souls that had lost their way and now searched for the light and its warmth.

Stepping down from the porch, the dewy grass bathed and prickled her feet. Something warm and slick slithered across her toes, and she gasped and leaped back onto the porch.

From where she stood, she could see the Noman house silhouetted against the night sky like an ancient dinosaur. A single lighted window shone back at her like an enormous luminescent eye. She turned away.

What was keeping him? He had left to walk the old woman home almost an hour ago. Before leaving, he had come into the bedroom to wake her. He had kissed her forehead and had promised, "I'll be back in five minutes. I don't want to leave you alone." But he did leave her, and worse, he even forgot about her.

Even though she felt better, she resented his staying away for so long. What if she passed out again? What if this time she hit her head? But she wouldn't. From somewhere deep inside her she knew the fainting episode was over, at least for today. She felt strong, almost like her old self before Burnwell ever entered her life.

She sat down on the wooden steps and thought about how she had passed out earlier without any warning. She wished she could remember exactly what happened, but the memory eluded her. She did recall waking up in Tom's arms as he passed the smelling salts under her nose, but there was something else— something about Eliza Noman. But what? She saw . . . damn, she hated her.

Tom had carried her upstairs and placed her on the bed where she had drifted in and out of sleep. After he woke her to tell her he was going, she had stayed in bed waiting for him to return, but by 10:30, she became restless and went downstairs.

She waited and waited and waited, but still he didn't return. She wanted to go up to the Noman house to see what was keeping him but decided against it. Instead, she went out onto the porch to wait further.

With a feeling of longing, she sighed deeply then plopped into one of the webbed loungers that the previous owner had so kindly abandoned. She strummed her fingers on the flimsy aluminum, got up, then paced the length of the porch before sitting down once again.

Where was he?

She took a deep breath, pulled the chair closer to the screen and focused on the sky where stars twinkled like chips of diamonds laid out on a jeweler's black velvet. She noticed how they seemed to merge and form clouds of light. She was soon able to pick out the North Star, the Big Dipper and the Little Dipper. She needed a book on astronomy to be better able to identify the other constellations. It would be fun being able to locate the planets and constellations. Since she knew the night sky changed with each season, it would be a challenge.

Just then she heard Tom whistling. It was the same innocuous tune that got on her nerves. She had asked him a thousand times where he had heard it, but he just said it popped into his head.

As he stepped onto the porch, she flashed him a dazzling smile, but he seemed aloof, and her smile soon faded as she watched him drop into the adjoining chair. She winced as the aluminum scraped against the wood.

"You're looking better. I'm glad to see you up and around," he said, coolly. "Sorry I took so long at Eliza's. We got carried away."

"Eliza?" She made a face and wrinkled her nose. "Why on earth are you calling her Eliza?"

Tom looked puzzled. "Because she asked me to call her by her first name. Why else?"

Kristen laughed half-heartedly. The closeness that had developed between them in one day was unusual. After all, they had just met!

All day she had watched them, feeling left out. Now she felt even worse. "She certainly has gotten *your* attention today."

"Jealous?"

"Hardly," she said. She thought for a moment. Yes, damn it, I am jealous. She couldn't explain why, but she really was. "Well . . . maybe a little." She laughed at herself for being so childish. She had no reason to feel as she did. "Should I be?"

"Maybe," he said jokingly.

Her head swiveled toward him. He was suppressing a smile, but not very well. The corners of his mouth were starting to turn up, and she noticed the twinkle in his blue eyes. Finally the smile won, and he faced her and raised his eyebrows up and down.

Kristen rolled her eyes. "What is it with you two?"

"What do you mean?"

"I don't know. There seems to be some sort of bond between you."

"I hadn't noticed." He paused and looked as if in deep thought. Then he said, "She's so fascinating." He shrugged. "Don't you think so?"

"More rude than fascinating—and snoopy. She reminds me of an old witch. You know the type, the kind you meet on Halloween. Just give her a broom, a black cat, and—"

"Whoa. Take it easy. She's just an old lady."

"And a senile one at that."

Her attitude surprised her. She hadn't meant to be so cruel, but waiting for Tom to come home had irritated her. She got up to stretch.

"What took you so long anyway? You could have carried her home in less time."

"I can tell you're feeling better," Tom said.

"Don't get smart. I just don't care for her. She's a snoop."

"All old people act like that, at least all those I've ever met."

She looked down at him and wondered why he felt he had to defend her. The old bitch seemed capable of doing that all by herself. Kristen opened her mouth to say something in her own defense, but quickly closed it. She decided it was best to say nothing further. He was enamored with Eliza Noman, and nothing she said would change that. She couldn't understand why. Hell, she couldn't even understand why she disliked her so much. She just did.

"Maybe I'm tired and grumpy," she lied. "I'm going for a shower. Care to join me?" She bent over him and nibbled his ear, needing some reassurance of his love.

Tom swatted at her as if she were a pesky fly. "I'll be up in a few minutes."

"Suit yourself," she said, feeling hurt and rejected.

She opened the door and went inside. Immediately she went to the newspaper on the countertop. Funny, she hadn't seen it earlier. It would have given her something to do, perhaps lessening her irritation. She picked it up and scanned the headline:

LOCAL BOY VANISHES
Fourth Child to Disappear This Year

She carried the paper to the dim light near the sink and began to read.

Early this morning Burnwell police suspended an all-night search for Scott Benson, age 14, of Hemden Circle, believed to have vanished in the vicinity of Willow Road late yesterday evening. The boy was reported missing at 10:00 P.M. by his parents, Roger and Margaret Benson. He is the fourth juvenile to disappear in the area since March.

According to Mr. Benson, his son spent the day with a friend, Billy Wilcox, and was expected home by 9:30. The Wilcox boy indicates that Scott left before dark, approximately 7:30, bicycling in the direction of Willow Road.

Kristen put down the paper. She didn't want to read anymore. She didn't want to know. But the black and white photo of Scott Benson smiled up at her, beckoning to her.

Crime didn't occur in the country. That's what Tom had said over and over again, but if he was right, then why was this boy's picture taking up half the front page? And what about the other children?

She avoided looking at the picture and once more began to read.

When asked about any clues to the boy's disappearance, Police Chief Milton Walters replied, "We found the Benson boy's bike at the top of a seventy-foot tree, bent in half around a branch. It's impossible to determine how it got up there."

Kristen felt overwhelmed with confusion. It all seemed a terrible joke. "How the hell could a bike end up at the top of a tree?" she asked herself out loud.

She looked at the boy's photo, then traced her finger over the outline of his jaw, his nose and his eyes, until goosebumps broke out on her arms and spread over her entire body. She folded the paper in half.

She had never met the boy, but she had a strange, uncanny feeling of kinship with him. It was almost as if they had something in common.

Her entire body shuddered as she stared out the window above the sink. The night was so terribly black; within such darkness anyone, or anything, had free reign.

She thought about the boy and the other missing children and wondered if some maniac, posing as a student, lived nearby. Again she shuddered. She didn't want to think about it, but the thoughts flooded her mind as if a dam had just burst.

Where on Willow Road? Their home was on Willow Road. How close did it happen to where she was?

From behind she heard the creak of the screen door and, frightened, turned around to find Tom.

"I thought you were going to shower."

She let out the breath she had been holding and stared at him, unable to speak. Finally she managed to whisper, "Did you see the paper? A boy . . ." She heard the quiver in her voice and swallowed hard before trying again. "A boy disappeared out here last night."

"Yeah, I read about it. I'm sure they'll find him holed up at a friend's. You know kids at that age."

Yes, she did know kids at that age. She had spent the past three years working with them at the center and had grown accustomed to their quirks, their unpredictability, and even their smart-assed attitudes. But it didn't make her worry less about them or even dislike them. They were young and still had a lot to learn. In time, most of them would become responsible adults—most, but not all. Some were destined at birth to never fit into the mainstream.

She hoped Tom was right and that the boy had decided not to go home. Maybe he had had an argument with his parents and wanted to give them a scare to teach them a lesson, but something inside her told her that wasn't the case at all.

Something awful had happened to Scott Benson. Of that she was certain.

She looked up at Tom. Her eyes were stinging as she forced back her tears.

"Don't look at me like that," he yelled.

"Like what?"

"Like I should go out to look for him. You and those big brown puppy eyes."

The tears pushed hard behind her eyes, and she turned away from him and looked out the window again. Whenever something happened to a child, whether she knew the child or not, it ate at her insides.

While working at the center, she had had tremendous problems controlling her emotions, especially if a child came in who had been abused. She wanted to punish the abuser herself and make him suffer as much.

She remembered Jessica Conrad, a timid, scared eight year-old who had been brought in for counseling. She had huge red welts covering her body and had suffered a concussion, all at her father's hand. The girl's mother had died giving birth to Jessica's younger brother, and Jessica had been forced to assume the roles of mother, maid and child.

47

Her father beat her regularly, but that day he had had a bad day. Dinner wasn't ready when he came home, and he went crazy. It was a miracle that he hadn't killed the child, and if a neighbor hadn't heard her screams and called the police, he may have.

But people like him seldom picked on anyone except children. They wouldn't dare risk a confrontation with someone who could retaliate.

Of course, this wasn't the case with the Benson boy—he had simply vanished—and more than anything, she wished and prayed and begged that Tom was right.

She felt Tom's arm come around her.

"Come on, Kris, you're getting too upset. I think if you get some rest you'll feel a hell of a lot better."

"What about the police finding his bike in that tree?" she said, prying herself out of Tom's arms and turning around to see his face.

His mouth shifted to one side, his eyes avoiding hers. "Maybe he left it on the road and it got hit by a truck and that's where it landed." He shrugged.

But she knew he didn't believe his own explanation; it only was his way of calming her down.

"What do *you* think happened to the bike?" he asked. Instead of waiting for an answer, he said, "Guess you think Big Foot showed up and wrapped the bike around that limb like a Christmas ornament, then he carried the kid to his lair or den or whatever."

Annoyed, Kristen shook her head. "Don't be

ridiculous. But since you're such a smart ass, explain what happened to the other kids."

"Maybe they ran away from home. I don't know. That's what the police think." He paused, watching her. "Didn't you read the entire article?"

She shook her head. She had simply scanned the beginning. Suddenly her face felt warm, and she tried to turn away from him.

"Ah, just look at those tomatoes on your cheeks. You know, you shouldn't overreact unless you have all the facts. You allow your imagination to fill in the blanks." He gripped both her shoulders and stooped to her level. "Guess I'd better fill you in. Not once in all four instances did the police find any traces of violence—not a shred, not a strand of hair, not one drop of blood."

"Oh." Her cheeks grew warmer.

"So, my dear wife, what do you say about that?"

She didn't answer, because even though they didn't find any evidence of violence, it didn't mean that four children were alive and well. All it meant was that they couldn't explain the disappearances, but since she didn't want to spend the entire evening arguing, she said, "Well, maybe I did overreact." She smiled weakly. After all, she had no proof other than her own gut feeling that something awful had happened to those kids, and if one didn't have solid, tangible evidence, one would be unable to convince Tom Roberts of anything. Tom discounted gut feelings, intuition, ESP and the like. He more than discounted it; he laughed at it. It was a product of his analytical approach to everything.

"You've been overreacting a lot lately—ever since I accepted the position at the college, come to think of it. Living in the country really has you spooked."

Again she didn't answer. There was no need in confirming the way she felt.

"Well, I'm going to do my best to show you how wrong you are. The day will come when you'll be glad we moved here. The city will become just a bad memory. I promise."

He put an arm around her waist, another under her knees and picked her up. "We'll start by carrying you over the threshold."

Kristen giggled and rested her head on his shoulder. Of course, it wasn't the threshold of the house he meant but rather the threshold of the bedroom.

As soon as he put her down, she undressed and hurried into the shower. A few minutes later, he joined her, a thick, soft sponge in his hand.

"Thought you'd like some help," he said, grinning as he got into the shower with her.

As they stood under the pulsating spray, the day's tension oozed from her and gurgled down the drain. This was what she had wanted and needed. It had been so long since they had been close, and when she thought about it, she couldn't even remember the last time they had made love. It had been more than a month.

Under his gentle scrubbing and massaging, she relaxed. And when he turned her around to face him and kissed her and pulled her to him, she realized how much she had missed him.

His hardness pressed against her, and a few moments later they were one.

FIVE

THE GRANDFATHER CLOCK AT THE BOTTOM OF THE stairs chimed twice. On the bed Tom stirred and rolled onto his side. Outside, a low, thick, gray fog blanketed the ground, and at the Noman house, a lighted third floor window beamed in the darkness.

Feeling tired, lonely and troubled, Kristen focused on the window. She had been up for over an hour, had wandered through the darkened rooms, had taken two aspirin and a glass of warm milk, but still sleep would not come.

She was alert; her body felt charged with electricity. Every time she closed her eyes, the picture of Scott Benson flashed in her mind. His disappearance had upset her more than she realized.

Sighing, she shifted in her chair and looked at

the lighted window. As she wondered if Eliza
Noman was awake or had just forgotten to turn
off the light, she saw a dark figure appear before
the window. It was the old woman, her frail
body framed by light. She was dressed in something very frilly and flowing.

Kristen pressed her back against the velvet
wing chair. She didn't want to be seen, although
there really was little chance of that happening.
Was her neighbor also disturbed by the boy's
disappearance?

She inched forward to look out again, but to
her dismay, the window was now dark. She felt a
pang of disappointment. She wanted to share
the lonely hours with someone—anyone.

Kristen tugged the pink terry-cloth robe tightly around her and thought of Eliza Noman. It
was odd that the old woman was awake. Most of
the elderly she knew were in bed by nine, ten at
the latest. But, of course, there were always
those who had trouble sleeping, those who
spent most of the night keeping watch, though
for what she never knew. Maybe they knew
something about the night. Maybe they were the
chosen few who protected the world while it
slept. Was she also chosen to stand guard? If so,
she wished she knew what to look for. To her,
the night was peaceful, calm and safe without
anything to guard against or fear.

The pills and the milk were having an effect;
her lids suddenly felt heavy, and she closed her
eyes. In the background, the steady, hypnotic
tick . . . tick . . . tick . . . of the clock drifted
farther and farther away. Slowly, gently, her

head rolled to her shoulder, and finally she fell asleep.

Shades of purple streaked the sky. Dense trees bordered the road on either side. A light summer breeze caressed her face and tickled her nose.

There was the hoot of an owl, the throaty caw of a raven and the steady hum of the crickets. From behind came heavy breathing.

The boy appeared on her right, riding his Schwinn. His face, his clothes, his entire body looked as it did in the newspaper photo—black and white. He contrasted with the lush green foliage around him. When his arm reached out to her, she stretched to meet him. Their fingertips brushed, and suddenly, as if by magic, he burst into vibrant color.

His hair turned a pale blond, and his eyes became two sparkling blue ponds. When he grinned, she saw the shimmering silver braces on his teeth. His Schwinn turned an apple red.

He passed her quickly, gaining first one bike length and then another. His head swiveled in her direction and, laughing, he urged her on. Kristen agreed to the challenge and pedaled fiercely until they rode side by side. Then laughing and taunting, she pushed past.

She labored to the top of the steep incline, then glanced back at him to see him flash a smile. He was gaining on her very slowly.

She released the brake and descended the hill at breakneck speed.

The wind shifted. The sweet floral air turned

sour, and the rancid smell of death hung around her.

There was a scream, angry and inhuman. A winter chill slapped her face.

Something was coming. She felt its presence and heard its raspy breathing. They had to hurry.

She turned to look at the boy whose eyes were wild with panic, his lips stretched taut over his braces. She motioned for him to hurry.

The distance between them seemed to grow. She tried to slow down to allow him to catch her, but the brakes had no effect and she zoomed out of control.

A scorching hot breeze carried the smell of blood in the air. She heard the scream, this time a child's scream—Scott Benson's scream. She hit the brakes over and over again until she gained control. She skidded in a half circle and now was facing uphill.

The boy was gone.

Above her she heard a *whoosh*, and when she looked up, something bright and shiny was coursing across the night sky. At first it appeared as a blur, then little by little she realized it was Scott Benson's bicycle, whizzing through the air. It hit the top of a tree, then twisted around a sturdy branch.

Where was the boy?

Immediately, she went back to where she had last seen him, stopped and got off the bike. She moved cautiously toward a low moan that came from the side of the road. It had to be the boy, but when she reached the spot and looked down, she released a silent scream.

Eliza Noman lay flat on her back. Her eyes were a molten orange; her lips were pulled back exposing teeth that were no longer human but three inch fangs.

The old woman rose up from the shallow ditch, her body stiff and unbending, her arms at her sides. As she came to her feet, she turned to Kristen and spoke, not with her lips but with her mind.

"Here is the boy you seek," she said. "Look. Look and you will see."

The figure of Eliza Noman began to fade. In her place stood Scott Benson—battered, bruised, his neck ripped and torn, a jagged hole in his chest where his heart was supposed to be.

Terrified, she backed away. The boy followed and extended his arms to her.

"Help me. Please. Help me," he pleaded as tears tumbled from his eyes, washing clean rivulets down his bloodied cheeks.

Kristen took one step toward him. She would help him, but what could she do about his lost heart? How could she find him another?

She threw her arms around his broken body, and as she slowly pulled him to her breast, he screamed, not a boy's cry for help but that of an animal.

Instinctively, she jumped back.

The boy had disappeared, and once more Eliza Noman had taken his place. She was laughing, taunting, beckoning her. She floated toward her, her arms up, her hands extended like hooked claws.

Kristen's feet felt frozen to the macadam. Slowly Eliza Noman drifted closer, and then only a foot away, she stopped and released a maniacal laugh as she raised her hand to touch Kristen, missing only by an inch. She did it again and again, with Kristen recoiling each time, until . . .

She jumped. Her body was trembling, and she was drenched with perspiration. Her eyes popped open, and then she knew it was a dream—thank God, a dream. She threw her head back, panting and trying to catch her breath.

Through the bedroom window, the first gray light of dawn shown through. On the bed Tom slept undisturbed. As she got up from the chair, she heard a rooster caw in the distance.

Holding back her tears, she stumbled from the room and staggered down the stairs where she collapsed on the living room couch.

The tears were warm and salty as they ran down her cheeks and into her mouth. It was difficult to breathe. The dream had been so real, so lifelike that she felt certain she had witnessed the boy's fate.

But it was only a dream. And Scott Benson wasn't dead—just missing. And Eliza Noman was no more than a foolish woman who was a danger to no one but herself—or was she?

Kristen didn't really believe that about the old woman. There was more to her than she allowed people to see. But she had seen something earlier, something that she couldn't recall, something that chilled her very soul. When

Eliza Noman had looked away from Tom when they were eating, what had she seen? She couldn't remember. God, how she wished she did.

Curling up into a fetal position, she snuggled into the couch. She felt afraid, even terrified, not only because of the dream but because of the enormity of her move to Burnwell. The terror was all pervasive. She wished she could go home, home to her old apartment, home to her place of birth, but that was impossible. Her place was with her husband, and here was where she would have to stay.

Besides, she was exhausted and in desperate need of rest. Everything was getting to her. It was only a dream and an overactive imagination.

But no matter how she tried to rationalize her feelings and reassure herself with psychological reasoning, she still lay awake, curled up into a ball, until the full morning sun illuminated the room.

SIX

"YOU MUST HAVE GOTTEN UP EARLY. THIS PLACE looks great," Tom said as he shuffled into the kitchen.

Kristen put the last stack of dishes on the shelf, then turned to face him. She watched him stagger to the coffee machine. He was dressed in his usual sleeping attire, a pair of red jogging shorts and an old Temple University tee shirt that had half a dozen holes scattered throughout. Its bottom was stretched out like a tent.

"I couldn't sleep knowing I had so much to do." She didn't want to tell him about the bad night she had had or the upsetting dream. It had taken her a long time to calm down, and the last thing she needed was a lecture or argument from him. She could just hear his usual stern response. "Dreams," he would say, "are a twist of the mind. Only a fool would take them seriously." Maybe so, she thought, but they still could be upsetting, especially when they were as real as the one she had this morning.

She tried to forget about it but couldn't. She decided that if she worked at straightening the house, she would feel better. So that's exactly what she had done, until each box in the living room and kitchen had been emptied and its contents put away. The work did make her feel better and take her mind off the dream, at least for a while.

"Want to go exploring today?" he asked, leaning toward her and kissing her cheek. He poured himself a cup of coffee.

She nodded as she watched him plop into one of the chairs. He reminded her of a rumpled teddy bear, his dark curly hair poking out in all directions, his blue eyes misted over from hibernation. She envied him and wished she too could have slept until 10:00.

"We have to find a grocery store, unless you want to eat stale donuts and leftover pizza tonight."

"Donuts stale?"

"Uh huh." She wrinkled her nose then shook her head as he reached for one.

He paid no attention to her warning and bit into the glazed cruller. "You weren't kidding," he mumbled with his mouth full. He rolled his eyes, took a huge gulp of coffee and threw the donut back into the box. "What time do you think you'll be ready?"

"As soon as I shower and get dressed. Half hour."

"Good. Maybe I can pick up some decent food on the way."

"Good idea. I could use a balanced meal," she said, heading for the living room. Going out was the best thing for her; it would help her to forget the nightmare. As she went upstairs she wondered if the dream had any significance to the boy's disappearance but quickly dismissed the thought. *It was a dream.* She told herself that over and over again all morning long, but somehow it didn't sink in.

She hurried to the bedroom, made the bed, then got into the shower. When she finished, she dressed in a pair of pink cotton shorts and a white blouse. She began to stare out the bedroom window as she buttoned the blouse and noticed the blur of color surrounding the Noman house. She moved closer to the window to admire the flower garden.

It was magnificent. There were reds and pinks and oranges and yellows in a variety of round and square and oblong flower beds. From where she stood, she couldn't make out all the different types, but the whole arrangement of the garden brought back memories of a trip she had once taken with her mother to Longwood Gardens in Pennsylvania.

At one end of the garden she saw Eliza Noman puttering near a circular bed. The woman was dressed in a baggy pair of blue jeans and a bright orange sweat shirt covered by a blue calico apron. On her feet were the red leather Reeboks.

Her hair looked wild like a bleached out piece of steel wool.

Kristen couldn't help but smile. The old woman's taste in clothes was atrocious.

The bed she was working on was still mostly a brown circular patch of dirt which she was filling with something crimson. Kristen lifted the window higher, thought of calling out to her but decided at the last second not to. She remained near the window and watched, taking deep breaths of the fresh morning air.

Another flower bed, she thought, hardly seemed necessary. Not counting the new addition, the woman had at least 50 beds that covered the entire five acres. There were thousands of flowers, and she wondered how her neighbor could keep up with the work and manage to keep things so beautiful.

She focused her attention on the house. It was enormous, with three floors, large spires, and porches that circled halfway around it. It too was well-kept, a truly magnificent structure.

As she remembered last night's dream, she felt a tightness in her chest. She couldn't understand why Eliza Noman had appeared to her as more of a beast than a woman. Although she had no great love for her, she certainly didn't dislike her to such an extent.

But there was something else, something she wanted to remember. She had seen it and sensed it, right before she fainted last night. But what . . . ?

Suddenly she felt the tightness in her chest grow and began to feel dizzy. It was difficult to breathe, and she swayed, falling backwards onto the bed. Her head was spinning, her heart pounding hard inside her chest. For no apparent reason, she felt terrified. It was as if something was buried deep inside her and couldn't get out.

She forced herself to sit up on the edge of the bed and tucked her head between her knees and waited for the spell to pass. Her mind reeled with thoughts of Scott Benson, Eliza Noman and the dream. There was a connection. What it was she didn't know, but there definitely was something going on.

She tried to be rational and reason it out, to attribute the dream and her fainting and her uneasiness to anxiety caused by the stressful relocation. But the feeling of doom and destruction overwhelmed her.

She was simply having a panic attack. Or was she?

Something evil infected this place. Scott Benson was one small part of it, as were the other children. But what could be more overwhelming than their deaths?

The thought startled her. No one said they were dead. They were only missing children.

But they *were* dead! She knew that like she knew the color of her own brown eyes. She also knew that more was to come for the children of Burnwell and for herself. It would be far worse than anything she had ever encountered before.

But how did she know this? Wasn't it just her imagination? Wasn't that what Tom would tell her?

She heard Tom's footsteps padding up the

steps. She could hear him whistling that strange tune, a tune she had asked him about, a tune he had no explanation for, a tune she hated.

By the time he entered the room, the dizzy spell had passed and she was on her feet. Her intuition, her gut feeling, warned her to say nothing about the episode. Instead, she gritted her teeth and continued to get dressed, pretending nothing was wrong while trying to ignore the tune that effected her the same way fingernails being scraped over a blackboard would. As soon as she found her purse and a pair of sandals, she hurried out of the room, away from him and his irritating song.

SEVEN

THERE WAS A LOW WHINE AND AN UNEVEN CHUG, and Eliza Noman jumped to her feet. Her head bobbed from side to side like a startled bird.

She turned and looked at the blue Honda, listening as the car settled into a comfortable hum. Squinting against the blinding reflection of the sun on the car's chrome, she saw Tom and Kristen sitting inside it.

She watched as they pulled away from the house. She felt exuberant that he had followed her suggestion about spending the day becoming familiar with the area. For she had planting to do and didn't want to be disturbed, not even by him, no matter how much she loved him.

Beside her feet lay the remaining boxes of bright red petunias, waiting for her touch. She looked down at them and shook her head. There were still two dozen left to plant and already her arms and legs cried out for rest.

Digging the circular bed proved too strenuous for her fragile body, but she had no choice except to continue. The risk was too great to put it off another day.

She stood waiting and watching until the Honda turned onto Willow Road before removing the soiled canvas garden gloves and the blue apron. She placed them neatly on the ground near the petunias and turned toward the house. Almost unable to lift her tired legs, she trudged over to her bed of herbs.

Stooping and rubbing the small of her back, she examined the nightshade. Then she turned her attention to the cubina root and smiled. Both were doing exceptionally well, their leaves a deep lustrous green, the bushes full and healthy. Soon they would become her ally.

Closer to the edge of the sidewalk, she reached for the camomile, thyme and rosemary, picked a handful of each, then headed inside. These she would place in her microwave to dry for her bath. She would soak away the grime of the garden and soothe her aching body.

Once inside, she filled a tall glass with home-made lemonade, then retreated to the coolness of the back porch. She sat in the white wicker rocker and surveyed her garden.

The daisies, phlox, gladiolus, marigolds and zinnias were in full bloom as well as the roses. It was all her handiwork and difficult not to admire. As she sat rocking, sipping the cool lemonade, she planned her future beds.

Before the growing season ended she would add another bed of roses, then one of mums. Then her plantings would be complete, unless, for some reason, she'd be forced to add another.

Setting the lemonade down on the glass-topped table, she squirmed out of the chair and limped to the edge of the porch.

She stared at the Roberts' house and thought about Tom—handsome, virile and so much like Louis. If she didn't know better, she would swear they were brothers or otherwise related. Maybe that was possible. Maybe Tom was a descendant, a great-great-nephew. After all, Louis had died so very many years ago—76, to be exact. It had been on May 21st, a dreaded day.

But wouldn't it be wonderful, she thought, if he and Tom were somehow related? Oh, yes.

She couldn't believe her luck. When she had bargained for a neighbor, she had never expected it to turn out so perfect—well, almost perfect—but that was how her father worked. He gave her what she asked for but always for a price.

The first time she struck her bargain with him, she gave him her soul, but it had been worth it. When he asked for sacrifices, she acquiesced. The price for Thomas, she already knew, would be his eternal soul.

Of course, her father always threw in some adversity. This time it was Kristen Roberts.

Yesterday, she had sensed the girl's dislike for her, but it was for the best. She, too, felt no love for Kristen, but she had also sensed something more. Kristen had a gift, a gift that could prove troublesome.

She knew the girl was too weak and naive to pose a serious threat, but she had to make sure that she never gained strength. Since the fool had no knowledge of her own ability, she also had to insure she never gained such knowledge. Then she would be able to crush her, crush her beneath her foot as easily as a robin's egg that had fallen from its nest.

She turned away from the house and hobbled down the porch steps towards her unfinished planting. Completing the garden work today was going to be more of a chore than Kristen Roberts would be.

It was past her time. The previous neighbor had ruined her schedule and in the process almost ruined her. This was her last chance, her only chance of survival.

But she needed two more sacrifices to be able to complete the final ceremony. Getting them would be difficult since the police were swarming the area, looking for the missing boy. She would have to let the ruckus die down before she could strike again.

Then, with the help of her father, she would become young again. She grunted. Why did he always make it so difficult? And why had she been so foolish to agree to aging naturally before she could return to her youth? She had struck the bargain so very many years ago, and it had been his express wish. Also it didn't raise suspicion. She was allowed to live with others and didn't have to move as often, only once every 60 years. But if the ceremony wasn't complete by the autumnal equinox . . .

Sighing, she stared at the loose dirt. She had to get back to work and not waste time. This morning she had seen fresh animal tracks.

She took a deep breath. Such a risk she couldn't abide. No matter how much her body ached, she had to finish today.

EIGHT

AFTER SPENDING AN HOUR RIDING THROUGH THE countryside, the dream, the foreboding, even the dizziness had passed and were soon forgotten. Kristen saw fields of sprouting corn, young cabbages and tiny potato bushes interspersed among the rolling green hills. The smell of manure was so thick in the air that it stung her nose. The sights, the smells and the solitude lulled and soothed her.

On the way back to town, they stopped at a dairy farm and in the adjoining store gorged themselves on banana splits and thick shakes. She felt at peace with herself and all that surrounded her.

They were crossing the covered bridge, the planks rumbling beneath the car's weight, when

Tom took her hand in his and pressed it to his lips.

"What do you think? Still feel we made a mistake?" he asked.

"No," she said, "not at all."

The beauty of the area had left an impression.

Beneath the bridge she could see the crystal clear brook. An abundance of robins, cardinals and blue jays fluttered from tree to tree, while rabbits, squirrels and chipmunks darted through the fields.

She noticed the lack of pollution, the lack of soot clogging her sinuses. She felt at peace with the world around her when she saw how all living things existed in harmony.

Maybe she hadn't given it a chance, she thought. Maybe she should.

"I never felt so attuned with nature," she said, looking at Tom and smiling. She never felt as relaxed as she did right now.

Tom kissed her hand again, his eyes brimming with love and his face beaming with contentment.

Soon they were back on Main Street, and Tom drove straight to College Hill Road, the narrow tree-lined street that led to the campus.

"Grand tour today," he said and winked at her.

Kristen laughed. She was eager to see the place where he'd be working, and she felt a twinge of excitement as they drove past the wrought-iron gates of the Randolf Sebastion College.

She found the drive through the sprawling 14 acres nostalgic, reminding her of her own college days. She envied the students who reclined on the grass and stretched out beneath the giant trees. Some studied, some socialized, while others, those who had moved into the sun, worked on their tans.

Most of the buildings were old but well-kept. There were also new additions to the campus, where the buildings had a modern boxlike shape.

Tom pointed to the Psychology building on the right, an ultramodern, four-story, white brick structure with aqua trim. On the left side of the building, she saw the counseling offices and decided to apply there for a job as soon as she finished getting settled. With any luck, she'd be employed by the fall semester.

Tom exited the campus on Sebastion Road and continued on for a few blocks, turning right onto King Street, a narrow two-lane street with lush maple trees. It reeked of faculty residences. He turned left onto Elm where Burnwell's only shopping center was located and pulled into the parking lot where the weekly Farmer's Market was in progress. Some of the farmers, those who didn't bother to erect stands, sold their produce from the back of pickup trucks.

"Let's get some fresh vegetables," he said excitedly, as he got out of the car. "We better not waste too much time inside. I'd hate to come out and find them gone."

Kristen suppressed a smile. He sounded like a little boy who had just entered a toy store. She, too, was eager to have fresh produce, but it wasn't quite as important as he made it seem. She grabbed his arm to keep him from wandering toward the stands and finally ended up pulling him through the parking lot to the Super Fresh store.

"We need other things, too," she said, yanking on his arm and dragging him through the automatic glass doors. "I won't waste time. I promise."

"Just make sure we don't miss them. I'd give anything for a home-grown tomato."

Kristen smiled. "Okay, okay." She stood on her tiptoes and kissed his cheek. "Come on, nature boy," she teased as she reached for one of the metal shopping carts, "let's get started."

"So you folks bought the Simpson place. Guess that makes us neighbors," said the bronzed and weathered farmer.

Kristen guessed his age to be near 60. He wore a blue and green plaid shirt and a faded pair of coveralls. When he handed Tom his change, she noticed how the veins on the back of his hands stood out like gnarled blue ropes.

George Howard leaned over the stand and whispered to Tom, "No need to come into town. Stop by the house if you've got a hankerin' for some home-grown. The tomatoes are doing fine this year. Beans and snap peas are, too. Shame you missed the strawberries, best I've had in years, but the blueberries are almost ready." He looked at Kristen and winked. "They'll make some delicious pies and muffins. By the way, that cornfield bordering your land is mine. When it's ripe, just help yourself."

"Thanks," Tom said. "That's real nice of you."

"Just being neighborly."

"I haven't picked corn since I was a kid." His eyes drifted dreamily past the farmer.

"Grow up on a farm?"

"No, I lived next to one. I grew up near the outskirts of Lancaster."

"Then you can appreciate home-grown." George Howard turned to Kristen. "How about you, little lady? You from Lancaster, too?"

Kristen shook her head. "Philadelphia."

The old man nodded, his gray eyes twinkling. "You'll learn soon enough that country life is better."

"That's what I've been telling her."

"Well, it takes some getting used to," he said.

Kristen said nothing. She felt as if she was being brainwashed. The country was beautiful, and she had spent an hour riding through it, enjoying its splendor. But it would take an awful lot to feel comfortable.

Maybe the city didn't have the rolling fields or the nature trails, but it did have something. Why else did so many crowd there?

To her, the world was divided into two types —city dwellers like herself, who loved the hustle and bustle, the crowds, the opportunity, and country folks, which included Tom, George Howard and Eliza Noman, who loved the quiet, the open spaces, and, unfortunately, the boredom.

"Now don't forget to stop by," George Howard said. "My wife's gonna be tickled when I tell her we got new neighbors." He was looking at Kristen as if directing the invitation only to her.

She interpreted his remark as an invitation to see his wife because she gets lonely out here all by herself. And that was the sum of what he said next.

"She gets lonely. Can't get out much. Arthritis keeps her down."

Kristen agreed to visit. If Mrs. Howard was half as nice as her husband, she wouldn't mind. She also had the feeling that if she didn't stop by, George would come and get her.

On the way home, driving along Willow Road, Kristen spotted the Howard farm. It sat on a small incline set back from the road; a full acre made up the front lawn. It was a large three-story home with white shingles and a red barn to its left. In front of the barn she saw a black 1968 Chevy Impala that sparkled in the afternoon sun like a polished onyx. Looking at the house with its gray shuttered windows and flimsy lace curtains, its flower-bordered walk and flower-filled window boxes gave Kristen a warm, homey feeling. She decided to definitely stop by the first chance she got.

After dinner, grilled steaks and an enormous salad made with the fresh tomatoes, Tom made a startling proposition to take a walk in the woods out back.

The thought unnerved her. "It'll be dark

soon," she said, having no intention of exploring that gloomy domain.

"It doesn't get dark until nine. Come on, we have three hours. You're not chicken, are you?"

"No. It's just that—"

"Sure you are," he interrupted. "You're chicken. Don't worry so much. There's nothing out there to get you. Besides, I'll be there to protect you." He wrapped his arms around her waist and nuzzled her neck.

"And who's going to protect you?" she said irritated, pulling away from him.

Kristen knew that the only way for her to get over her fear would be to face it. She had to go into the woods and find out for herself what was out there. Unfortunately, she wasn't ready to do that, at least not yet.

When Tom tried to grab her again, she ran into the living room. He quickly caught up to her and gently threw her down onto the couch.

"Say yes," he commanded.

When she shook her head from side to side, he began to plead, "Please. Don't make me go alone."

Kristen took a moment to think. The last thing she wanted was for him to go alone. What if he got lost? What if something dreadful happened to him? What if he needed help?

The decision was made. "Oh, all right," she said. "But not far. And only if you promise we'll be back before dark.

"I promise," he said raising his right hand as if to swear. He allowed her to get up from the couch, and as she headed for the back door, he yelled, "You can't go dressed like that. You can't walk through the woods in shorts and sandals. At least put on a pair of jeans and sneakers."

She whirled on him and stuck out her tongue. He was right. She couldn't go into that thick, murky, damp place dressed as she was. In no time her legs would look as if she had been attacked by a cat, and her feet would be all torn and bleeding.

She let out an exasperated sigh then stomped up the steps to the bedroom, praying she hadn't made a mistake by agreeing to go. But she knew he would have gone alone, and it was far better to be out there with him than to be at home waiting for him to return.

As she slipped into a faded pair of jeans and an old pair of sneakers, she found herself wishing for a special outfit, the kind the astronauts wore to go up in the shuttle, to keep all the creepy crawlers as far away from her skin as possible. She giggled to herself at the thought of it. She was being ridiculous, overreacting to the unknown.

She reasoned that maybe it wouldn't be half as bad as she imagined. The drive through the country had helped ease her fears, and maybe this short hike would do the same. At least that was what she hoped. She hated being so close to the woods, but she also knew she had little choice. Unless some developer bought up the land or an act of God wiped it out and replaced it with green fields, the woods were there to stay.

As soon as she finished dressing, she bounced down the stairs to her impatient husband.

"Let's check on this side. Maybe there's a path." Tom pulled her after him.

The underbrush had been too thick, and it was impossible for them to step through it or over it. And without realizing it, they had crossed onto the Noman property.

"There's one," Tom yelled excitedly, pointing to the narrow opening.

From the appearance of the path, it was obvious that it had been used frequently.

"Guess we're not the only nature lovers around here." He ducked beneath a protruding branch.

Kristen followed him quietly, the back of his leather belt locked firmly in one hand. She could tell from the way it had been trampled that the path was used often. She felt afraid, but mingled with that fear was a strange exhilaration. She stepped over a small thorny bush and stared into the dark woods. Again she felt a tingle of excitement.

Around her she could hear the songs of what seemed to be a thousand birds. To her right she heard a rustle coming from beneath the bushes. She stopped and pulled back on his belt. Then the entire bush shivered as if alive. She gasped.

"Come on, Kr—"

Before Tom could finish his sentence, a shrill voice screeched, "Where the hell do you two think you are going?" The voice was so high pitched, it sounded as if it could shatter glass.

Kristen released Tom's belt and turned around to see Eliza Noman standing at the beginning of the path, glaring angrily at them.

Tom moved to his wife's side.

"Hi, Eliza. Kris and I were about to do some exploring," he said cheerfully as he nudged his wife with his elbow. "Maybe you'd like to join us."

"I suggest you stay out of there." Her voice had dropped an octave but was still earsplitting. "It's not safe in there. You'll get hurt." When she looked at Tom her face softened a bit, not much but enough to be noticeable.

"Come on out, and don't be foolish." She reached for his arm and literally yanked him onto the lawn. Kristen followed in silence, afraid to speak. "No one ever goes in there. It's too thick, too dangerous."

"Well it looks as if someone di—" Again Tom wasn't allowed to finish his sentence.

"Never mind. I know what I'm talking about," she screamed.

Kristen stared at the old woman, who paced restlessly back and forth in front of them. She reminded her of a soldier walking the perimeter of her territory.

Right then she realized that they had accidently crossed onto Eliza's property. She couldn't help but wonder if she was really protecting them—and from what? No sooner had she thought that when the old lady grabbed her arm and roughly led her back to her own yard. Her strength was amazing, a far cry from that expected of an old woman.

Once they were as far away from the path as possible and on their own land, Eliza waved a finger in front of Tom's face. "I'm surprised at you, Thomas, taking your pretty wife in there. You should know better." With pursed lips she glared at him. "Last year, Mr. Simpson, the previous owner of your house, went in there and didn't come out. A few days later they found him dead. He had been attacked by wasps and poisoned. I'm sure I don't have to tell you what his body looked like, but if you want me to, I will. I just think its unnecessary to scare little Kristen here by such descriptions. Knowing that it happened should be sufficient."

She shook her head violently, like an angry, rabid dog. "I want you to promise me you won't go in there again." She stopped as if waiting for their answer, but neither said a word. "I said, 'I want your word, Thomas.'" She whirled on him, and for a moment Kristen thought she was going to pounce on him.

They both shook their heads, too unnerved to say a word. Their mouths hung slack, their eyes wide.

Kristen noticed that Eliza Noman's face had turned a deep plum. She definitely was angry, that much was certain. Would the woman have a stroke?

Finally they nodded their heads and made their promise.

She smiled and said, "Good." She turned and stalked up the incline to her house. They waited until she entered the back door before moving.

Kristen looked at Tom and shrugged. She

slipped her hand into his, and they walked toward their home. It was difficult to understand the old woman. Why had she become so livid? A simple statement about the danger of the forest would have been sufficient. Now, more than ever, she feared the woods. If what Eliza Noman had said about Mr. Simpson was true, and she was quite sure it was, she had no intention of ever going exploring—and she intended to make sure Tom didn't go either.

With that in mind, she followed Tom into the house. She had hoped to spend a quiet, romantic evening with him, but from the look of anger on his face, she knew they would not.

NINE

LATER, AFTER THE SUN HAD SET, TOM SAT ON THE porch, cradling a bottle of beer in his lap and ignoring the pleasant sounds around him. He was fuming with anger and was glad Kristen had gone to bed. They had almost gotten into a fight because of her I-told-you-so attitude, but he still hated to admit that she had been right about the Noman woman. The old lady did act as if she had a few screws and bolts missing.

Gulping the remainder of the beer, he reached into the half-empty six-pack for another bottle. The rage and embarrassment he had felt when Eliza approached them on the outskirts of the woods still lingered. The way she had yanked him out, as if she owned the damn woods, infuriated him. "Did she own them?" he wondered. He wasn't sure, but even if she did, that was no reason to treat him like a little boy. His father had always done an excellent job of that.

Since he had grown up in the country, he had spent most of his childhood romping through the woods and exploring, and he sure as hell knew how to avoid a wasp's nest.

But to make matters worse, what bothered him the most, was that she had scared the hell out of Kris, who was just beginning to relax. If she hadn't come along, maybe Kris's fears about moving here would have finally been dissolved or at least lessened to a tolerable degree. He had seen the look on her face, one of stark terror, when she first spotted the woods out back. All he wanted to do was dispel her fears by making her face them, but Eliza screwed up that quickly enough.

Damn the old bitch! Damn her to hell!

Kris was right. The only solution to that nosey old bitch was complete avoidance, and he planned to do his best to keep her out of their lives. No wonder she had complained about that Simpson guy. He probably decided to do the same after she drove him nuts.

He took a swig of the warm beer and leaned his head back on the metal frame of the lawn chair. It was only 10:30, plenty of time to finish the six-pack and maybe start on the other one he had bought in town. Tomorrow he'd drive back for an entire case, but for now, the two would do just fine in helping him get a buzz on and allowing him to relax enough to sleep.

He guzzled the beer, placed the empty bottle in a straight line against the base of the screen and reached for another. The buzz he was trying for was already taking effect.

It was 2:00 A.M., and the lights at the Roberts' house had finally gone out. Eliza was sure Tom finally had gone to bed.

Earlier, she had sneaked down to the house, circling it as quietly as a cat. She had peeked around the side of the porch to see him sitting there, drowning himself with beer. She had spent the following hours sitting near the window, watching and waiting until the house was dark.

She had lost her temper with him and now regretted it. She had seen the anger in his eyes after she had chastised him about going into the woods. Somehow she would find a way to apologize, to show him that she wasn't as bad as his wife wanted him to believe.

But the fear she had seen earlier in Kristen's eyes made it worthwhile. The story about Simpson's body in the woods, dead from bites, had shook the girl to the core. If only she knew the entire truth . . .

The encounter with Kristen and Tom had proved that she had been right about the girl's weakness. Nothing pleased her more than to see Kristen cringe with fear. Kristen Roberts would not pose a problem, and once she begged Tom's forgiveness, he would be charmed by her admittance of guilt. All would be as she intended, as it should be.

She moved from the window and finished

packing a blue Samsonite suitcase. She slammed it shut and locked it. Tonight, she was forced to travel. A friend needed her help. It wasn't right that she had to leave just when things were taking shape at home. Sometimes she hated Agatha Crenshaw, that stupid, willful woman. If only she would have heeded her warning, then she wouldn't be forced to clean up her mess. What made it worse was that this wasn't the first time she had to extricate Agatha from her self-made dilemmas.

She picked up the overstuffed suitcase from the bed and flung it across the room, like an empty tissue box. Controlling her rage was becoming increasingly difficult. She watched as the suitcase bounced off the mahogany doorframe and out into the hall where it came to rest on the red and black carpet.

If it wasn't for Agatha, she would have been more patient with Tom and wouldn't be facing a major setback in their relationship.

Getting control of her temper, she stomped out into the hallway and picked up the suitcase, then hurried downstairs to the garage. This time she would teach Agatha a lesson and make her pay dearly for her mistake.

She lifted the trunk to the black, four door Mercedes and flung the suitcase inside. She slammed the trunk with such fury that the car bounced on its shocks.

She got into the car, started it and pulled out onto the drive. When she got out to close the garage door, she pushed it down with one hand, banging it so hard against the cement that it caused a hairline crack in one of the windows.

She then heaved the door, making sure it had locked. She jumped back into the car and sped away from the house onto Willow Road.

By morning she'd be in New York, and the fun, the pleasure that was her due, would begin.

TEN

THE AIR CONDITIONER IN THE NARROW SIDE WIN-
dow of the living room hummed comfortably,
releasing pleasant cool air. From the corner of
her eye Eliza could see Agatha bustle around the
lemon-yellow kitchen, preparing a sumptuous
breakfast feast fit for a queen—and *she* was the
queen.

On the dining room table was a bowl of fresh
cantaloupe cut into neat little cubes. A mountain of grapes sat in a silver tray. There were
sliced grapefruits in a sparkling crystal bowl
and crystal goblets containing orange juice,
freshly squeezed by Agatha's own hand. She
knew how to treat her guests.

Eliza Noman turned to the window and
looked down at the lush green foliage of Central

Park. The treetops were so full they resembled giant pompons. The sidewalks were bustling with pedestrians, and traffic was getting heavy as the rush hour drew near. Over the hum of the air conditioner, she heard the blare of horns each time traffic threatened to come to a halt.

For the life of her, she couldn't understand how anyone could live with such bedlam. From where she stood, the streets looked as if they were filled with ants. She wished she was back in Burnwell, sleeping late, rejuvenating her body for what was yet to come and enjoying the clean air, the quiet and the solitude.

But the girl, Alyssa Brandon, was here, asleep in the large master bedroom. Agatha had given up her own room because of the girl's demands.

Her fury started to build, and she took deep, heaving breaths and let them out slowly, trying to defuse. She was eager to meet this young woman, this whore, more eager than even poor Agatha could dare imagine.

Tired of the sight of frantic humans, she moved away from the glare of the window and eased into the soft plushness of the white velvet couch. Agatha's apartment was decorated to perfection. Gold brocade curtains hung flawlessly from each window. Black marble-topped tables reflected the golden brass lamps as if they were mirrors. The thick white carpeting was set ablaze by the morning sun that streamed into the room.

To Eliza the room, the entire apartment, was too perfect, too neat and too sterile. It seemed as if it belonged in an elaborate showroom or on the pages of *House Beautiful*. Of course, she did admire Agatha's excellent taste, but the woman lacked the ability to make a house feel homey. What the place needed was a little clutter—a magazine not in the brass basket, a spot on the immaculate rug, a smudge on one of the tables, or a few knickknacks out of place, maybe scattered around instead of neatly positioned in the lighted glass cabinet.

Sighing, she turned her attention to her friend who still hopped around the kitchen while humming to herself, as if she hadn't a care in the world. Eliza Noman shook her head. How could her best friend be such a bubblehead? The girl could have, possibly may have already, ruined her, even ruined them all.

With eyes as cold as arctic waters, Eliza watched her friend glide around the kitchen.

Agatha Crenshaw was a handsome woman in her early forties, or so she claimed. She had blond sculptured hair and enormous brown puppy-like eyes. When she moved, she appeared to glide across the floor. Her legs were lean and shapely, and her height was five foot eight. At the moment, she wore a blue silk robe that barely came to the top of her thigh.

No wonder she always got into trouble, Eliza thought. She still acted like a teenager, rather than the mature woman she was.

Suddenly she felt an urge to kill her best friend—to get up and rush into the kitchen and grab her throat and put an end to the woman's foolishness once and for all—but she didn't.

Through the years they had been like sisters.

Eliza, the older of the two, had instructed and guided her beloved Agatha. No matter how many mistakes her friend had made, she had been easily forgiven, but Agatha never learned from her mistakes. She always returned to her flighty ways and, as a result, burdened others with the mess.

Now, the chore of correcting her errors was becoming tiresome. The ability to forgive was waning. Agatha, with her exotic tastes and her inability to heed warnings, was becoming increasingly dangerous, and soon she would not only destroy herself but the others as well. Something had to be done!

Eliza still could not understand why Agatha preferred women. It seemed so unnatural to her own persuasion. Agatha claimed that the roughness of men and their lack of sensitivity had driven her to her quirk, as she so aptly labeled it.

Eliza knew it was more than that, but still she had never been able to figure out. Maybe she had had a bad experience and decided not to give men another chance. All men were not insensitive; many were like her Louis or like her Tom. It wasn't even Agatha's sexual orientation that caused the problem; it was her choice in companions that was atrocious. It was as if she sought out the worst women she could find, the ones who were eager to take advantage.

"Breakfast is ready, darling," Agatha said, interrupting Eliza's thoughts.

Eliza smiled and nodded, then got up and shuffled into the adjoining room. She sat at the head of the dining room table, her rightful place, and watched as Agatha spooned a mound of creamy scrambled eggs onto her plate.

The table had been set to perfection. The crystal goblets, the sterling silver flatware and the scrolled silver trays all sparkled in the sunlight.

A table set for a queen, she thought. How fitting!

As she picked up a pale yellow napkin and placed it across her lap, she heard a soft rustling coming from behind, moving closer and padding across the plush carpeting. Her back stiffened, and she strained to listen. A second later a voice, reminding her of smooth pearls, reached her ears.

"Well, well, well, don't tell me your mother's visiting today. How wonderful!" said the sarcastic disembodied voice as it approached.

Eliza looked up from her plate as Alyssa Brandon sauntered into the room—naked. She saw the beauty of her alabaster skin, her watery, pale blue eyes, and her waist-length raven hair, tinged with blue. As she bent over the table and popped a plump grape into her mouth, Eliza noticed her firm, high breasts and her flat, tight stomach.

Drowning in envy, she watched the porcelain doll slip into the white velvet dining room chair and motion for Agatha to serve her.

"You woke me up," she snapped. "You know I sleep until ten and look," she pointed to the clock on the wall, "it's only nine." She flashed an angry look at Eliza. "And who the hell are you? Let me guess . . . Gee, I really don't care."

Agatha stood behind one of the chairs, a look of terror on her face.

Eliza focused on her breakfast, taking small bites of her French toast. She watched as Agatha handed the brat a large crystal goblet of papaya juice. It was impossible to understand what her friend had seen in this girl to bring her home and even to suggest initiating her into their group. The girl undoubtedly was beautiful, but there were thousands of beautiful women out there. Why couldn't she ever find one whose beauty was more than superficial?

Alyssa gulped half the goblet of juice, then leaned back against her chair.

Eliza's eyes drifted to the girl's breasts. Oh, to have breasts that firm and round again. She averted her eyes and looked at Agatha who was propped up against the table, staring at Alyssa and drooling with passion.

The girl smacked her tongue against the roof of her mouth repeatedly before speaking. "That tasted funny." Her brows crunched together, and her nose wrinkled. "What'd ya do, bitch, spike it?" She looked at Eliza then back at Agatha. "I want you to know I know exactly who your mother here is. I also want you both to understand that as long as you keep me, and keep me well, you'll have nothing to worry about." She paused and faced Eliza once more. "I'm well aware that you're the Queen Mother. I heard Aggie call you yesterday." She shook her head and laughed. "Queen Mother, my ass." She picked up her hand and tapped her index finger on her temple. "I have it figured this way. Since

I'm not a little kid, I have nothing to worry about from you perverts.'' This time she released a hearty laugh, throwing her head back and revealing a set of perfectly straight, brilliantly white teeth. Again Eliza felt a pang of jealousy.

"Well, daaarlings, I'll be at Bloomies most of the day. As you can see I have nothing to wear.''

Eliza watched as she pushed away from the table and stood up. In an instant her legs buckled beneath her and she dropped with a muted plop onto the thickly cushioned chair. Her eyes popped open wide as if she had made the most shocking discovery. Eliza couldn't help but snicker.

"What the hell's going on . . . ?'' Her voice slurred, then garbled like a phonograph record that was being played at too slow a speed. She slumped back into the chair.

Eliza reached for her hand and squeezed it hard, listening to the tiny bones crack beneath the skin. She leaned closer to look into the girl's eyes.

"Nothing to fear, dear? How could you be so foolish to believe that?''

Alyssa opened her mouth to answer, possibly to scream, but no sound came from behind the pale lips. Slowly, her eyes glazed, and just before her head dropped to the table, a single tear escaped down her cheek.

The papaya juice with her special mix had done what she had intended. She was so pleased with herself and her ability to play chemist that Eliza giggled and clapped her hands with glee.

She had won; she always won.

"Eliza, darling, please be gentle with her. Do what you must, but do it quickly. I do love her so. I can't bear to know she suffered." Agatha's eyes overflowed with tears. She brushed at them quickly with a baby pink, satin handkerchief that she had taken from the pocket of her robe. As she headed from the room in the direction of the bathroom, she continued to plead, her voice trailing off with her sobs.

Fool! Eliza thought. Of course she would do what she had to do, but certainly not quickly. Oh, no, there would be no mercy for this money hungry little bitch.

Feeling the rage build inside her once again, she took a series of deep breaths and buried her anger. A moment had passed before she was able to pick up her fork and dig hungrily into her breakfast.

Afterwards, she moved into the living room where Agatha was curled up in an easy chair watching some boring talk show. She moved to the couch, hoping to take a nap to help pass the day. As soon as darkness fell, she would take care of the chore she had been called upon to do, a chore poor Agatha found too difficult to perform. And now, for the first time since Agatha had called, Eliza felt more pleasure than she had in a very long time.

ELEVEN

BEHIND A THICKET OF BIRCH TREES, ELIZA SAT ON a large rock, waiting.

The night was black. Thick clouds covered the moon, ozone filled the air, and on the western horizon jagged streaks of lightning illuminated the sky. A storm was approaching, and although she still couldn't hear the rumble of its thunder, she knew she had less than an hour before it arrived.

Suddenly she heard the click of the car door and the rustle of the silver lamé evening gown that Agatha had insisted upon. She stood up and moved forward to watch the girl stumble from the Mercedes. She sneered as Alyssa Brandon tripped closer and closer to the pit's edge.

Eliza Noman had taken the Hazleton exit off Interstate 81, knowing full well that the deep pit, a result of years of coal mining, was located beside Route 309. She had been here before on similar business.

No one ever ventured down into the old coal pits which descended some several hundred feet into the earth. A fall into such an abyss was usually fatal. Even if one survived the fall, escape was virtually impossible.

With eyes that easily saw in the dark, she watched the dazed girl stumble and fall to her knees, releasing mouselike squeals before getting back on her feet. She could hear her tortured sobs drift through the air.

The herb mix she had prepared had done the trick. Alyssa had been compliant, offering no resistance from the moment they had departed. She had obeyed her every command, never imagining what awaited her here. But now, as the powerful potion wore off, the fun was just beginning. The fear, the stark naked terror of one who finally has realized her life was about to end and that there was no escape, was also ready to begin.

Eliza felt her own impatience; the fool was taking too long. If she didn't tumble over the edge soon, she would be forced to offer some assistance. She had promised Louise and Jenny Kacher that she'd be at their home in the Black Mountain by 2:00 A.M., and it was almost 1:00.

During her drive from New York, she had thought of her dear friends and had decided to spend the week with them. After taking the Hazleton exit, she had stopped at an Amoco station and called them from a nearby phone booth. Of course they were excited and said she would be more than welcome.

Jenny and Louise Kacher were also part of her family, as was Agatha, but they were much younger, twins who could pass for 35, which, of course, they were not. Their exact age was unknown to anyone but themselves and Eliza, but they were lovely girls. Jenny, a reddish blond, was statuesque and lithe with crystalline blue eyes; Louise was a redhead with blue eyes, but shorter and plumper. Both enjoyed life to the fullest and were fun to be with. Unlike Agatha, they preferred men, young men, men in their late teens to early twenties. They bragged constantly about their affairs.

The reason for her visit had little to do with any blunders as it had with Agatha. It concerned her own future. They had plans to make before the sisters came to, her home in Burnwell, before the ceremony could begin.

Some of the others would come, too, though not Agatha, of course, since she was too much of a bungler to be trusted with such delicate matters. But Dorothy Lassur from Miami, Becky Tocks from Los Angeles, and Emily Gregory from Detroit, who would take Agatha's place, would all come. Only the best of the select society had been chosen. Then, once they were together, they would speak of Agatha. She was certain that they would all agree with her solution to the woman's stupidity and recklessness.

The girl's scream suddenly broke the silence. She could hear her slipping, sliding over the loose shale at the edge of the precipice and clawing at the sides of her future grave. Eliza knew she had finally stumbled over the edge.

She stepped out from the cover of the trees and hurried to the side of the pit. When she looked down, she could see the silver dress reflecting in the blackness. How she enjoyed this part of the solution to Agatha's most recent problem.

When the girl cried out for help, Eliza Noman giggled. No one, except for the two of them, would hear her screams. Most everyone in this small town was already asleep. Her giggle erupted into a loud cackle, and she clapped her hands together and held them to her breast and danced with glee.

Alyssa Brandon lay motionless on the small ledge which jutted out over the cavernous pit, no more than three feet away from a sheer drop to the bottom. Her arms and legs were burning from the sharp jagged pieces of coal that had ripped her ivory skin. Dazed and half-conscious, she tried to figure out where she was. She tried to move but stopped as the coal dust shifted beneath her weight. Her body ached, and her left hand, the one Eliza Noman had crushed, was swollen, bleeding and useless. When she lifted it to her eyes, she saw the shiny satin scarf, Agatha's scarf, bound tightly around it.

From above she heard the laugh that sounded like cracking glass. She cringed and pushed her body against the black wall of the pit.

Abruptly the laughter ceased. She held her breath and listened for movement, with each second her mind becoming more and more alert.

She remembered sitting at Agatha's dining room table and the ugly, grotesque woman who had been there. The Queen Mother, she had called her. She had been frightened by the woman's piercing stare.

She remembered Agatha handing her the juice and drinking it. Finally, she remembered the numbness that had started in her chest and worked its way into her arms and legs.

Had they poisoned her? Did they plan to kill her and dump her body into some makeshift grave? Yes, that had to be it. But where were they now? Was that them, or one of them, laughing? Did they linger close by or had they gone? Why was she dressed in an evening gown? Was all this because she wanted the good life at the expense of a horny, kinky bitch who could well afford it? The questions rambled aimlessly through her head, but no answers were found.

She strained to listen. There was no sound except for the swirling wind of the impending storm.

Certain that they were gone, she turned slowly onto her side. The grit on the ledge shifted slightly beneath her with each movement.

Digging the fingers of her right hand into the coal dirt she found a stable hold with her right foot. Her left foot rested on a small rock that jutted from the side. A second later the ledge she had been resting on collapsed, and she could hear the loose dirt fall into the bottomless pit.

She held on tight, then slowly, steadily, inch

by inch, pushed her body upward, digging first with her hand, then with her left foot, then with her right foot. She winced with pain as the loose dirt forced its way beneath her nails. Her broken hand throbbed as she tucked it against her chest.

She knew she was close to the top because she could feel the freshness of the air. She stopped to rest before the final assault.

The ledge had been barely 20 feet from the top. If it had been any farther, she couldn't have made it.

Her body began to tremble and shudder from the pain and the realization of her predicament, but her will was strong. She now was thinking of revenge and that kept her going.

In the distance was a low rumble of thunder. The air felt electrified.

"Almost there. A few more feet. Just a few more," she repeated over and over. "Then I'll see to it that the old hags really get what's coming to them. They're going to pay through the nose for this." She pushed up another few inches and repeated her oath of revenge.

Then for the first time she heard it, crying out in the night.

It was a scream, sounding like that of a hungry, wild animal. It caused her to cringe and hug close to the side, to press her body into the dirt.

It was unlike anything she had ever heard before. And at that moment she knew that she had to hurry if she was to get away.

Burying her toes into the dirt and moving as if

she were mounting an incredibly steep staircase, she pushed up and up and up. Finally, she
stretched out her hand, and beneath her bleeding fingertips she felt the pit's edge. She rested
her cheek against her arm and sighed with
relief. She had made it.

But when she opened her eyes and looked up,
she drew a jagged breath.

Directly above, intently staring down at her,
were two molten orange eyes. She withdrew her
hand and remained motionless as the animal let
out a howling cry. It threw back its head and
revealed to her the three-inch, curved fangs
lining the inside of its mouth. It was impossible
to avert her eyes or to move. So stunned, so filled
with terror was she that she didn't feel the coal
begin to crumble beneath her toes.

And when the creature lifted a mighty paw
and extended the razor-sharp claws, she still
could not turn away.

With one swift swipe, the claws tore open her
face and slashed quickly across both eyes.

Blinded, with blood streaming down her face
and her nose partially torn off, she felt her body
automatically recoil. The dirt broke loose, and
she slid silently over the ledge, tumbling and
bouncing off the sides to the bottom.

The beast snarled and watched the human
doll drop and fly through the air. It listened for
her screams and heard her body thump when
she hit bottom.

Picking up its paw, the same one it had used to
rip open her face, it licked it clean. Once fin-

ished, it released a triumphant scream, then started down the pit, effortlessly locating the crags and abutments of the stripping hole until it reached bottom where the girl lay dead.

By the time it had reached her body, it started to rain.

TWELVE

THE WEEK OF JUNE 29TH PASSED QUICKLY FOR Tom and Kristen. They finished unpacking, painted the living room and dining room an antique white, then did the master bedroom a pale shade of pink. It was so pale, in fact, that it appeared to be more white than pink. Only when viewed from a certain angle did the slight blush appear, but Kristen was pleased.

Afterwards, Kristen busied herself organizing closets and drawers, wiping the peach window-paned wallpaper in the kitchen and hanging curtains. She also spent time in the garden, planting pink and white petunias, trimming the evergreen shrubs in the front and pruning the few rose bushes that bordered the sunny side of the house.

Tom mowed the lawn with the tractor that had been left in the garage by the previous owner, so instead of taking days to do the three acres, it took only four hours. He was grateful Mr. Simpson's estate had thrown the John Deere into the deal.

On Tuesday of that week, they received a greeting card from Eliza Noman, postmarked from New York. The card was decorated with a flurry of lilacs and roses on the front. Inside was a short note.

Had to leave because of a sick friend. Hope you kids don't miss me. I, of course, miss you. Can't wait to get home.
See you soon.

Eliza

Kristen giggled as she read it. She hadn't missed her one bit. As a matter of fact, she was relieved she didn't have to put up with her.

Tom felt a tinge of regret. Even though he was angry with Eliza for giving him a hard time about going into the woods, he still missed her. He didn't understand it, but he was attracted to her, regardless of her age.

Kristen and Tom enjoyed their time together. Their love blossomed, then bloomed. They became closer than they had been in months, and if anyone would have observed them, he would surely conclude they were newlyweds.

As with all things, the week of renewed love came to an end. On Monday morning, Tom headed for his new job, his very first position at a college. That morning he lingered in his wife's arms at the front door, then reluctantly headed for the college.

His first class, Psychology 101, was at 8:00 o'clock. It wouldn't be a problem. While working toward his doctorate at Penn State, Tom had taught an elementary psychology course, and it had been a breeze.

When the bell in the hall chimed, he left his cramped office and headed for room 310. The classroom was full. He stepped behind the desk and picked up the roster sheet.

"Okay, ladies and gentlemen, let's get started. I'm Dr. Roberts. Now let's find out who you are. When I call your name, grunt or something."

A few chuckles rose from the back of the room. Some of the tension of getting acquainted had been broken. He glanced at the typewritten sheet.

"Tammy Aster."

"Here."

A chunky dark-haired girl with expressive brown eyes replied.

"Jennifer Becker."

A blonde, brown-eyed beauty, whose pink shorts revealed her long, shapely legs, raised her hand. She had on a revealing, bright pink, halter top.

"Aimee Clark."

Tom's heart skipped a beat. Aimee Clark was beautiful. She had long golden hair, huge blue eyes, a flawless complexion and full, pouting lips. She had the body of a goddess, accentuated by the strapless tube top and the tiny white shorts that exposed her long, lean, perfectly sculpted legs.

He swallowed hard, then averted his eyes. He couldn't deny his attraction to her, but he also couldn't allow that attraction to interfere with his job. He was the professor, she the student— and that was the way it had to stay. Otherwise, he'd risk losing his job.

He avoided looking at Aimee Clark and continued to take attendance. When he finished, he wasted no time getting started with the class.

"Since this is an introductory course, some of the topics we're going to cover are the Biological Connections to Behavior, Sensation and Perception, Motivation, Learning and Memory, and Personality, to name a few. Psychology is a fascinating field. I'm sure you'll find the material interesting."

He listened to the few sighs, then continued. "We'll start with the brain."

For the next 60 minutes, he taught them about brain functions and how certain types of brain damage, such as strokes and lesions, effected behavior. By the time the bell outside the door rang, he felt exhausted. He hurried back to his office, grabbed a cold can of Pepsi from the small refrigerator, propped his feet up on the desk and relaxed.

The office would be his haven where he could get away from the rigors of teaching disinterested students. It was small yet cozy. He had a large wooden desk, a soft padded chair and an entire wall of bookcases. The refrigerator was one of the perks of the job. He'd add a coffee machine and a radio and make it his home away from home.

He closed his eyes. A picture of Aimee Clark flashed in his mind. For a moment, he allowed himself to fantasize, then he blocked her out of his thoughts by opening up his notebook and reviewing his notes on Statistics, his second class of the day. The class was at 2:00, and it would be more difficult to teach since most students had a rough time with them.

He finished his soda and threw the can into the green metal wastebasket beside his desk, then started making more notes so that he could present the material easily and efficiently. The last thing he needed was some disgruntled psyche major running to Dean Jensen, the head of the Psychology Department, complaining that Dr. Roberts didn't know what he was doing. It was his first job, and he was on probation for a year. The last thing he wanted was to screw up.

THIRTEEN

AFTER TOM HAD LEFT FOR THE COLLEGE AND AFTER she had finished breakfast dishes, Kristen donned a pair of walking shorts and sneakers and a cool yellow blouse and headed for George Howard's farm. During the past week she had grown acquainted with the area and felt the two mile walk would do her good. Her fear along with her nausea and dizziness had simply vanished, and as she strolled up Willow Road, she found herself enamored by the countryside around her.

Tiny yellow butterflies drifted out of the fields and fluttered around her like petals on the breeze. From a tall tree she could hear the cacophony of what seemed like a thousand birds, and as she watched, robins and sparrows darted repeatedly across her path, settling for only a moment before taking off again. The air was fresh and clean, unpolluted. It smelled of flowers and fresh grass and, occasionally, manure.

In the eastern sky, the sun had risen, a promise of the scorching heat that was yet to come later in the day. Kristen stepped up her pace, wanting to be home before noon. Walking briskly and perspiring, she languished in the patches of shade offered by the full trees that bordered the road.

Within half an hour, she was waving to George Howard, who was perched atop a massive green tractor. She turned into the dirt drive, passing a miniature house-shaped mailbox that read THE HOWARDS across the top. George got down from the tractor and headed toward her, greeting her as she reached the top of the drive.

"Welcome, little lady," he said with a twinkle in his brown eyes. "I was beginning to fear you wouldn't come. Glad to be wrong."

"We've been busy getting settled."

"I bet. Moving must be a chore. Never did it myself, but I don't envy those who have." He looked past her towards the road. "Your hubby isn't with you?"

"He started work today."

"Miss him, huh?"

She nodded.

"Then you walked up alone. Must mean you're getting used to our neck of the woods."

Smiling, she answered, "It's a pretty area."

"Sure is." He breathed deeply as his eyes scanned the horizon. "Hope you've come to meet the missus."

"I have—and for some fresh vegetables, too."

George smiled down at her warmly. "Got a basket out back. Pick what you like. No charge."

"You can't do that. I have to pay you."

"Absolutely not. Neighbors don't pay. Friends neither. Come on, follow me."

They strolled around the side of the old, white shingled house, acting as if they had known each other for years. From this close, Kristen noticed the house was in need of repair. The frames around the long narrow windows, of which there were many, needed painting. The shutters, once a glossy black, were faded to a dark gray. Even the screen porch at the back had tape over the numerous holes. A few yards from the porch was the barn, weathered and beaten. It was a sickly gray and had two immense wooden doors that appeared to be falling off their hinges. To one side of the door she saw a few wide brush strokes where someone had started painting the barn red, then apparently changed his mind. Coming from inside the barn were a series of cackles and squawks.

George swung open the squeaky screen door leading up to the porch, wiping his muddy boots on the knobbed rubber mat before going up the steps.

"Rosie," he called, his voice excited. "Rosie, we have company, so get yourself presentable."

"I'm always presentable, George Howard," a small voice called out from inside. "Now you just bring our company in."

He turned to Kristen and winked. "Okay, here we come." He touched Kristen's elbow and ushered her onto the porch, then went to the door leading into the house and nudged her inside.

Rose Howard sat in a motorized wheelchair near a sunny lace-curtained window. She was lovely.

"Look who's here." He pushed Kristen farther inside. "This here's our new neighbor, Christy . . . Christine . . . um . . ."

"Kristen. Kristen Roberts. It's nice to meet you, Mrs. Howard," she said as she approached the woman and extended her hand. "Oh, I'm so happy to meet you, too, Kristen," she said as she clasped Kristen's hand between her hands. "Please do me a favor, though, and call me Rose."

She smiled at the 60-year-old woman who indeed was lovely. Rose had chestnut hair with streaks of glittering silver; it was permed short and curly. Her eyes were brown and sparkled with a zest for life, and she had a tiny nose with just a slight bulbous appearance at the very end.

On her lap was a lacy bundle from which dangled a long thread leading to a ball of white thread. Tucked into the ball was a thin crochet hook. Kristen couldn't help but look at the wheelchair, the metal spokes glinting in the sunlight. Beneath the mint green house dress and pink slippers, she surmised by the condition of the woman's twisted hands that the frail Mrs. Howard was riddled with arthritis.

"Please sit down," Rose Howard said, her gnarled fingers struggling to tuck her crochet work into a pocket alongside the wheelchair.

"What are you working on?" Kristen asked. "It's beautiful."

"Oh, this?" Rose said, picking up the delicate handwork and displaying it. "I'm crocheting a doily. I love doing all kinds of needlework. It helps keep these old fingers from getting stiff."

Kristen studied the doily. Its intricacy amazed her. Creating something so lacy from a ball of thread fascinated her. When she was a little girl, her Aunt Helen had taught her the basics of crochet, but she had never pursued it.

"Would you like me to teach you?" Rose asked. "It's very relaxing, and it's fun, too. An added bonus is that when you finish a piece, you have something beautiful to show off."

Kristen nodded and handed the doily to Rose.

"Good. We'll get together next week. Now, I bet you'd like a cool glass of homemade lemonade." Rose put the doily inside the wheelchair's pocket, then pressed a button on the arm of her chair and swung around to face the refrigerator.

"Rosie makes the best lemonade in the state," George bragged, hurrying to beat his wife to the refrigerator door. "I'll serve. You enjoy your guest."

Rose smiled up at him and hit the buttons again, swinging around, then moving toward the kitchen table. One of the ladder back pine chairs had been placed against the wall so that her chair could fit easily by the table. "Make sure you use the better glasses, dear. The blue ones

112

with the frosty white flowers."

"Yes, ma'am," he said looking past his wife and winking at Kristen once again.

Kristen smiled back at him. When she first had met him, she knew she liked him. Today she liked him even more. As for his wife, she simply adored the woman. There was a gentleness, a kindness, a cheerfulness that was contagious. "Please don't go through too much trouble on my account." She felt guilty watching George bustle around the room.

"No trouble," he said.

"None at all," Rose chimed. "I'm just tickled pink you came. We don't get many visitors too often out here." She hit the buttons again and darted to the pine hutch against the wall. She retrieved a variety of floral tins, took out a blue plate and filled it with cookies—chocolate chip, oatmeal, peanut butter and double fudge. Holding the tray on her lap, she crossed the kitchen slowly, then placed the plate in front of Kristen. George served the lemonade.

It was tangy yet sweet, and it had a distinctive orange flavor mingled with the lemons. The cookies were luscious, and she found herself unable to refuse a second, then a third and even a fourth. While she munched on the chewy treats, Rose and George divulged tidbits about their life. The farm had belonged to his father, and they were married for 40 years. They had two daughters—one lived in Harrisburg, the other in Los Angeles—and they had four grandchildren, three boys and a girl. George expressed dismay that he had no son to take over the farm, but he hoped someday a grandson would show some interest. Rose also was raised on a farm. She met her husband at a church social, but they couldn't marry until she was 20 because she had to care for her sick mother.

Kristen told them about herself, her family and Tom. She confided her fears about moving to the country, and her concern about Scott Benson and the other missing children. Rose and George also expressed their concern, but had nothing to add about the strange disappearances.

But when she mentioned Eliza Noman, they bristled.

"It's not good for you and Tom to get involved with her. She's a strange woman. You'd do best to stay away," George warned.

Rose's face clouded, and she appeared disturbed. "Please, Kristen, she's not a very nice woman."

"Well, she seems to take to Tom more than to me. Frankly, I don't care for her. She's awfully nosey, but maybe that's because she's lonely," Kristen said.

"Nosey? Lonely? Simpson thought she was more than that, and so do I."

"You mean the Simpson who owned our house? Eliza told us an awful story about that poor man being found dead in the woods from wasp bites. Just thinking about it gives me the creeps. I'm never going in there."

George nodded, grimly. "Good girl. It's no place for a city girl who's not used to the dangers of the forest."

Kristen agreed, wholeheartedly, but since George had brought up Mr. Simpson's opinion of Eliza, she had to know more. "So what did Mr. Simpson say about Eliza? I guess he knew her well, since he owned the house for ten years."

A scowl formed on George's face, and he shook his head. "Simpson didn't say all that much. He just thought she was odd."

For some reason, she felt George was keeping something back about Eliza which disturbed her. It wasn't only Simpson and George who thought Eliza odd; she did, too. She wanted to probe deeper, but before she had a chance to say a word, Rose broke in.

"Let me show you my home. I get so little chance to show off George's handiwork."

Kristen smiled, then took the grand tour.

Before leaving the kitchen, Rose pointed out that George had made the pine kitchen set and the matching hutch and jelly cupboard. He also made the drop-leaf coffee table and end tables in the living room.

Kristen loved the hurricane lamps, the burnt orange Early American furniture, and the delicate floor-length lace curtains. The multicolored braided rugs also caught her eye, but the most exquisite piece of furniture was the handmade chest in the bedroom. It was stenciled by George with violet curlicues and hearts and flowers.

Rose's handmade doilies and needlepoint pictures were displayed everywhere. Kristen found the skill of her arthritic hands impressive.

The Howards were good, earthy people who made her feel comfortable, and when she finally left, sometime after noon, she felt sad.

As she gave Rose a hug, she promised to visit often. It was people like the Howards who would make her stay in Burnwell bearable.

FOURTEEN

WHEN KRISTEN RETURNED FROM THE HOWARDS, she knew Eliza Noman was back from her trip. Even though she hadn't seen her, she sensed her presence. It felt like a thick blanket covering her, shrouding her, trying to smother her, and as she made her way up to the house, her arms filled with bags of peppers, beans and tomatoes, she could swear that she was being watched. She looked up at the tremendous Victorian and studied each window but saw no one.

Overcome by a feeling of unease, she hurried into the house, her stomach churning, her shoulders bundling into knots. Obviously she wasn't the only one who thought Eliza was weird. Rose did, George did, and so did Mr. Simpson. Sooner or later, she would make

George tell her everything he knew about the old woman.

She intended to visit often. Spending time with them would help her adjust to Burnwell. They had been like a soothing tonic.

As she started dinner, she imagined sharing lazy summer cookouts, autumn harvests, snowy winters and, of course, Christmas with her new friends.

While she had been walking home, dodging frantic bumblebees and snowflake butterflies, the feeling of well-being was all pervasive, until she realized that Eliza had come home. Then the same odd foreboding returned.

But she didn't want to think about it. She was content to concentrate on people like Rose and George. So as she continued to prepare dinner, she relived her visit with them while eagerly awaiting Tom's return from his first day at the college.

Later, during early evening, she and Tom sat on the porch sipping lemony iced tea from huge 16-ounce tumblers. They stared out at the haze covering the back lawn and at the forest bordering their land, saying little, just enjoying the nearness of each other. Strong portents drifted and lay suspended in the humid air, portents that Kristen tried to dismiss. When she couldn't, she tried to understand them.

Then she did.

Eliza Noman appeared at the bottom of the steps leading up to the porch. Her presence made every hair, every nerve in Kristen's body stand on edge. Why? She had no idea, but she wished the old woman would keep her distance.

"Hi, kids. Thought I'd stop by to let you know I'm back." The old lady was dressed in a denim skirt and a blue and white striped pullover, with the hightop Reeboks on her feet.

Kristen noticed her arms hugged a box filled with apothecary-type bottles and colorfully wrapped cubes. Her first reaction was to get up and go inside to avoid her, but that would be rude, and the last thing Kristen Roberts could ever be was rude to anyone.

Feeling obligated to say something, Kristen swallowed hard. "Hope you had a nice trip," she said, trying to make conversation.

"Yes, I did. And how have you two been doing? I bet you're all settled in."

"Uh-huh." Kristen took a sip of tea. She couldn't understand why the woman felt it was okay to drop by at anytime. Surely she had to notice she wasn't welcome.

"Did you get my card?" Eliza Noman asked, her brow furrowing with concern. Though she directed her question to Tom, he didn't give her a single look.

"Yes, we did," Kristen answered, feeling the strain of trying to make conversation with someone she detested. "I hope your friend's illness wasn't too serious."

"Unfortunately it was—and still is."

"Really? What's wrong with her?"

"Why don't you open the screen door and let me come in so I can tell you. I'm too old to be standing out here like this."

Kristen blushed. She and Tom were being rude, but still she regretted asking about the old woman's friend. She knew that once she allowed her onto the porch, they'd never get rid of her. And to think she had been looking forward to a quiet evening with her husband alone.

"I brought you some special things."

Feeling embarrassed, she got up and opened the door. Eliza Noman hurried onto the porch. She placed the bottles on top of the mesh table that was positioned between the chairs and sat down heavily in the lounger that Kristen had been using, right next to Tom.

Exasperated, Kristen sighed, then unfolded a small lawn chair and placed it directly opposite Eliza. She watched the old woman study Tom.

For a few moments there was silence, broken only by the chatter of the many birds nesting in the surrounding trees. Suddenly Eliza leaned over toward Tom and placed her hand on his bare arm. He pulled away and rubbed his arm briskly, still avoiding looking at her.

"What's wrong, Thomas?" Her voice quavered, her eyes on the verge of tears. "Have I done something to upset you?"

He continued to rub his forearm as he turned to her, opening his mouth as if to speak, but before the first syllable even came out, she hushed him.

She said, "I know. You're angry because I scolded you about going into the woods."

He gave her a wry smile.

120

"Oh, Thomas, I was only concerned for you. Please don't be angry." Pulling a yellow lace handkerchief from the pocket of her denim skirt, she dabbed at her eyes.

Kristen had the impression that the old woman was playacting. She saw no tears, not even one.

But Tom melted, and Kristen watched as he did. His jaw relaxed, his eyes softened, and a tender smile creased his lips. He fell for the act. "No need to cry," he said, patting her hand, then retrieving his own and massaging his fingers, just as Kristen had done the first time she had touched her. She knew Tom felt the same ice.

"I'm not mad at you. I just had a rough day."

"Thank you, Thomas." She pretended to be sobbing. "I don't know what I'd do if you were angry. You're like a son to me."

Since neither paid any attention to Kristen, she sat back and rolled her eyes. She shook her head and thought, What a performance. This lady belongs in the theater. She suppressed a laugh that was building inside her.

"Look what I brought for you," Eliza said, excitedly. She reached for the box on the table and picked out a bar of what appeared to be soap, wrapped in orange paper. "And for you, too, Kristen. I hope you enjoy these as much as I do. They're all handmade." She handed Tom the neatly wrapped bar, then also handed one to Kristen which was wrapped in green.

Kristen waved the soap under her nose. Tom did the same. Hers smelled like cucumbers. But there was another smell, a strange underlying odor, barely noticeable, that she couldn't identify.

"Smells great," Tom said and handed the soap to his wife.

She brought it to her nose and took a whiff. It had a spicy fragrance but also a strange odor beneath the spice. She smelled them both again. Yes, there definitely was a slightly offensive odor to both.

"I'm glad you like it. I was so unsure about the fragrance," Eliza said to Tom. She reached into the cardboard box and pulled out one of the apothecary jars. "Look, there's aftershave and cologne to go with it."

Tom took the bottle from her hand and popped off the top. "Spicy. I like that." He recapped the bottle and placed it inside the box. "Thanks. That was really nice of you." He smiled warmly at the old woman before asking, "Care for a tall glass of iced tea?"

"Wonderful." She released a shrill cackle.

After he got up and went inside to the kitchen, the old woman turned her attention to Kristen. "How do you like yours?"

"It's nice. Reminds me of cucumbers." She forced a smile. She didn't like it at all and probably would never use it, but there was no point in telling her that. Sometimes little white lies are necessary. They hurt no one.

Eliza Noman giggled. "Of course it does, dear. It's made from cucumbers. Gives you a radiant complexion." She took two bottles from the box. "Here's a bath oil to soak away the tension and an after-bath splash, too.''

Kristen smelled the contents of the bottles. The bath oil was a green liquid, thick and rich, made from cucumbers, and once again the faint odor beneath stung her nose. ''Thank you,'' she said. ''It wasn't necessary to br—''

''Hush. It was. I'm just delighted to have such good neighbors. I wanted to do something for both of you.''

Kristen smiled. She put the bottles on the table. As she did, she couldn't help but notice that none of the items were labeled. Curious about their origin, she asked, ''Where on earth did you find such unique scents? I really would like to know in case I want more.'' She was lying though she didn't know why, but at the time it seemed appropriate. Something about the toiletries bothered her.

''Don't worry, dear, I can get more. And it won't cost you a thing.''

''Really?''

''Yes. A dear friend of mine makes them.''

''The friend who's sick?''

''No. Another.'' She paused. Kristen could tell she was becoming annoyed. ''You see, my friends and I have our own specialties. One makes bath products, another scented candles. I make potpourri, herb wreaths and luscious liquors. We trade.''

''I suppose it's like a hobby.''

''Yes, you could say it's a hobby.''

''And the friend you visited, what does she make?''

''Agatha never did crafts.''

"You sound disappointed."

"I am, but it doesn't matter. I still love her."

"You said her illness was serious."

Eliza Noman nodded, then stared past her into the woods. "She had a malignancy that had to be removed."

"Oh, no! Will she be all right?" She felt a wave of shock. A malignancy reminded her too much of her own father and his death from cancer.

"I don't think she has much time left."

"I am sorry."

"I am, too."

At that moment Kristen was sure the old woman would burst into tears. She could sense her sorrow and grief as if it were her own. But when the old woman smiled a wry, almost wicked smile, Kristen was baffled.

"Let's not talk of such sadness. Surely there must be something else to discuss," Eliza Noman said.

That was the second time she refused to talk about something painful. The first had been her lost love, Louis. Maybe she didn't dwell on things that made life difficult.

But what about the smile? She had done the same when she had spoken of her mother. Maybe the old woman was senile. She certainly appeared old enough for that.

Kristen just couldn't understand the woman. She was so unlike the Howards. And as she mentioned her visit to them, she couldn't help but sense that Eliza Noman disapproved. She wondered if the relationship between her and

Rose and George was strained.

It was a relief when Tom returned with the iced tea along with a bowl of chips. She was uncomfortable talking to Eliza and felt grateful when he told her about his day at the college. Kristen sat watching Eliza's interest and listening to her husband's details of his first day for the second time.

It seemed strange that the old woman hung on his every word and how she looked at him with such adoration. Maybe she viewed him as a son, but she looked at him like a lover.

Soon after, to Kristen's surprise, the old woman said good-night, even over Tom's protests. Before she left, she invited them to dinner, insisting she owed them a meal and would be crushed if they refused. They set the date for Saturday.

Tom promised they'd be there, then hugged her gently as if afraid to break her brittle bones. At that moment, by the look in his eyes, Kristen knew he had forgiven the old woman for her humiliating tirade in the woods. She also saw something else, a relationship that she didn't know existed previously. There was an unmistakable love that seemed to surround each of them like a cloud. Even though she knew that she shouldn't feel threatened—after all, the woman was old enough to be his grandmother —she did.

And as she watched Tom escort her to her home, she couldn't keep from wondering what it was about Eliza that upset her. She was old and fragile. She was trying her damndest to be neighborly. Sure, she had an eye for Tom, but it posed no threat.

Maybe it was Kristen herself. Maybe the paranoia about moving to the country had generalized and now included Eliza Noman.

Hell, she had no reason to dislike her—but she did. Damn, she disliked her more than anyone she had ever met. But why?

She picked up the gifts and went inside. There was no reason to drive herself insane about the woman. It just happened that way. Some people you liked; some you didn't.

It was a personality thing, she supposed, and there was nothing you could do about it. When two personalities didn't mix, it was just tough luck. Nothing more to it than that.

She deposited the toiletries in the bathroom closet, but she had no intention of using them. As for Tom, he could decide for himself.

Afterwards she showered and settled in for the night, Eliza and her gifts already forgotten.

FIFTEEN

ON WEDNESDAY OF THAT WEEK, TOM RETURNED home late from work. Worried that he had gotten into an accident, Kristen rushed outside as soon as she saw the New Yorker turn into the drive. When he pulled up to the garage, she saw he had a sly, devious look in his eyes and a grin on his face that seemed to say, "I know something you don't know."

After he got out of the car, she kissed him and hugged him, glad she had been mistaken about an accident, glad he had returned to her in one piece. Tom laughed as he gently removed her arms from around his neck.

"I have a surprise for you," he said. "Now close your eyes and don't open them until I tell you to."

She did as he asked. Listening to him open the

car door and hearing him hum, she knew he was up to something and could hardly wait to find out. She sensed him coming back toward her, then felt him nudge her arm with something smooth and hard. Her hand rose and touched a sharp corner like the edge of a cardboard box.

"You can open your eyes now."

She did. Then she released a squeal of delight. She had been right about the cardboard box, but it was what it contained that sent her into giggles.

"Tom, it's adorable. For me? Thank you." She kissed him hard on the mouth and took the two month-old collie from the box and cuddled it. She nuzzled her nose in its soft, downy fur, then held the dog up and away from her. "What should I name him?

"Her." Tom shrugged. "It's up to you."

Scratching the back of the animal's neck, she rattled off different names in her mind—Lady, Duchess, Lassie—and then it came to her. Amber. She would name her Amber because of her golden fur.

The dog was precious and cuddly and wonderful. Her long pointed snout had a streak of white running between the eyes. Coming up from beneath the dog's jaw and down the chest and belly was more of the white fluff. The tips of her paws were also trimmed with white. Kristen adored the little bundle of fur.

"Where did you get her?" she asked. "She's so perfect."

"One of the faculty had a notice on the

bulletin board. He was giving them away, and I thought we needed a dog.''

"I'm glad you thought so." She placed the puppy on the manicured lawn. Once more she hugged and kissed and thanked Tom. They both joined the dog on the grass while it romped around them, staying there for almost an hour until dinner.

Later that night, after they made love, Kristen lay in bed thinking how wonderful life was. She was getting accustomed to the area and the near perfect life they were now living. For the first time she felt glad they had moved.

But what she didn't know was that the near perfection she now enjoyed, the tenderness and the love of her marriage, was soon to end.

What awaited Tom and Kristen, especially Kristen, was disaster.

SIXTEEN

WEARING A WHITE COTTON SUNDRESS AND LOW
heeled white leather sandals, her hair clipped
back from her face with two pearl barrettes,
Kristen walked arm in arm with Tom toward the
Noman house. It was Saturday night, the night
of the big dinner. Kristen had been nervous and
reluctant to go. She had reservations about
leaving Amber alone, locked in the laundry
room, but with Tom's coaxing and pleading and
reminding her that not going would be rude, she
finally agreed. No matter how hard she tried to
like the old woman, she still felt uneasy in her
presence, but since they were neighbors, she
would force herself to associate.

She turned and looked at Tom, admiring his
crisp white slacks and his powder blue short
sleeve shirt. He looked so handsome it made her

feel like a princess being escorted to a ball. "You look wonderful," she said, "like a prince."

"Why, thank you, my lady. You look kinda wonderful yourself."

Kristen giggled. She felt a small wet splat on her shoulder, then another on her nose. "I just felt two raindrops. We'd better hurry."

She looked to the west where heavy black clouds rolled across the sky, getting closer with each second. The wind picked up and whipped through her hair. The towering pines that rimmed the front of both properties swayed and ruffled like huge feather dusters planted in the earth. The woods looked darker and more ominous than she had ever seen them. From deep inside the forest came a low whooshing sound as the winds approached gale strength.

All day the local weatherman had predicted a violent thunderstorm caused by a fast moving cold front approaching from the west that would collide with the humid, hot air that had been trapped in a stationary front for the entire week. At first, Kristen welcomed the promise of relief from the oppressive heat, but as the storm approached, she became frightened of its intensity.

Suddenly, a jagged streak of lightning flashed, followed by a loud clap of thunder, Large raindrops pelted her, and they started to run, the cold rain stinging her bare arms.

Holding hands, running, darting between flower beds that turned Eliza Noman's lawn into an obstacle course, they laughed as they tried to outrun the downpour. Around them the flowers had closed their petals, and those that were hit by the huge drops lay flat, some stems already broken.

Kristen hopped up onto the porch, brushing the rain from her shoulders, then shaking her auburn curls and fluffing them. Tom joined her, laughing and gasping at the same time. "We just made it," he said.

"I think you're right," said Eliza Noman.

Turning away from the storm, Kristen looked behind her. The old woman was standing on the other side of the blue wooden screen door, grinning.

"Come inside. It's not safe to stand outside when it's lightning."

No sooner had the word passed her lips when another clap of thunder boomed, causing Kristen to jump nearly six inches off the wooden porch. She held her small hands against her chest as if to quiet her pounding heart and turned to see another blinding streak of lightning flash downward and disappear behind the trees. The accompanying boom was almost instantaneous. She heard a crackle and a sizzle and realized that something nearby had been hit. She grabbed Tom's arm and yanked him toward the door. "She's right. We better get inside."

When Eliza Noman pushed open the door, Kristen was taken by how lovely she looked. She was dressed in a pink, short sleeve, silk brocade shirtwaist. A large round garnet brooch with dozens of tiny stones was pinned to the "V" at her neck. She wore earrings to match, and on the index finger of her right hand was a ring of the same design, covering the finger to the first knuckle.

The old woman stepped aside as Tom held open the door and allowed Kristen to enter. The strong, sweet floral aroma of gardenias stung and burned her nose as she passed her. Obviously, the woman had drenched herself with perfume. Kristen tried to avoid getting too close as she stepped nimbly into the kitchen.

What she had expected to see upon entering Eliza Noman's home was a coal stove, no kitchen cabinets and maybe a few old dilapidated sideboards but, instead, she saw that the entire kitchen had been remodeled—and quite recently, too.

A pint-sized Litton microwave oven sat on top of the white and gold speckled countertop. There was a Jenn-Air range and an almond double-door Westinghouse refrigerator. The oak cabinets had glass doors that had been etched with butterflies and roses. The entire room had been decorated in earth tones—beiges, ecrues and almonds—set off by blue flowered wallpaper that covered the walls from the ceiling to the oak, narrow-slatted paneling that started halfway down the wall and ended at the floor. The floor was covered with dark blue wall-to-wall carpeting.

In the center of the room stood a round, light oak table with ladder back chairs. An almond vinyl tablecloth was on the table, and a 12-inch cobalt blue pitcher, filled with gigantic daisies, stood in the middle. A matching sugar and creamer had been placed to one side.

A series of wooden shelves had been mounted on the far wall where blue and amethyst bottles, containing liquids, had been placed in neat rows. Kristen stepped closer.

"They're my homemade vinegars, dear," said Eliza Noman as she moved toward Kristen. "On this shelf," she waved her hand toward a series of cobalt blue and amethyst containers, "I keep my dried herbs." She moved to a corner shelf. "These are my salad dressings. I make them myself with things from my garden."

Intrigued, Kristen studied the bottles and jars, then smiled. "I guess they come in handy."

"Of course. They taste good, too."

"I'm sure they do," Kristen answered, turning to face Tom who was also inspecting the jars and their contents. Kristen scanned the large kitchen and concluded that there had to be at least 100 homemade specialties. They were not only on shelves, but were also jammed against the back of the countertop, inside some of the cabinets and inside the oak hutch against the wall. Another of the old woman's obsessions, she thought. What on earth did one do with so much vinegar and salad dressing?

"Believe me, I use them all."

Kristen nearly jumped out of her sandals. It was as if she had just read her mind. "I bet you do."

"You'll see how they can spice up a meal very shortly. Especially my chicken Wellington."

So that was what she smelled, what caused her mouth to water. It smelled luscious. Suddenly she was ravenous and wished she had had a snack before they had left. She prayed dinner wasn't far off. The old woman had said seven o'clock, and it was now ten minutes before the hour. The worst thing would be if she kept them waiting and salivating for any length of time.

At Eliza Noman's request, they followed her through the hallway leading toward the front of the house. The walls were cluttered with photographs of every size and shape, framed in ornate silver and brass. Most of the pictures were black and white and were of people of a bygone era. The few that were in color seemed to be from the 1950's. Kristen stopped and examined them, but before she had the opportunity to get a good look, Tom, who was coming up behind her, placed his hands around her waist and gently pushed her forward. She glanced over her shoulder to see him mouthing the words, "Don't be so nosey."

She turned up her nose at him and continued into the living room.

It was as if she had stepped over the threshold of time and catapulted back 100 years. "Oh, how beautiful," she cried, surprising herself by the emphasis of her own voice. "Miss Noman, this room is magnificent."

"Thank you, dear. But I do wish you'd call me Eliza. All my friends do."

Kristen smiled and nodded, glad that not only Tom was allowed the privilege of addressing her by her first name. She strolled around the room which reminded her of a more romantic time. It gave her a warm, comfortable feeling.

Beneath the long bay window was a tufted cranberry couch with gold fringe; a matching loveseat was directly opposite with a mahogany coffee table separating the two. There were rose and pink tapestry side chairs on either side of the mantled fireplace, and a similar footstool was placed before one, trimmed in scrolled mahogany. On the end tables, also mahogany, were domed crystal oil lamps that had teardrop prisms dangling from their scalloped shades.

The hardwood floor, polished to a lustrous glow, had a fringed burgundy rug placed in the center. Figurines, Hummels and Laddro, lined scrolled shelves along one wall. On a long table beneath the side window stood gleaming silver vases, at least eight inches tall. She picked one up and found it was made of solid silver. On the other end of the same table was a black marble sculpture of a cat. To Kristen, it seemed out of place, belonging more in an Egyptian tomb rather than in a Victorian living room.

Turning from the cat, she scanned the entire room. In every corner, in every nook and cranny, and on every table and shelf stood something valuable—brilliant diamond-cut crystal ash-trays, vases and bowls that brimmed with flowers and potpourri, porcelain flowers consisting of an iris, a pink rose, a white lily, an orchid. There was a cranberry colored hurricane lamp, a tea light, and a swan-shaped candy dish. They appeared to be a set. The entire room was an antique collector's paradise.

Floral oil paintings in various shades of pink and in ornate gold frames hung on the walls.

Above the polished, wooden-framed fireplace, on whose mantel stood two tremendous crystal and brass lamps, was a portrait of a young man and woman. Kristen stepped closer. She studied the dark-haired man in the portrait, his ruffled shirt, the black waistcoat, his aquiline nose, the sapphire eyes. He looked familiar, and she sensed that she knew him—or knew of him.

Then she focused her attention on the woman seated in front of him. She had green luminous eyes and thick golden hair that tumbled to her shoulders in soft waves. She wore an emerald green gown, trimmed at the neck and at the cuffs with a band of white fur.

The woman seemed familiar also. She definitely knew her. It was the eyes. Never had she seen eyes so green until she met Eliza Noman. Was this Eliza in her youth?

"That's you, isn't it?"

Eliza smiled softly. "Yes, it is. I was very, very young at the time."

"And beautiful, too," Tom added as he stepped closer to the portrait.

Just then Kristen felt her heart flutter. She looked at the man in the picture again and looked at Tom. They had the same color and curl of hair, the same dreamy blue eyes and almost the same nose. If the man had had a mustache there would be little difference between them. She studied the portrait more closely and concluded that the one major difference was that Tom was taller and more muscular. For some reason that made her feel better.

But still it was unnerving to see two men,

unrelated—born how many years apart? a century?—resemble each other so much.

"I see you've noticed," Eliza said, breaking into Kristen's thoughts. She stood beside her and stared up at the portrait. "I saw the resemblance the first day I met Tom."

Kristen said nothing.

"What resemblance?" Tom asked, looking first at his wife and then at Eliza. "What are you talking about?"

"The resemblance between you and the man in the picture," Eliza answered.

Tom looked back to the portrait and appeared to study it for a minute. "I sure don't see it."

"It's there," she said. "Am I right, Kristen?"

Kristen nodded. She found the whole thing kind of spooky. In one way it alarmed her, but in another, it explained why Eliza was so attracted to Tom. She recalled when they met and how they seemed unable to take their eyes off each other. She was sure she had felt electricity pass between them that first day. It had given her an eerie feeling then, but not quite as eerie as now.

It was only coincidence, she told herself. Hadn't she heard that each person had a double? Well, she had just viewed her husband's. But who was this man?

In a whisper, as if afraid to speak, she asked, "Who is he?"

Eliza turned away from the portrait and looked at Kristen for a moment. Her eyes were misting over as she released a sigh and replied, "That was Louis, the man I told you about."

"Oh," Kristen whispered.

"He died many years ago."

Kristen said nothing. If she believed in reincarnation, which of course she did not, she'd swear Tom *was* Louis. But that was nonsense. She had been brought up as a Catholic and been taught there was an afterlife, not reincarnation. Nevertheless, the similarity in appearance certainly led to some interesting speculation.

Finally Eliza broke the silence that had temporarily claimed all three. She walked briskly to the hallway that led into the dining room and returned wheeling a brass oval serving cart filled with bottles of assorted liquors on the bottom shelf. On the top shelf was a glass pitcher, three delicate crystal glasses and a cut crystal ice bucket.

"I made martinis. I hope you'll join me in one before dinner. We can toast to my new neighbors and friends—and Thomas's success at the college."

Kristen and Tom nodded in unison. Although she would have preferred a glass of white wine, a martini sounded like a good idea. The portrait was very disturbing and caused the muscles in the back of her neck to knot up. Here was one more mystery surrounding the life of Eliza Noman with which to contend. She needed to relax.

She sipped the drink which soon caused the desired effect. Sitting back on the couch and sinking deep into the plump cushions, she found herself getting a little light-headed and hungrier. Eliza sat with Tom on the loveseat, chatting once again about his job. Then the phone on the Chippendale table began to ring.

The old woman stared at it in anger, but instead of answering it in their presence, she excused herself and scurried off in the direction of the kitchen. Kristen looked at Tom and shrugged. He did the same to her. They sat for some time before getting up and treating themselves to another drink.

"If she doesn't hurry with dinner, I think I'm going to get drunk or sick from the booze," she whispered, then giggled before popping a green olive into her mouth.

Tom also went for the olives. "I agree. I'm starved. Maybe you shouldn't have any more to drink. You know you have no tolerance for the stuff, especially on an empty stomach." He paused and ate a few more olives. "Maybe I shouldn't either. The last thing I need is a damn headache."

Feeling giddy, Kristen wandered through the living room, still sipping her drink, still admiring and maybe envying Eliza's treasures, but she avoided looking at the portrait. She walked into the front hall and peered into the foyer. An ornate brass mirror hung on the wall. The floors, also hardwood, were polished to the deepest glow. The front door, leading to the massive porch, was beautiful, a frosted oval glass set into a satiny wood and etched with flowers. From beyond the door she could hear the steady drum of rain and see the outside gloom.

A few feet from where she stood, halfway between herself and the door, were a pair of etched, frosted louvre doors with the same floral pattern. Curious, she raised herself up on her toes and tiptoed across the bare floor toward them.

"Where the hell are you going?" Tom's hoarse whisper called to her.

She turned to him and put an index finger to her lips. "Shhhhh." She continued down the hall.

"Kris, come back here!" His voice sounded a little louder. "Kris! Jesus," he said, louder still.

She kept going. When she reached the doors, she saw that they had been left ajar, and she slipped into the room without a sound.

The walls were lined with books, and she stepped closer to see what taste Eliza had in literature. What she saw surprised her—Balzac, Shakespeare, Dickens, Poe, Hawthorne, all packed tightly into the recessed wooden shelves. There had to be well over 200 books.

Nearby was a burgundy leather easy chair, a brass floor lamp beside it. On the opposite wall was a matching loveseat. Positioned in a small alcove created by the triple windows, curtained in lace and heavy cranberry drapes, was a rectangular mahogany desk. Kristen stepped closer to the desk and examined the cluttered desk top. There was the usual—phone bill, light bill, a statement from Central Bank—but the unusual also stood out and caught her eyes. An ornate brass inkwell, a feather fountain pen and a letter opener that resembled a stiletto with a pearl and ruby handle were scattered on the desk top.

Then there was the book, the size of a sheet of typing paper, a half-inch thick and bound in black leather and trimmed in gold. Each corner had a small gold filigree sleeve, and she wondered if it was karat gold. She looked for a title or an author, but found neither. She reached to pick it up, hoping to examine it more closely, but quickly pulled back her hand. The damn thing scared her.

She stared at it for a moment, then with the tip of her index finger, she flipped it open. Its heavy leather-bound cover made a thump on the desk. She held her breath and looked at the door, sure Eliza had heard.

When no one came, she began to study the single loose-leaf page before her; it was hand-written. Squinting in the dim light, she saw the signature of Agatha Crenshaw at the bottom of the page written in the strangest shade of ink she had ever seen—a crusty reddish brown. She tried to focus on the text, but she couldn't make it out. The words were foreign and unusual. She couldn't even pronounce them. She mouthed each syllable as a child would when learning to read.

"Sue . . . dom . . . sa," she said, pausing to repeat it in her mind. "Suedomsa," she said aloud. She continued to struggle with the first sentence. "*Suedomsa te lisserg eret timeorp oge.*"

She shook her head and looked outside at the pouring rain. She repeated the sentence. It still didn't make any sense. What language was it? It wasn't French or German or Italian. It wasn't Latin either. She had been exposed to Latin as a girl at the Catholic school she had attended.

She flipped to the next page, hoping it was more readable. It wasn't.

"*Suedomsa te reficul eret timeorp oge.*" Except for the third word being different, the lines of the second page were identical. But the words meant nothing to her. Eliza's signature was scrawled at the bottom with the same ugly reddish brown ink.

She turned the page. It had a list of names scrawled on it. The writing appeared to be Eliza's. Beside the names were addresses:

Louise Kacher—Black Mountain, PA
Jenny Kacher—Black Mountain, PA
Becky Tocks—Los Angeles, CA

She scanned the next page and the next, until she reached the end. Each page contained a list of names and addresses of people from all over the country, from all over the world. It certainly was an odd address book. The names were not listed in alphabetical order or in any order that she could tell.

Puzzled, she turned back to the first two pages, laying the loose-leaf page with Agatha Crenshaw's signature beside the bound page containing Eliza's signature.

What did it mean? What—

"Where's Kristen?" The voice of Eliza Noman shrieked. "Thomas, where is she?" Kristen could hear the panic in the old woman's voice.

"Huh?" Tom sounded groggy. "I guess she got lost looking for a bathroom."

143

Thank you, Tom. She tucked the loose page inside the book and closed it gently, making sure nothing appeared disturbed.

"A bathroom? Why didn't she ask me? Which way did she go?"

"That way." Tom sounded less groggy.

Picking up her drink, Kristen slipped through the narrow opening between the doors just as Eliza stomped into the hall. The woman was livid.

"Where have you been?" she screamed. Her blazing eyes bored through Kristen.

Frightened by the woman's appearance, Kristen stumbled over her own words, "I-I-I-"

"Speak up!"

"I was looking f-for a b-bathroom." The sight of Eliza terrified her. She had never seen anyone so angry. Her eyes were dark and piercing, her mouth snarled as if she were a wild animal.

"Why didn't you just ask?"

Kristen took a ragged breath and let it out slowly. There was no reason to be so afraid of this old bat. And who was she to talk about asking permission to go through one's house? Didn't she snoop through all they owned on the first day they arrived? Yes. A thousand times yes. "You were on the phone. I didn't want to disturb you."

Eliza Noman narrowed her eyes and looked like a cat ready to pounce. Kristen knew the old woman suspected she was lying. Then with a grunt, she turned from her and focused on the partially open louvre doors. "Were you in there?" she growled.

"No." Kristen avoided the woman's fiery glare. "I just peeked inside. I thought it might be the powder room."

"Hmmph." Eliza Noman stomped toward the small room, flung open the doors and then went inside.

As Kristen watched her inspect the room, she noticed the woman's fury mount. It seemed as if she was making a big fuss over nothing. Or was she? Was there something in that room that she wanted no one to see? Was it the book? Automatically, Kristen's eyes moved to the desk where it lay.

"Were you snooping around my desk?"

"No! I told you I was looking for the powder room!" Her denial lacked sincerity, and she suspected the woman knew she was lying. What difference did it make if she had read the book? She had no idea what it was about. The damn thing made no sense. It was gibberish.

Eliza Noman took a small gold key from her pocket and unlocked the top drawer of the desk, threw the book inside, slammed the drawer shut and locked it. She checked the lock twice before jamming the key back into her pocket. She remained behind the desk, faced the ceiling with her eyes closed and took several deep breaths, trying to compose herself.

"The powder room is off the kitchen," she said as she approached Kristen, her eyes still dark with anger. "Come. I'll show you. And when you're through you can help bring dinner into the dining room. That is, if you don't mind."

"I don't mind at all."

Embarrassed, Kristen turned and followed the old woman toward the living room where Tom stood silently. As she passed him, he nudged her ribs with his fingertips, then shook his head.

Tom was annoyed with her, Eliza was furious, and she felt ashamed that she had spoiled the evening. As she stepped into the tiny blue powder room, she glanced over her shoulder. Eliza glared at her, and Tom continued to shake his head. She closed the door behind her and sighed.

Getting through dinner was going to be difficult, if not impossible.

Without a sound, Kristen slipped into bed. Beside her, Tom snored lightly. She didn't want to wake him when he was in such a bad mood.

When they returned from Eliza's, he was still annoyed with her. He had lectured her about being a snoop. "You bitched about Eliza snooping, then you do the same thing. If she wanted to give you a tour of the house, she would have offered."

Kristen nodded and agreed she had been wrong, but still, she couldn't understand why Eliza had made such a fuss.

She followed Tom into the laundry room where Amber awaited their return. Tom went straight for the pup. She was so excited to see him, that when he picked her up, she let loose a yellow spray all over his white slacks.

He dropped the dog and yelled, "Pisshead! Look at my pants."

The entire front of his white pants was soiled. Kristen suppressed a giggle.

Exasperated, Tom stripped them off, then threw them at the washer. They hit the side and fell in a heap on the floor. He breathed deeply, then said, "I've got to take another damn shower." He stomped out and up the steps to the bathroom.

Kristen picked up the slacks and pretreated the stains, then decided to let them sit until morning. She hugged Amber and nuzzled her soft fur with her nose, then took her into the kitchen.

She needed some Maalox. Eliza Noman's dinner was tasty, but it was boiling in her stomach. The old woman used entirely too many spices and herbs—on the chicken, in the green beans, in the salad. She overpowered the food, instead of complementing it, and everything, including desert which consisted of vanilla ice cream drowned in homemade liqueur, had a tangy undertaste. Maybe the banana that Eliza and Tom shared was different, but her strawberry was awful.

Even now, hours after dinner, after a large dose of antacid, she lay next to Tom with a queasy stomach, listening to the patter of rain on the roof. She rolled onto her side, pulled the covers up under her chin and curled into a ball. From the condition of her stomach, she expected to have nightmares.

And she did. All night a wild, ferocious beast with sharp, serrated fangs chased her. Then, toward morning, she dreamed of Scott Benson, the boy who had vanished. He showed her his wounds, pleaded for her help and warned her of danger.

Tom's dream was better. A blonde woman with green cabochon eyes and rosebud lips, more beautiful, more exciting than any he had ever met, came to him.

Just before dawn he woke up, panting, out of breath, his shorts stained with semen. He got out of bed, staggered to the dresser drawer for a clean pair of shorts and went into the bathroom to change. Disoriented and not wanting Kris to see, he washed the soiled shorts in the sink. He tried to understand the dream but couldn't. He went back to bed.

Unfortunately, neither told the other of the dreams. If they had, they might have been able to stop the horror that awaited them.

SEVENTEEN

THE RAIN CONTINUED TO FALL, A STEADY DRUM-
beat upon the roof and the parched earth. Eliza
sat in the white wicker rocker near the back
door, certain the girl had been in the room and
had seen the book of names. Troubled, she
twisted and wrung her hands.

She was slipping, getting careless. Never in
her long life had she been so careless. Never.

She had been so excited about Thomas's visit
she had simply forgotten to lock the book away.
Before bed, she had to remember to remove it
from the desk drawer and take it to the attic
where she could store it away in an even safer
place. She couldn't forget, not again.

She stared out into the blackness, the outline
of the tall trees rimming the woods out back;
she listened to the rain and gave its soothing

patter her complete attention until the tension, caused by her own stupidity, flowed from her.

Leaning forward, she caught a glimpse of the Roberts' house, Thomas's house, and smiled.

She took a deep breath then leaned back and began to rock, back and forth, back and forth. Even if the girl had seen the book, she reasoned, the fool would have no understanding of it. Still it was no excuse for her own mistake. Now, more than ever, she would have to be meticulous about such matters. She had no choice, lest she lose it all.

But the evening had gone well, and if it hadn't been for Agatha's intrusive call, it would have gone better. After she realized that Kristen had snooped, it had been difficult to control her rage, to keep her poise in front of Thomas.

The best part of the evening came when she saw his own annoyance with his wife for her insolence. It had been a pleasure to watch Kristen's discomfort.

Nothing could satisfy her more.

Getting up slowly from the rocker, her muscles and joints stiff from age, she shuffled to the far side of the porch and stared at Thomas's house. It was 2:00 A.M. The outline of the house was silhouetted against the black and gray clouds; not a light was on. He was asleep, and so was she. By now both were locked in dreams. Thomas would dream of a woman who looked as Eliza did when she was young, the way she appeared in the portrait, the way she would look again.

As for Kristen, her dreams would not be as pleasant. Instead, they would be filled with terror, a premonition of what was yet to come.

Tonight the herbs would work their magic. The banana and strawberry liqueurs and the toiletries she had given them contained the special mixtures—a touch of nightshade and cubina for her, a dose of Paris for her beloved Thomas. The dinner also contained traces of each, and if they used their gifts as she intended, the dreams would come often, making her task easier.

It was unfortunate that Kristen hadn't worn the toiletries. If she had, her nightmares would be more intense.

But Thomas had worn the cologne. He had reeked of its spicy aroma, and it pleased her. He had to apply the scented herb everyday, as did his fool wife.

But if the bitch refused to use it and the cubina didn't get into her system, she would find another way. She had many alternatives, maybe not as safe but just as effective. Feeling smug, she went inside. All was going as planned with only one small hitch—the book. Kristen had seen the book. How she hated that girl, hated her very name.

Without turning on any of the lights, she went into the study, retrieved the book from the desk drawer and headed up the steep staircase to her bedroom. She would put the book away properly in the morning. Tonight it would stay on her nightstand.

She was elated at the progress she made during the evening. In three short weeks the others would arrive to help complete her task, just as she had once helped each of them. Then she would be whole and revived, and for the second time in her life, she would be able to enjoy the sweetness of true love. Life was good. Her father had been kind to send her Thomas.

She waltzed down the long hallway to her bedroom in pitch darkness, seeing with the eyes of a cat, humming a strange tune, the same tune Kristen so often heard her husband hum.

By the time she opened her bedroom door, she was singing the words of her haunting melody:

> Come with me,
> Come with me
> into the night.
> Stay with me,
> Stay with me,
> past morning's bright light.
>
> Forever awaits,
> and there's no time to waste.
> So please come with me now
> before it's too late.

"Please, Thomas, I need you. If we don't hurry, it will be too late." She stood by the open dark window facing the Roberts' house, the rain gently soaking the dark rose velvet drapes. She directed her attention to the small bedroom window where he slept. She probed his mind with her thoughts and left them there. She closed the window and placed the book on the lace-covered nightstand beside the bed. She undressed, still singing her song softly, while her mind reached out to her love.

EIGHTEEN

JULY HAD WHIZZED BY, AND IT WAS THE FIRST week of August. Kristen was relieved that not one child had been reported missing since Scott Benson. The pattern of a child disappearing each month since March had been broken. Unfortunately, no progress had been made with any of the cases, and it upset her. She wanted the police to find something, anything, but the paper continued to print "no new leads."

This morning, Tom had left early for a faculty meeting, his second summer session already in progress. As soon as he walked out the door, she started on her usual Friday routine, cleaning the entire house.

As she worked in the bedroom, she heard a chattering that resembled a flock of excited geese, coming from the direction of Eliza

Noman's. She hurried to the window.

Five women of various ages, dressed in frilly summer dresses, gathered on Eliza's front lawn. A polished ivory Cadillac Seville was parked in the drive.

One of the women, the youngest, who appeared to be in her early twenties, carried a huge, white, wicker basket with pink lace draped over its top. Chills coursed through her.

Suddenly her stomach quivered, and nausea set in. Her temples throbbed, and her heart pounded inside her chest. Her eyes blurred, and she felt dizzy. Slowly she backed away from the window and stumbled to the bathroom. She threw up repeatedly, then sat on the floor, resting her back against the tub.

She pulled her knees up to her chest and cradled her head in her hands. She wished for Tom, then smiled, wryly. What good would he do?

Since their arrival in Burnwell, Tom seemed to be going through some sort of personality change. He had become so withdrawn and sullen that it was starting to drive her crazy. It was difficult to talk to him with his monosyllabic answers. It was impossible to get close to him. Some days when he returned from work, she found herself wishing he hadn't. Maybe the pressure of the job was the culprit.

Last week his mother had called to invite them for the weekend. Tom had always enjoyed spending time at his parents; he loved the Lancaster area. He loved lolling around the pool until the wee hours of the morning and the debates with his father about world affairs. But, to her surprise, he had refused. Not only did he refuse, but he became belligerent to his mother, a woman whose sweetness and understanding deserved better. Of course, she was devastated and sobbed uncontrollably, while Kristen made excuses for him. She remembered the conversation vividly.

"Please don't get so upset, Mom. It's his job. Really, it had nothing to do with you," she explained.

"Are you sure, dear?" asked Mrs. Roberts. "He never yelled at me like that before. Not ever."

"Well, it's the pressure. He's trying to do his best. I'm sure as soon as the year of probation is over, he'll settle down. Maybe even by fall things will lighten up for him, and then we'll come."

"Oh, I hope so."

"We will. I promise." But it was an empty promise. When she hung up the phone, she wondered if lying to his mother and not telling her of the change in him had been justified.

But what else could she do after he had screamed at the woman that he had no intention of driving all the way to Lancaster—not now or ever? He told her he was too busy.

That was when she grabbed the phone out of his hand and shoved him aside. How could he scream at his mother like that?

Lately, there was a lot about him that puzzled her, especially the nastiness he seemed to direct at everyone, including her—everyone, that is, except Eliza.

He acted as if he cared for neither his family nor his wife. She hoped it was a silly passing phase.

As for having the time to visit his family, he would have lots of time if he didn't spend so much of it at Eliza's. But he wasn't the only one to blame. The old lady constantly called with the excuse that something needed repairing like a window, a door or a faucet. Maybe the woman should hire a handyman. From the elegance of her house, she could well afford one.

Usually, when Tom returned home from Eliza's, after taking an entire evening to repair something, he talked on and on about Eliza, enamored by the old house, the old Mercedes, her travels, her this, her that. Once, when Kristen had foolishly asked him to talk about something else, he became furious. As a result, she decided to say nothing about his obsession, hoping it, too, was simply a passing phase.

Suddenly, squeals of delight and laughter came from the direction of the Noman house. Unable to squash her curiosity, she stood up and peeked out the bathroom window. When Eliza emerged from the house, the women squealed and acted as if they were having an orgasm. She hugged each of them, then focused on the basket. They all did.

Kristen stared at the basket, and once again her stomach turned. A cold sweat broke out on her forehead, and the dizziness returned. She backed away from the window, then threw up.

She stayed on the bathroom floor and rested her back against the tub, listening to the woman's chatter. She wondered who they were and what they were doing at Eliza's. More importantly, what was inside the white wicker basket that caused such a stir? Just the thought of it sent chills through her.

Suddenly their chatter ceased, and she assumed they had gone inside. Maybe it was good Eliza had guests. Now she'd have Tom all to herself. She hoped they stayed an entire week or two. Better still, they could stay for a month, a year or forever.

To add to her sudden good fortune, tomorrow evening she and Tom planned to attend the annual faculty barbecue held by the Psychology department. They would meet new people, hopefully, some their own age. They needed to make friends. Tom needed to break away from Eliza, and the party would be a good start.

Feeling better, she got up from the floor, then headed to the kitchen for a dose of Pepto Bismol. She blocked Eliza and her friends from her mind and concentrated on the forthcoming party.

NINETEEN

THE FOLLOWING MORNING, KRISTEN WOKE UP EARLY and scrambled out of bed. She had been assigned salad duty for the evening's barbecue and intended to make the best potato, pasta and bean salads Tom's colleagues and their wives had ever tasted. As she slipped into a pair of shorts and tee shirt, she turned and watched Tom, who lay listless in bed, staring at the ceiling. Then the phone rang, and before she had a chance to get to the night table, he picked it up. His mood immediately changed; he became excited. It seemed as if he was being informed that he had won the Pennsylvania lottery.

"Eleven. Great!" he said. "We'll both be there."

Kristen moved closer to the bed and watched as he placed the phone in the cradle. "Be where?"

"Eliza wants us to come for brunch to meet her friends."

Frowning and scowling, she shook her head. Damn that woman!

"I can't. I have salads to make for tonight."

"So. Make them when you get back."

"I have to start them early or they won't come out okay."

"So what?"

"So what?"

Her eyes opened wide with surprise. How could he be so callous? These people were the ones he had set out to impress. She stared at his grinning face, and for an instant, she felt like balling her hand into a fist and slugging that smile right off his face. He was becoming more impossible with each passing day.

"What's so important about salads?" He got out of bed and strolled to the chest of drawers for a clean pair of shorts. "Huh? What's so important?"

"It's important to me that I don't make an ass out of myself in front of your coworkers."

"Oh, I see. But you'd rather make an ass out of me in front of Eliza and her friends."

"What are you talking about?"

"I told her we'd be there," Tom said, the pitch of his voice steadily rising.

"Why didn't you ask me first?"

"I didn't realize I needed your permission. Look," he paused and shot her a sly look, "if you don't go to Eliza's, then you can forget about tonight's party."

Anger bubbled up inside her, adrenaline pumped through her arms and legs, and she felt her body tremble.

"I mean it, Kris." He stalked toward her. His eyes were dark and threatening, his lips pulled back over his teeth in a snarl.

She stepped back, fearful that he was about to attack her, to take one mighty swing and send her sprawling. She had never seen him so angry, not once in the five years they had been married.

He stopped inches from her face and glared into her eyes.

"You have three hours to make your goddamn salads. I suggest you get to it."

Turning from her he headed for the door, brushing her arm with his muscular forearm as he past. She lost her balance and stumbled against the mattress, then turned and watched him stomp into the bathroom.

Blackmail! That's all it was. He knew how badly she wanted to attend the barbecue, and he was using it against her. Bastard!

She waited until he closed the bathroom door and turned on the shower before grabbing his pillow from the bed and pounding her fists into it. "Bastard! Bastard! Bastard!" She cried out over and over until, finally, the anger was released. She wondered if he would have hit her. Probably. She had never seen him so . . . violent. Exhausted, she picked herself up from the bed and headed to the kitchen. What was happening to him? Another word of protest and he would have belted her for sure. But worst of all, for the first time since they had met, she was afraid of him, afraid someday he would do just that and shatter every bone in her face.

The walk to Eliza Noman's was done in silence with Kristen trailing a few feet behind. Up ahead, on the wide porch, she could see the six women sitting in the wicker chairs around a circular white table.

Although curious about them, she hated them, especially Eliza Noman, for driving another wedge in her relationship with Tom. And, for the first time in their marriage, she hated him, too.

She had hurried to finish her salads, then with only ten minutes to spare before the brunch, she stuffed the huge bowls into the refrigerator and quickly changed into a pale yellow sundress. She had only enough time to hurriedly apply some makeup and brush her hair. Tom had stood at the bottom of the staircase, providing a countdown and complaining that he had no intention of being late.

She tried to keep up with his long strides, jittery from being rushed. The August sun blazed down on her and caused her to perspire profusely. Tiny rivulets of sweat trickled down the sides of her face.

Why was he doing this to her? It was unnecessary and cruel.

"Tom, wait. Please slow down."

He didn't answer, just kept his pace, then increased it as if to spite her.

Damn you! She thought. Then without another word, she slowed down, not caring if he became angry.

A moment later, he was five feet ahead of her, then six, then ten. He obviously didn't mind, and neither did she. It was impossible to keep up. The day was too hot and humid to run a race to Eliza Noman's.

Slowing down to a stroll, she sniffed the air around her and felt something was different. It seemed as if something dark and ominous wafted on the breeze. She took a long, slow, deep breath, filling her nostrils, her throat, her lungs with the fetid air. She wanted to gag. It smelled like . . . like . . . what? She didn't know.

Strange! The weather was beautiful—hot but beautiful. Not a single cloud marred the azure sky. The air was now filled with the fragrant scent of roses that occupied the various beds around her feet. But there was also the trace of the disgusting odor.

Something else was different. It was too quiet.

She looked around her, scanning the landscape, the numerous flower beds, the towering pines out front, the dark woods bordering the back of their properties, the houses. Everything appeared as it should be.

But a feeling of impending doom gnawed at her stomach as a dog would gnaw at a bone. For a moment she paused and listened. And then it hit her hard, as if a wall of steel had been placed before her and she unwarily had walked into it. Everything was not as it should be.

For the first time since her arrival in Burnwell, there was silence—total, complete, unadulterated silence. Not a single bird chirped, not a solitary bee hovered and buzzed among the flowers, and when she looked around her, not even a butterfly danced in the air. Odd. The ground and the air were usually filled with swarming insects, often to the point of annoyance—except for today.

Kristen couldn't make sense of the change. She felt as if the birds and insects were hiding and were afraid to venture out.

She looked up and saw Tom mount the low wooden steps amidst the squeals of the awaiting women. The distance was still too great for her to make out much of their looks.

Then it hit her, harder than before. This time it felt as if she had hit that steel wall at 50 miles an hour. There was no mistake about what she felt. It was danger. For some reason, she felt danger all around her.

Cautiously, she neared the porch, avoiding the inquiring eyes of those seated around the table. When a few turned around to look at her, the feeling of being in grave danger increased and clawed at her throat. Suddenly, she wanted to turn and run and hide, as the birds and bees and butterflies had.

As she mounted the porch steps, her legs felt heavy and weighted. Her heart thumped inside her chest, and her temples throbbed and felt as if her entire head would explode.

Run! A tiny voice in her head warned her to run.

But she didn't run. She continued her climb and the women lapsed into silence.

"Girls, I want you to meet Thomas's wife. Her name is Kristen."

She wasn't certain, but the introduction seemed a bit sarcastic. The other women said nothing.

"Isn't she lovely? Just like a doll," Eliza continued.

Kristen stopped on the top step and listened as if in a shrouded fog to a variety of responses, wearing her best "I'm so happy to be here" face.

"Yes," one said.

"Of course," another agreed in a deep, husky voice.

"She is lovely, Eliza," said another in a sexy, come hither tone.

The danger signal flashed inside her head, a light like that seen on a highway after a terrible accident. It flashed behind her eyes and told her to grab Tom and run. Run as fast and as far as you can and never, ever return.

She turned to look at Tom who quickly lowered his eyes.

Run! Run! Run!

She held her ground, and mounted the final step and smiled warmly as the introductions began.

Seated near the table, flanking Tom on both sides, were the Kacher sisters, Jenny and Louise. Both nodded curtly when Eliza introduced them. Then they focused their attention on Tom. Kristen guessed their ages to be mid-thirties. Even though they were seated, it was easy to see that Jenny was taller and much thinner. She had large, round blue eyes and reddish blond hair that cascaded to her shoulders in loose waves.

Her sister, Louise, was short and plump, with tremendous breasts and hair that was a cross between bright red and brassy orange. She, too, had blue eyes that twinkled and sparkled as she looked longingly at Tom. To Kristen, it seemed as if she would swallow him whole. The sight of them so near him made her cringe.

Emily Gregory stood near Eliza. She appeared to be in her late fifties; her face showed its age and had a leathery texture to it like Eliza's. She wore a loose-fitting chiffon dress with a bright floral print of muted greens and blues. Her eyes were amber, her hair a blue-gray. She gave Kristen a sweet, warm smile. "I'm pleased to meet you," she said. "It's good to know that Eliza has such a nice neighbor."

The introduction to Emily made Kristen relax. Unlike the Kacher sisters she was down-to-earth and unthreatening.

Dorothy Lasur stood away from the others, leaning against the wooden picket railing. She, too, smiled warmly at Kristen and further dispelled her fear. The woman had dark brown eyes and hair and appeared to be in her early forties. She was plump and quiet and seemed shy. When Kristen made eye contact, she quickly began staring at the wooden floor.

The final introduction was Becky Tocks, the exact opposite in personality of Dorothy Lasur. She was outgoing, cordial, well-mannered and exceptionally beautiful. She certainly was the youngest of the group, barely in her twenties, and wore a brilliant white, strapless, terry cloth dress. She was barefoot.

Becky extended a hand to Kristen who marveled at the girl's bronze, baby-soft skin. Her eyes were dark, the color and size of ripe black olives. Her long, waist-length golden hair was pulled back from her flawless oval-shaped face and clipped up into a high ponytail at the crown. Her lips were a natural pink blush that puckered into a cupid's pout. "How wonderful it is to meet you," she said to Kristen. "You must tell me all about yourself." Her eyes smiled and twinkled with warmth, her voice sounding as smooth as cream.

Kristen felt the fear drain from her completely. She now felt foolish and wondered what had even caused her to feel threatened. It had to be her imagination. These women, except for the Kacher sisters who seemed a bit oversexed, were absolutely harmless. And Becky Tocks was the most harmless of all. She liked her but couldn't help question her association with the others. She was so young and so beautiful. Surely, she had better things to do than spend time with these other women.

"I adore your dress," Becky continued. "Would you te—"

"Oh, Eliza, how do you rate having him as your neighbor?" Jenny Kacher squealed, interrupting all conversation. "He's soooo wonderful!"

The exaggerated pleasure in Jenny Kacher's voice caused Kristen to whirl on her heel and face the woman. She drew in a breath, ready to pounce. Both sisters were running their hands up and down Tom's chest. And what made it worse was he looked as if he was enjoying it. He was blushing, of course, but neither protesting nor resisting. Anger swelled inside her. What kind of women were they?

She was his wife, and they were practically seducing him in front of her.

She opened her mouth to speak—no, scream —but before she had the chance, Eliza rushed to his side. Her arm shot out, and she shoved Jenny Kacher aside with such force, the woman nearly fell on her ass. Then she positioned herself beside Tom and linked her thin arm through his.

"That's enough," she shrieked, glaring at Louise Kacher, who cowered and quickly retreated to her sister's side. "I'll have none of that! Behave yourselves! He's not about to become one of your playmates, I can assure you."

Awestruck, Kristen stared as the two sisters backed away even farther until they were almost sitting on the low railing. The color of their faces drained until it became positively chalky. They were scared, truly scared, and neither of them dared meet Eliza's glare. Jenny was the first to speak, her lips quivering as if she was about to burst into tears. "I'm sorry. I guess I got carried away." She glanced at her sister. "Yes. I suppose I did, too," Louise said sheepishly. "It was just a joke. Please, don't get so an—" "The joke is over," Eliza interrupted in a booming voice.

The sisters winced as if they had been slapped

hard across their faces. Kristen couldn't believe how terrified they were of this old, old woman. Even though she didn't appreciate their fondling of her husband and was grateful to Eliza for putting an end to it, she couldn't understand their fright.

She looked at Eliza who kept shooting them angry glances, glances that would kill if they were bullets. The other guests fidgeted with downcast eyes. Something was very strange about all these women except for Becky Tocks, she concluded. But even she was rather odd to associate with the likes of the Kacher sisters, Eliza Noman and that Gregory lady. What was the connection?

"Girls, let's not quarrel," Emily Gregory said. She caught Eliza's eye with her own, and for a moment it seemed as if some silent communication was taking place. It lasted only a moment before the woman continued. "Maybe we should have something to eat, don't you think? I'll pour the tea." She moved to the table, and for the first time Kristen saw the feast that had been prepared.

There were huge, round pastries with fruit fillings of cherry, blueberry and strawberry. A large oval tray heaped with croissants and bowls of fresh bananas, grapes and sliced oranges cluttered the table. There was a dish of petits fours, another of baklava, and still another containing a round, braided, poppy seed ring. On another long folding table that was covered with lacy cloth was Eliza's good china, silverware and diamond cut crystal. Nearby, in its own stand,

was a bottle of champagne chilling in an ice-
filled silver bucket. What elegance, Kristen
thought. The brunch appeared fit for royalty.

Kristen watched Eliza release her grip on
Tom's arm and take a series of deep breaths.
After a few seconds, her face seemed to lose its
harshness. "You're right, of course, Emily."

Emily Gregory looked up from the table and
smiled warmly. "Maybe Thomas would like
some tea."

"Yes," he answered and sat down, waiting to
be served. As Eliza seated herself beside him, he
looked at Kristen, then quickly dropped his eyes
to the food before him. Emily Gregory's hands
trembled as she poured the tea into a fine china
cup.

Louise and Jenny Kacher moved from the far
end of the porch and skittered past Eliza, taking
the two seats on the opposite side of the table.
They didn't lift their eyes once. Instead, they
stared at the croissants and their plates like two
children who had been scolded.

"How about you, dear?" Emily Gregory said
to Eliza, but got no answer.

"Kristen, tea?"

"Yes, thank you." She moved toward the table,
hoping to seat herself on the opposite side of
Tom. She wasn't hungry, but she would nibble
to be polite. She had to be near her husband.
She felt the need to protect him.

At the same time, Dorothy Lasur took the
chair situated between Louise and Eliza, a barri-
er to prevent any further antagonism.

The mood had definitely changed, and

Kristen felt it was time to go home. Something ominous lurked, polluting the air like a thick smelly fog. As she passed Becky Tocks, hoping to reach Tom and nudge him to leave, Becky grabbed her arm, "I'd like it if you would join me and Emily under the gazebo. Please."

She hesitated, looked at the young woman and noticed she was the only one who seemed unafraid of Eliza. "Well, I . . ."

"Of course she would," Eliza broke in. "You two go on, and Emily'll bring a tray." She smiled warmly, but her eyes, those fierce green cabochons, narrowed to thin slits.

Kristen was about to protest, to tell Eliza to shove it because she wanted to stay close to Tom, when Becky shoved a small plate into her hands, a buttery brioche in its middle. She grabbed Kristen by the shoulders and whisked her from the porch.

When they were a good distance from the others, Becky said, "I know you wanted to stay near your husband, but now is not the time to give Eliza a hard time."

"Why?"

"It just isn't," Becky replied, as she cast a nervous glance over her shoulder. Then she put her index finger to her lips.

"I bet you and I have a lot in common," Becky said, tiptoeing through the spiky grass in her bare feet. They were nearing the gazebo located 50 feet to the left of the house. Kristen didn't know Eliza had a gazebo, but it was pretty, white and lacy, with small benches painted the same shade of medium blue as the house. A round wooden table stood in the middle.

"You must tell me where you bought that dress," Becky continued. "I simply adore it."

"Thank you," Kristen said trying to keep tabs on Tom and the others on the porch. She nearly tripped on the steps. "I, uh, bought it in, uh, Wanamakers, in, uh, Philadelphia." She stopped and stared at Tom sitting amidst the four women. He looked ridiculous, like an overgrown kid. He didn't belong. She didn't belong.

Becky grabbed her arm and pulled her up under the gazebo's dome, then directed her to sit at the far end. For a brief instant, Kristen had the urge to belt the girl and give her one hell of a right hook to the chin. She didn't like being manhandled, pushed, told what to do and where to go. Although she had no quarrel with Becky —in fact, she liked her a lot—she couldn't help but become irritated by her pushy behavior.

Once seated, she noticed she could no longer see Tom or the others. It made her uncomfortable.

She was about to get up and move to a better vantage point when, above the continuous chatter on the porch, above the sexy inquiring voice of her companion, came a cry. It pierced the still August air and hung there for a few moments.

Kristen turned her attention to the direction of the sound which seemed to have been an upstairs window. All was silent.

Feeling uneasy, she shifted in her seat and looked questioningly at Becky, who was undisturbed.

But there had been a cry, and it sounded so familiar. It sounded like a . . .

It came again, louder and shriller.

There was no doubt. Only one thing could release such a pitiful wail.

"Did someone bring a baby?" she asked Becky, who suddenly stiffened as if someone had inserted a steel bar up her spine.

Becky smiled weakly. Then avoiding Kristen's eyes, she said, "A baby? Oh, no. Why on earth would you think that?"

Kristen was shocked by the answer. Was she deaf? Or did she view her as a moron? An idiot could see that the girl was lying, her cheeks taking on a definite blush, her lips drawn in a thin line across her teeth.

"Well, that sure sounded like a baby."

"What?"

"That cry or wail, or whatever you want to call it."

"Oh, that. Well, it's one the Kacher cats. They take those animals everywhere. Just between you and me, this one is as wild as they are." She smiled, then covered her mouth with her hand. "Now be quiet. Here comes Emily. She'd have a fit if she knew I was talking about the sisters."

Kristen watched the older woman marching toward them, a silver tray filled with tiny tea cups in her hands.

She thought about the cry. It *was* a baby. Even though she listened for another wail, it never came.

She again felt overwhelmed and wanted to

leave. She didn't want to associate with these women and didn't want Tom to, either. But she knew that until he decided to leave, she was stuck and was forced to make the best of the situation. Besides, if she rudely declared she was leaving, he would prevent her from attending the faculty party. Of course, he couldn't actually stop her from going—she still had the Honda— but it would be quite uncomfortable without him, especially since no one had ever met her.

She knew she had made a mistake by allowing him to bully her into coming to Eliza's stupid brunch, but since his recent behavior was so unusual, so unlike the Tom she knew, she felt intimidated by his demand. Never again would she allow him to pull this sort of thing on her.

The evening's festivities proved as trying as the brunch. After hurrying home from the Noman place at 2:00 and adding the final touches to her salads, she showered quickly, dressed in a pair of white cotton shorts and a crisp, mint colored blouse. With only seconds to spare, they arrived at Robert Jensen's house.

The Dean's home reminded her of an old English estate. It was a large two-story Tudor with diamond-paned windows and a heavy wooden front door that was rounded at the top. In the middle of the dark, polished door was a knocker of heavy brass shaped like a lion's head.

The grounds were magnificent, surrounded by an evergreen hedge that rose to the height of at least ten feet. There were Japanese maples, oaks, spruces and firs dotting the landscape. Out front were huge rhododendrons in bright pinks and orchids against the house, while out back were the rose gardens, daisy patches and beds of giant golden zinnias. Kristen was impressed.

On the flagstone patio that led from the lower level of the house through two sliding glass doors, her hope of meeting people their own age vanished. Most of the couples were in their late forties or older, some very near retirement.

After half an hour, she realized she had little in common with the other faculty wives, who had spent most of their lives riding on their husband's coattails, raised their children and now spent most of their time at quilting bees, shopping trips and afternoon teas. Not one had a career nor any interest in one.

They were pleasant, cordial, talkative and nosey, but worst of all, they were patronizing, not blind to the fact that she was so much younger than they. What bothered her more than anything was their gossip.

Whenever one of their friends, it didn't matter which one, excused herself to the little girl's room or wherever, the remainder of these best friends acted more like enemies. They talked about the absent one's dress and how terrible she looked. They talked about her makeup and how poorly it was applied, or how much jewelry she wore. They talked about her housekeeping which was too clean and prissy or too sloppy.

Kristen excused herself from the group and decided to mingle with the men. However, they weren't much better, mostly insulting and childish. It seemed as if they never let those who weren't their equal on the academic social ladder forget their standing. Tom mingled, too, and appeared oblivious to the entire situation.

Toward evening's end, Kristen found herself alone. Enjoying her solitude, she sat at the padded leather bar in the dark-paneled family room, watching the circus through the sliding glass doors and drinking one drink after another.

So much for developing a new circle of friends. She knew that if it weren't for Rose and George Howard, there would be no one for her in Burnwell. Oh, there was Eliza, but she was more interested in Tom. She didn't try to kid herself that the old lady gave a damn about her, no matter what Eliza had said about being her friend.

Then there was Tom. He used to be her friend before Burnwell, but he no longer cared. He acted as if she was in his way. He was rude and insulting and treated her as if she hadn't a brain in her head. How quickly he forgot that she had graduated from Temple with honors, summa cum laude. He had grown away from her, no longer needing her. He spent more time with Eliza than with her.

She took another sip of her vodka and orange juice. She had been hitting the booze heavily, feeling sorry for herself. She knew it, but *someone* had to feel sorry for her.

She looked out through the doors. Tom was talking to Jensen, laughing and yucking it up like two old buddies. It was hard to believe that there ever was a time when she could confide in him, when he listened and understood her needs and feelings. Mostly he ignored her or just pretended to listen. Whatever had happened to him was a mystery, a mystery she no longer felt compelled to solve.

She was alone—no doubt about it. She was alone in a place called Burnwell, and it would please her to no end if the town burned down to the ground.

Taking a huge gulp of her drink, she thought about going home. It would be wonderful to see her mom and her sister, to feel loved again. Maybe tomorrow she would call and make plans for a visit. She hadn't been in Philadelphia since June, and oh, how she missed her family. Of course, they wrote and called periodically, and she did the same, but it was no longer enough. She needed the physical contact. She needed to be needed.

She thought about Tom. If he didn't soon return to his old self, the tender, loving man she married, she would . . . would . . . leave him. No, she didn't want to think about that. It couldn't come to that. No matter what, she still loved him and knew inside her heart that she always would.

Outside, the chatter of the gossiping wives grew louder. The last rays of sunlight came filtering into the room, illuminating the glasses and bottles on the shelves behind the bar. She smelled the aroma of hamburgers grilling, the fat sizzling on the hot coals.

She was about to get up and mix herself another drink when a deep male voice startled her out of her self-pity. "Mind if I join you?"

She turned to face the intruder and saw a balding man with gray hair. He stood barely a foot from her shoulder. He grinned, exposing a set of tiny white teeth, the left front tooth being chipped almost in half.

"You look awfully sad for a party," he said. "Bet I can cheer you up in a minute." He winked, then climbed onto the black leather bar stool beside her.

"I'm Alan Kaspar," he said, extending his right hand.

She shook his hand, then introduced herself.

He gave her a warm smile. "You must be Tom's wife. Nice to meet you."

To Kristen, Alan Kaspar was the warmest person she had met at the party. She took a hard look at him and decided he reminded her of an elf, similar to one from Santa's workshop. He had soft brown eyes with flecks of gold that glittered in the fading light. He was short and muscular, and the tip of his nose was as rosy as his cheeks. He exuded a certain zest for life that couldn't be ignored.

"I'm the head of Parapsychology at the college."

"Oh. Interesting field."

"Yes, I know, a ghostbuster," he said, chuckling, "but it is interesting." He took a gulp of beer straight from the bottle. "I hope I didn't startle you. I mean, you don't mind my being here, do you?"

"Not at all," she answered, smiling. At least he

didn't have any pretensions about who he was, she thought.

"Do you always drift off by yourself at parties?"

"Not usually." She took a sip of her almost empty drink.

"Bad party?"

"Uh-uh. I just felt like being alone for a while."

It wasn't really a lie, since she did want to be alone. It was much better than being with the others.

"Should I leave?" He looked into her eyes, as if trying to read her thoughts.

"No." She focused on her drink, running her finger around the rim of the glass. No longer wanting to drown herself in self-pity, she really did want him to stay. It felt better.

"Tom's a welcome addition to our little family. Bright boy. He'll go far at the college." He took a large gulp of beer, draining the last of it. "Why so sad? I would think you'd be thrilled to know that you and your husband have such a bright future."

She shrugged. It didn't seem appropriate to tell him of her marital woes. She didn't know him well enough for that. Could she tell him what little use she had for the faculty wives, especially when one of them could be his? Hardly.

"Don't let things get you down. Relocation is a difficult experience. Give it time, and everything will work out. As for these people, don't let them

get to you either. They're all show. Phonies.
Know what I mean?"

Kristen couldn't believe what she had just
heard. How on earth could he be so perceptive
to know what she was thinking? Maybe it was
just a coincidence. It had to be. But then he
spoke again and her eyes widened.

"It's no coincidence. I have what you might
call a gift. I'm good at reading other's thoughts
though not all the time. It doesn't work with
everyone, only with special people, and I have a
feeling you're one of those special people." He
toyed with the empty beer bottle and shot her a
quick glance. He put the back of his hand to his
forehead, closed his eyes and said," Something
tells me Kristen Roberts and I are to become
friends—the best of friends. Misfits usually do."
He looked at her and winked, twirling the empty
bottle in his hands. "I need another drink," he
said with a toothy grin. "How about you?"

Still stunned by his remarks, she was only able
to nod. The man was amazing. How did he know
she felt like a misfit?

"Care for a burger? Something else? Sure you
do," he answered for her, tapping his temple
with his finger. "I'll be right back." He scanned
the bottles behind the bar. "Guess the vodka and
orange juice are outside."

She started to smile as she watched him
bounce toward the sliding glass doors and disappear into the small crowd. He did remind her of
an elf, maybe Santa Claus himself.

She didn't believe he had actually read her
thoughts. It had to be coincidence—

observation and deductive reasoning. That was about the sum of it. It didn't take a genius to conclude she was miserable and felt out of place. Why else would she be drinking alone? As for knowing what she was drinking, he probably smelled the orange juice.

One thing she didn't question was the fact that she liked him. Somehow, she knew he was right—they were destined to become friends.

When he returned, ten minutes later, he was carrying a large rectangular glass tray heaped with hamburgers, barbecued chicken, chips, potato salad, corn on the cob, beer, and an extra large tumbler of vodka and orange juice. She jokingly concluded he meant to get her drunk, then like some dirty old man, he would take advantage of her.

He placed the tray on the bar and once again climbed onto the bar stool.

"Don't worry, my dear, no one suspects a thing." he said in a hushed voice, gently putting his hand on her wrist. "I'm charitably referred to as eccentric. Dr. Kaspar lugging around a tray full of food doesn't raise too many eyebrows. You must have some of this potato salad."

At that moment, a jolt that felt like a bolt of electricity passed through her. She looked at him and noticed he, too, had experienced the same thing.

"See, I was right about you and me. Things'll be good between us."

Yes, he was right. Sitting there beside him and feeling the electricity from his presence convinced her there would be more between them than she could imagine. It was if she had known him for years. She felt peaceful and comfortable. How could it be? Could what she needed be him? For the first time in ages she felt love pouring in her direction, and it felt good. No, better than good, it felt wonderful.

They sat for a long time bent over the bar talking, nibbling on the feast he had purloined. She learned about him, his travels and his beliefs in the paranormal, of which she had no doubts. She confided that she also believed, and he was thrilled when she revealed her background in psychology.

By the time the party ended, close to midnight, Kristen felt refreshed, having thoroughly enjoyed her time with Alan Kaspar. She agreed to come to his office at noon on Monday to begin the process of confirming his suspicion that she, too, had a psychic gift, more powerful than she could ever dream.

TWENTY

UNDER THE GRIM SMILE OF A SILVERY MOON, UN-
der the watchful eyes of a million stars, six
women shed their hooded black satin robes.
They stood in a circular clearing where the
grass was green and lush, the texture of velvet.
Towering pines, gnarled oaks and a thick underbrush of burrs and brambles surrounded them
like barbed wire, protecting them from the
outside world. They were safe. No one would
dare venture this deep into the forest to find this
place of sacred rites.

They moved toward the center of the clearing,
one by one, smiling. Their nude bodies reflected
their various ages from the very old and shriveled to the young and firm. The six nude wom-
en formed a circle within a circle and joined
hands.

The ceremony was about to begin.

The focus of their attention was the roughly hewed stone and the object that lay upon it—a beautiful, innocent child only weeks old. The infant's eyes, wide and unseeing, were the color of the ocean. They stared into the starry sky with wonder, unwary and unsuspecting of the danger around her. The moon's luminous glow streaked down and smiled upon her, touching her tiny body with the dust of silver, giving her a surreal, ethereal quality, like an angel come to earth.

The six moved closer, tightening their circle, then bent over the child.

The baby girl, alarmed by the darkness and the strange blurred faces above her, wriggled and squirmed. Her face clouded, her mouth contorted, and then she released an ear-shattering wail. But as the women began to chant the ancient song, she soon quieted. They stepped back, and once again the infant was exposed to the light and smiled.

In unison, the women bent down and retrieved small jars from beneath the altar. The containers were only three inches in height and were shaped like tiny ginger jars. They contained a shimmering, clear, oily liquid that had been carefully prepared for this sacred night. All six popped off the lids and massaged the contents onto their skin, careful not to miss a single nook or cranny of their bodies. The chant continued.

Once certain that each had been sufficiently covered with the ointment, they proceeded to anoint the child, massaging the few remaining drops from each jar onto her tender flesh. She glistened and appeared almost translucent in the moonlight.

The dance began.

In a counterclockwise motion, the women circled the altar. Their chant filled the night, lulled the baby and was muffled to the outside world by the thick forest.

Round and round and round they went.

And with each revolution, their feet lifted from the ground until they were levitating inches above the plush green carpet.

Faster. Faster. Faster.

Higher. Higher. Higher.

The ground shuddered and rumbled, moving as if liquid. The baby, alarmed, cried and wailed and screamed until her face turned crimson, blue, then purple.

But the six could no longer hear the infant. They no longer saw the trees or the silver medallion suspended in the velvet sky. They whirled and whirled and whirled, a sparkling, lustrous blur. Slowly, they ascended 100 feet into the air, to the tops of the giant trees, and there they stopped, hovering, spinning and waiting.

Below, the earth split into a jagged fissure, starting at one end of the clearing and leading directly to the altar and the child. It opened and widened, resembling a large mouth waiting to be fed.

A figure cloaked in blackness oozed from this fissure and came forward. It touched a long, ragged claw to the baby's chest. The child fell silent. The ceremony was complete. The sacrifice accepted.

From beyond the confines of her bedroom, from deep within the forest, a cry intruded on her sleep. Kristen stirred and thought, a baby. No, a cat. The Kacher sisters had a cat.

Beside her, Tom breathed steadily. She touched his shoulder with her fingertips. She was home, in her own bed, safe. Content, she rolled over onto her side and faced the window. Dreamily, she watched the sheer curtains flutter in the warm breeze. Pulling the sheet under her chin, she closed her eyes and drifted off to sleep.

When the sound reoccurred, she stirred again. It was a baby's cry that wafted through the open window. But where could that baby be? There were no children nearby.

As the intensity of the cry increased, she opened her eyes, then smothered a scream with her hand.

Standing at the open window was a figure rimmed in a pale silver glow. She could not see its eyes nor its face, but she sensed that it had been watching her, waiting for her to wake up.

The slender, lanky figure stepped forward. Inch by agonizing inch, it limped toward the bed, toward her.

She drew the sheet tightly around her throat. Her heart pounded in her chest, and her body shriveled as if trying to vanish into the mattress.

The figure continued, inch by inch by inch.

She closed her eyes. It was a dream, and when

she opened her eyes it would be over. She reluctantly peeked. The figure was getting closer. She pulled the sheet over her head, trying not to be seen or to see it. Even tucked beneath the covers, cowering and cringing, she could still hear it, dragging its leg. She had to scream, to cry out to wake Tom, but her teeth were clamped together.

Then it stopped. The room became silent, and she sighed with relief. She didn't move, afraid to drop the covers and peer into the room. She held her breath and listened intently for any movement.

There was a tap on her shoulder, an icy prick that penetrated the bone. Her heart leaped into her throat. If she did nothing and pretended not to feel the touch, it would go away, whatever it was. It touched her again, and once more she did not stir, determined not to show any movement.

But when it spoke in a familiar voice and called her name, her body jerked in spasm.

"Kristen, you must come."

It knew her—knew her by name. Who or what was this creature in her bedroom? She had to know. She hesitated for a moment before slowly pulling the sheet from her face. She opened her eyes and gasped.

In front of her, looking down at her with eyes that burned like embers, was a boy, a boy she recognized, a boy she had met in a previous dream. It was Scott Benson.

From the dim light caused by the moonbeams streaming through the window, she could see he was as he appeared before—bloodied, battered and bruised. There was a hole where his heart had once been, and his throat was torn open.

In his arms was a bundle she couldn't make out. She looked back into his eyes, then at the bundle, then back into his eyes.

"You must come," he repeated and took a step closer. He offered her the bundle. "Please."

How was he able to speak to her? She dug her heels into the mattress and pushed away, banging into Tom's back. She wanted no part of the boy's offering. She wanted him to go away. She opened her mouth to scream, again to wake Tom.

"No! Please!" the boy pleaded. "You must be quiet. You must not wake him. I need only you."

"Why?" she managed to whisper.

"He would not believe. He would send you away, and we need you to help." He dropped the mangled mass he was holding onto the bed.

Alarmed, she brushed it to the floor.

"No! You must come. We need you."

Kristen looked up at his face. Tears formed in his burning eyes and turned the irises to a murky blue. It was a dream, a very bad and vivid dream. Why? Because people's eyes don't glow and don't change color. Besides, Scott Benson was dead. Or was he?

He picked up the bundle from the floor and once more offered it to her. She looked at it. It was her underwear, her jeans and her Philadelphia Eagles tee shirt. She felt her body relax, and her breathing became more regular.

As Scott Benson backed away from the bed,

she eased from beneath the covers and got up. There could be no harm, no danger in doing what he asked. She would go. She slipped the tee shirt over her lavender teddy and pulled on the jeans.

"Shoes, too," he ordered. "You'll need them."

If you say so, she thought, then retrieved her old Nike sneakers from beneath the bed. If this wasn't a dream, she concluded, then she had gone mad.

"Now come with me. It's almost too late. We must hurry."

Too late for what? She had no idea but followed him anyway.

Out of the house and through the narrow path, the same path that was located behind the Noman house, he led her into the woods. The story of the fate of Mr. Simpson, the previous neighbor, flashed into her head. She was very frightened of the forest.

But Scott Benson promised to protect her and remain by her side. Reluctantly, she entered.

The full moon made it easy to see; silvery streaks shot through the thick tree branches and helped illuminate the way.

As they walked along the narrow path, barely two feet wide in some spots, the canopy of leaves grew increasingly thicker. The light grew dimmer. Scott nudged her to go faster, which was difficult because of the protruding branches and rocks. She did the best she could while trying to appease this visiting apparition.

She concentrated on each step, feeling the warm, musty darkness envelope her. The distorted shapes of the foliage, the eerie sounds of scurrying creatures, the snapping twigs under her feet, the agonizing scrape of the boy's wounded leg caused fear to course through her body. She now regretted that she had agreed to the boy's pleas.

Finally, after what seemed a journey of miles, Scott Benson pulled her off the path behind a clump of bushes. He motioned for her to get down low so that she could see. Obediently, she knelt among the bushes.

Through a break in the bushes, she saw a circular patch of land that resembled a small, lush grove. It was highlighted by the moon, and she was able to see the dew glisten on the velvety grass.

But that was not all she saw.

Startled she recognized the five women who were visiting Eliza Noman, standing at the far end of the grove. Eliza was there, too. They were all naked. The older women, Emily Gregory and Dorothy Lasur, looked pitiful, wrinkled with sagging breasts, loose skin hanging from their arms and legs and protruding stomachs which had lost elasticity. Eliza was the worst. She sagged all over. Her skin hung so loose on her body that it resembled a spandex leotard five sizes too large. Louise Kacher, although not fat, had been cursed with huge thighs, a protruding ass and a round, puffy belly. On the other hand, her sister, Jenny, and Becky Tocks looked terrific. Jenny Kacher looked very sexy and voluptuous, her huge melon breasts bouncing as she laughed. Becky was simply beautiful with her tanned skin, firm, high breasts, long lean legs and a delicately curved back that flowed into her tiny, apple-cheeked buttocks.

Kristen's curiosity peaked as she wondered what they were doing so far into the woods, naked no less, at this time of the night. Maybe they were lesbians, part of some bizarre social club. Maybe that was why these women from such varied life styles and ages associated.

She opened her mouth to speak, but before she could utter a sound, Scott Benson tapped her on the shoulder. She turned to him and followed his slender arm, the index finger pointing like the needle of a compass at a strange stone located dead center in the clearing with something upon it. She squinted, trying to make out what it was, but the distance was too great and the stone was too elevated from her own stooped position.

Shifting her weight from one side to the other, her legs almost numb, she changed her angle to try to get a better look. There was a small white thing upon the stone, surrounded by a puddle of some odd looking reddish black liquid that dripped and formed a small pool at the base. Without thinking, she stood up.

In an instant, she felt Scott Benson's icy hand on her arm as he forced her back down. His strength was so great that her knees cracked when they hit the ground.

"Wait. They will see you. You're not like me."

She flashed a puzzled look at him. Not like him! And how was he? Her eyes fell on his battered face. In this light, he appeared more gruesome and grotesque than he did before. She turned away in disgust.

"You're not like me." His words echoed inside her head. "They will see you."

And what did it matter if they did? It was only a dream, a horrible, vivid, realistic dream. That would explain why she was in the dreaded woods in the middle of the night, her guide being a disfigured, missing boy who haunted her sleep as he did her first night in Burnwell.

"Close your eyes," he said. "Please. I want to show you."

She gave a visible shrug and did as he asked. She felt his icy hand press to the side of her head.

"No matter what you see, do not make a sound. If they know you are here, they will kill you," he said.

Kristen nodded. The side of her head felt as if he was holding an ice pack to it. It was beginning to get numb. If *they* didn't kill her, he would freeze her brain instead.

Through his cold touch, she saw. She saw more than she had bargained for. She saw what was lying on top of the stone. Her mouth flew open. She had to scream. She had to release the terror pushing up from deep within her, but before she could do so, he muzzled her with his other hand.

Tears rolled from her eyes, past her cheeks and down into the collar of her shirt.

On top of the stone lay a baby girl. And she knew, the knowledge washing over her like the rolling tide washes a beach, that it wasn't just a stone. It was an altar.

Suddenly, her stomach began to heave, and she tried to pull away. The boy pressed his hand more firmly to her mouth.

She had to scream, had to throw up, had to do something. Insanity threatened, beckoned, even welcomed her. What she saw was a tiny, innocent baby girl whose heart had been removed. There was a ragged, symmetrically round hole carved into her chest. The liquid surrounding the child was blood. Once more she struggled against the boy's grip. She wanted to see no more of the images.

He removed his hand from her head, ending the gruesome picture. "Enough," he said. His right hand remained over her frozen lips.

"Look!" he commanded, nodding in the direction of the women.

She brushed the tears from her eyes to clear her blurred vision. All six women approached the altar. As they walked, they draped the long, black robes over their shoulders, the fabric shimmering and billowing around them. Eliza Noman unfolded something dark and glossy. It took only a moment for Kristen to understand, truly understand.

What the old woman carried was a black garbage bag that could have only one use. She watched as Eliza opened it and, with one hand, grabbed the infant by its feet and dumped it inside the bag, head first. She spun the weighted bottom of the bag several times, twisting it closed. Then slinging the bundle over her shoulder like a sack of laundry, she turned and headed toward the path, the others following her in single file.

Kristen wanted to vomit. They had killed a baby! Her stomach heaved and wrenched, but with Scott Benson's hand still firmly clamped over her lips, sealing them shut, she felt certain he would allow her to choke rather than be detected.

She then realized that Becky Tocks had lied. Earlier today, when Kristen heard the baby's cry, Becky said it was a cat. Some cat! Bitch!

"Don't make a sound. Let them pass," he said.

She obeyed and remained huddled amidst the underbrush, the drooping limbs of the spruce shielding her as she watched the six file past. Each had a smug, defiant, wicked smile on her lips.

They did this, she thought. They murdered that child. What kind of beasts were they?

For the first time in her life, Kristen felt capable of murder—violent, savage murder in retribution for what they had done. She would kill them all, one by one.

She felt the adrenaline surge through her, the urge to chase after them through the narrow, winding path, but the boy firmly held her back.

"You can't confront them by yourself," he said. "They are protected by a power much greater than you, than themselves."

"I have to do something. What can I do?" she asked, tears filling her eyes. "Why show me this if I'm no match for them?" For a moment she thought about her other options. "Should I call the police?"

"No, they would not believe you. You have no proof, and I am the only other witness." His eyes moistened. "Now you know and now you believe. Soon you will do what must be done. The time of your fate is near."

"My fate? What about my fate?"

"You were drawn here for a purpose. You're the only one who can help me and the others."

"How can I help you? What others?"

For the first time since the beginning of this horrible nightmare, the boy smiled, exposing his silver-tracked teeth. "You can help us with your gift."

"I don't know what you're talking about. I have no gift."

"Yes, you do, believe me. You must use the power. It's greater than the one that protects those demons and binds us to them. You will be our savior."

Confused, Kristen turned away from him and stared at the sacrificial altar. Savior! Her? This kid had to be joking. He hadn't revealed who the others were. She had no idea who she was destined to save. At this point, overwhelmed at what she had seen and heard, Kristen started to question her sanity. "I must be going crazy. This isn't happening. It has to be a dream. Things like this don't happen," she muttered.

Scott Benson gave her another silver smile. "We'd better go back," he said, nudging her in the direction of the path.

As she stood up, thousands of pins and needles shot through her feet, up her legs and into her thighs. And for some time, as she headed in the direction of her house, she limped and stumbled until her circulation returned.

She didn't remember crawling into bed or recall that Scott Benson had taken her on a whirlwind tour of the faces of evil. Until, the next morning when . . .

A chattering and cackling came from outside, and she forced herself to open her eyes. The digital clock on the nightstand read 10:15. She had slept later than she had intended. She lay for a moment, listening to the noise and knowing it was Eliza and her guests. Such boisterous women, she thought, squeezing the pillow over her ears and trying to block out the sound. It was funny how well sound carried in the country where voices drifted untethered across the fields. These voices were entirely too loud and excitable.

Maybe they were having another brunch, or preparing for a Sunday picnic. Maybe they were . . .

And she remembered. With a jerk, she sat up and shook her head. She couldn't block out the memory. It flooded through her.

But did it really happen? she wondered. Or was it a dream? A dream. Yes, it had to be a dream.

Lying back down, she gratefully noticed that Tom was already up. She needed to be alone. She had to reconcile the incidents of last night.

It had been horrible, more horrible than anything she could ever imagine. Someone had killed a baby. No, that couldn't be. Who would do such a thing? But someone had killed something. A cat? The screeching, wailing, howling cat that the Kacher sisters owned? The one Becky said was as wild as they were?

She lay motionless, desperately trying to remember more. When she did, it was more than she really wanted to remember, but it was too late.

Scott Benson was there. He had taken her to the woods behind Eliza's house to show her what Eliza and the others had done. And he did show her. Oh yes, there could be no mistake about what she had seen—a baby girl that the six had murdered.

Now, lying in bed, it seemed impossible. It had to be a dream, another one brought on by the missing boy.

But even though she had to admit the women were an odd bunch, she couldn't believe they were . . . Satanists . . . devil worshippers . . . murderers. It was utterly absurd. Eliza was so damned frail and so damned old that she seemed incapable of doing anyone harm. It was more likely to happen the other way around.

The chatter outside continued, and she eased out of bed and crossed to the window. The day was bright and cloudless, already steamy and holding the promise of another August crusher.

In front of the Noman house, the five women piled into the ivory Cadillac. Eliza, dressed in a pale blue housecoat, stood by the driver's side watching. They said their good-byes, then the car pulled away from the house, moving slowly down the drive. The horn honked several times as the women waved and shouted their farewells.

Kristen stepped back from the window just as Eliza turned and looked toward the house. Although she hated to admit it, she was sorry to see the women go, dream or not. Except for the morning brunch, Eliza had ceased to be a nuisance. Now, with her friends gone, she'd be calling or looking for Tom again before the day was over.

Disappointed, she went to the closet for her pink robe. As she opened the doors, she gasped and took a step back. On the inside of the door was a full-length mirror, and in it she saw her reflection. A long scrape ran from her elbow, down her forearm to her wrist. The blood had dried and caked. When she touched it, she winced with pain. She examined it more closely. Where the hell . . . ?

Then she remembered. Last night, when she was with Scott Benson, she had caught her arm on a sharp branch that had protruded into the path.

Impossible! That was a dream, and one doesn't get injured in a dream.

Tom must have scratched her during the night.

Convinced of the scratch's origin, she reached for her robe. After slipping it on, she looked at the closet floor for her slippers. What she saw made her reel.

Her jeans and Eagles tee shirt were in a jumbled heap. Her Nike sneakers were caked with mud, pieces of leaves and pine needles.

She examined the tee shirt and found traces of blood.

Scott Benson had really come to her last night. "No. No, it can't be. Oh, my God, no!" she screamed and ran from the room. There had to be another explanation. She needed Tom. With his cold logic and analytical insight, he would be able to explain everything in rational terms.

He would ease her fears, she thought, as she ran down the hall and bound down the steps. He had to explain the nightmare or she surely would go mad.

TWENTY-ONE

"TOM, I HAVE TO TALK TO YOU ABOUT . . ."
Kristen made an abrupt stop in the doorway.
Tom was slumped over the kitchen table cradling his head in both hands.

"Are you okay?"

He slowly raised his head. His eyes were so bloodshot that the whites had disappeared. Black half-moons rimmed his lower lids.

"Yeah, I guess so."

"No, you're not. You look awful."

"Didn't get much sleep last night."

"Why?" she asked, wondering if he had the same awful dream. She drew in her breath, hoping he wouldn't tell her what she feared.

He shrugged and drained the last of his coffee from the cup. "Your behavior at the party got to me."

"I don't understand."

"Well, first you secluded yourself from the rest of the wives by going into the family room. Then you hooked up with Alan Kaspar."

"And?"

"For Christ's sake, Kris, I'm trying to make a good impression."

"The wives bored me to death. They were catty and gossipy. I had hoped to become friends with them, but I finally did find a friend —Alan."

"Christ. The man's a lunatic."

She couldn't believe what he had just said. Alan was far from a lunatic. He was a sweet, gentle, unpretentious man.

She poured herself a cup of coffee and sat down next to him. "He seemed okay to me."

"The way I understand it, he's obsessed with contacting his dead wife."

"His wife's dead? He didn't mention that to me."

"Why would he? It was probably his fault."

"What?"

"According to Alfred Bowser from Social Psychology, Kaspar blames himself for the accident." He took a gulp of coffee. "Kaspar had too much to drink at the annual faculty Christmas party. His wife was with him, but he wouldn't let her drive home. The roads were icy, and he plowed into a tree." Tom shrugged. "They had to cut her out of the car."

"Oh, my God, the poor man must be living with a lot of guilt. He shouldn't keep blaming himself."

"Well, he turned into a lunatic."

"Tom, don't be so cruel. He needs help. He has to accept his wife's death."

"No kidding. At first, people were sympathetic and tried to help him get over it, but now everyone at the college avoids him. They all laugh at him. He's into every crackpot supernatural idea there is. You can't take anything he says seriously."

Kristen said nothing. How could she tell him about Monday's appointment? He'd be furious. She decided to change the subject. "Did you take Amber out yet?" She reached for the puppy at her feet and stroked the back of its neck.

"You mean Pisshead? Yeah, about an hour ago."

"Don't call her that. She understands. When she gets a little older she'll bite your kneecaps." She giggled.

"So what's the story with you and Kaspar? I have a feeling you're not telling me everything."

She lowered her eyes. "Why do you think that?"

"I just do. Listen, I don't think you should get too friendly with him. It might look bad for me."

"How?"

"I don't want to be associated with him. He can screw me up."

"Don't worry. Alan Kaspar can't screw you up. Only you can do that."

"You and that lunatic are already buddies?"

"Something like that. I have a lunch date with him."

"Oh, Christ."

"I promise I won't cause you any embarrassment. And I won't involve you, either."

Tom shifted uneasily in his chair, deep furrows creasing his brow. "Is that what you wanted to talk about when you came in?"

"No. Something else. Something worse."

"Christ, what could be worse than Alan Kaspar? Go ahead, tell me."

"It's spooky."

"Already influenced by him?"

"No. It's about last night, after the party. You see, I had this dream. At least I thought it was a dream. Now I'm not so sure."

She paused trying to sort out her thoughts. Maybe telling him was a mistake, but she had to talk to someone.

Twice, she had dreamed about the boy, and if it happened one more time . . .

"Go on. I can't stand the suspense."

"Last night was the second time I dreamt about that boy Scott Benson."

"Scott Benson . . . Scott Benson. Who the hell is Scott Benson? An old boyfriend?"

"He's that kid that disappeared a couple months ago. Remember? It was in the paper when we first moved in."

She watched as Tom tried to remember. His logical, computer-like brain was retrieving the file. "Ah, I remember. So what was the dream about?"

She told him about the first dream—her bike ride out on Willow Road. She told him how he had vanished and then reappeared all bloodied and battered. Then she told about Eliza Noman appearing in the boy's place.

During the half hour it took to reveal the details of the two nightmares, Tom said nothing. He simply alternated between a frown and a smile. She told him about the boy's arrival in the bedroom, his appearance, and their journey into the woods where he led her to Eliza and her friends.

". . . and there was an altar in the middle with a dead baby on top of it. They had cut out its heart. Eliza and the others were naked." By the time she finished revealing the details of the dream, she was in tears, dabbing at her red, swollen eyes with a shredded tissue.

Tom nodded, took a deep, heaving breath and let it out very, very slowly through pursed lips.

"That was some story, one hell of a dream."

"I don't think it was a dream. Look at this." She picked up her arm and turned it so that the large scratch was visible. "I did that out on the path." She watched as he examined her.

"Could have done that anywhere. You better clean that out. Maybe I scratched you with my tossing and turning."

His nails were long, but not long enough to do that to her arm. "Maybe. But how can you explain my clothes?"

"You were probably doing some yard work, threw them on the floor and forgot about it." He examined her arm again, tracing his fingers along the side of it.

She quickly pulled away. "Don't poke at it. It hurts." He didn't believe a word of her story.

"Put something on it. I probably did it."

"Maybe I did it to myself," she said angrily as tears formed again and rolled down her cheeks.

"Look, Kris, you never really wanted to come here, but you did it for me. You were afraid. It's natural. The move was traumatic, and you suppressed your anxiety. Because you care about people, you empathize with this Scott Benson thing. The latent fear and anxiety are manifesting themselves in your dreams."

"Well, Eliza and her friends really bothered me yesterday. They were weird." She wiped the tears from her face.

"You're kidding. They were a great bunch of women." He paused. "They talked a lot about Eliza's garden and her plantings. Nothing wrong with that. They're a harmless bunch of women who enjoy gardening."

Kristen grunted. "Well, what about that baby I heard crying?"

"What baby? It was a cat. I saw it. Louise Kacher ran inside when it started to whine, then a few minutes later she brought it out onto the porch. Big white sucker."

He gulped his coffee.

"Oh." She had to accept his explanation. If he saw the cat, then it was a cat. "But that dream really upset me."

"It was only a dream. Forget about it. I had one last night, too."

"You did?" Was his similar to her own?

"Yeah. It was erotic. Guess I'm not gettin' enough."

Kristen smiled. Since the move, their sex life had been nonexistent. More than anything, she

205

missed that closeness, but she also missed not spending time with him. It wouldn't be a bad idea for them to go out and spend the entire day together, alone. Besides, getting away from the house would help her forget about the dream.

"How about if we drive to Carlisle or Harrisburg today? We can have dinner. See a movie."

"Why? I'd rather hang around here."

"Tom, please, I need to get out. This place, this town, is making me crazy. I need a change of scenery."

He didn't answer. A scowl formed on his face, and he took another gulp of coffee.

"Please."

"Well, maybe we can just drive into downtown Burnwell. Check out the shops."

"No. If you won't come with me, I'll go myself."

"It's up to you. I just don't want to go out. I have classes tomorrow." He got up, put his coffee cup on top of the counter and left the room.

Kristen finished her coffee, then headed upstairs for a shower. There was no point in going alone. She'd find something to do to take her mind off her dream.

TWENTY-TWO

"YOOO-HOOO, ANYBODY HOME? I SURE COULD USE some help out here."

Kristen stood in the laundry room, cursing to herself. She put down the puppy's water bowl then turned to the door, wishing there was some way to avoid her. But if she didn't answer Eliza's call, Tom would.

"Damn her," she grumbled. She had wanted to spend the day training Amber and working on the crochet patterns that Rose had given to her, not entertaining Eliza.

She took a deep breath, counted to ten, then went out to the screened porch. "What is it, Eliza?"

The old woman stood at the bottom of the steps, her hands holding two huge, rectangular silver trays, one on top of the other. Tucked beneath her arm was a bulging brown paper bag.

"Open the door, dear. I'm loaded down."

Shaking her head, Kristen stepped toward the door and held it open, allowing Eliza to pass through. She did the same with the kitchen door, then helped the old woman place the trays on the table. Both were filled with goodies—cherry and blueberry pastries, miniature donuts, croissants and cookies. They looked delicious.

"I brought you some goodies. Thought we could share a late brunch. Emily enjoys baking so much that she's swamped me with leftovers. I can't possibly eat it all myself," she said, emptying the contents of the bag. It was filled with tiny finger sandwiches in the shape of hearts and diamonds and clovers. "I'm really grateful that you and Thomas are here to help me out. It certainly promises to be another scorcher today. Well, fall isn't too far off. I can't . . ."

Kristen's eyes drifted to the old woman's mouth. It seemed to move with an animated motion, like a windup toy whose mechanism had jammed and was now unable to stop.

She tried to interrupt but finally gave up. Eliza talked so fast that she started to get the hiccups, but she continued talking. If she wasn't such an annoyance, she'd be comical.

Soon her voice changed from a distinguishable babble to a shrill buzz. Kristen could only stand by and watch her, wondering if she would ever shut up. Then she noticed something strange about Eliza—a vague, subtle difference.

The old lady seemed more vibrant than she was the day before. Her face glowed, and she looked younger.

She studied her features more closely. She was right. The deep furrows that ran the length of her face didn't seem as deep. Her hair, which had been fine and wispy, appeared thicker. The skin under her chin didn't sag as much.

How odd, Kristen thought, frowning. It couldn't be. No one in history had ever had the ability to reverse the aging process. There was never a fountain of youth and never would be one. And if someone did discover the key to the aging process . . . well, it would be a miracle.

Whether it was possible or not, Eliza definitely seemed younger.

"And let me tell you about the Kacher . . ." The old woman rambled on.

Kristen nodded politely, pretending to be interested, but her mind was on something else. She was thinking about the day Eliza had returned from New York. Then, too, she had seemed younger and more vibrant. Maybe spending time with her friends, with those who were much younger, had a positive effect on her. Maybe that was why she spent so much time with Tom. Eliza certainly appeared younger than the first day they had met.

But could companionship alone produce a physical change? Hardly. It had to be her attitude or the way the light filtered into the room.

". . . so I said to Louise, 'Thomas and Kristen just love your colognes and soaps'. And she gave me another bottle. She had it in her suitcase just in case she met some attractive man. Oh, she was pleased that you both liked them. She promised to send an entire dozen."

"What?" Kristen asked. She wasn't sure she had heard her right. An entire case of cologne and soap for her and Tom? For what purpose? She wasn't crazy about it to begin with.

"She's going to send you and Thomas all her bath products, her homemade toiletries." She pulled a bottle from her pocket. "I'm sorry I don't have one for you today, dear. She only had Thomas's with her."

"That's okay. I still have a lot left." She didn't want to tell her that she hadn't used it, not even once.

From the large paper bag, Eliza retrieved a bottle of banana liqueur. Kristin wondered how the old lady knew that Tom had finished both.

Thank heaven she didn't bring any for her. Unlike Tom, she found the underlying scent offensive, and the liqueur had a funny aftertaste.

"You are using it, aren't you, dear?" Eliza didn't wait for a reply. "I'd hate to have Louise go through the expense of sending more if you're going to let it go to waste."

Then you should have asked me first, Kristin thought. "It won't go to waste." She smiled weakly. She would give it to her mother or her sister or whomever cared for the scent.

Right then, Tom sauntered into the room carrying Amber in his arms. "If this little shit doesn't quit following me . . . Oh Eliza, I didn't know you were here."

Amber barked, then growled. Squirming out of Tom's arms and hitting the floor with a thump, she went for Eliza's legs. But when Eliza stomped her foot, Amber jumped away, still barking and growling at the old woman.

Eliza's face turned hard, her eyes blazing at the dog. She bent over and hissed at Amber like a cat.

Suddenly Amber tucked her tail between her legs, pulled back her ears and scurried out of the room, whimpering.

"That animal's neurotic," Tom called after her. "Maybe we should get a replacement. I can't take this shit."

Kristen ignored his remark and ran after the dog. Hell, she loved Amber and would train her even if it killed her and the dog. "She's gone, Tom. I can't find her. She was too quick for me. Where the hell did she go so fast? Amber!"

Tom and Eliza followed her, and she saw them shake their heads as if in disgust.

"So that's the pup you brought home," Eliza said, rolling her eyes. "Could've done better. Would've done better with none at all. Too much trouble."

Tom looked down at her and nodded in agreement.

"Hmmph. It's cute, but no matter. I hope you train it soon. It'd be a shame if it got out and started to dig up my flower beds and hurt itself. Should've gotten a cat."

Amber let out a yelp, then scurried out from behind the floor-length drapes and up the stairs to the bedroom.

"I don't like dogs," Eliza said in a huff, narrowing her eyes at the scampering, terrified animal. "They're too destructive."

"Eliza, she's just a puppy," Kristen shot back, recognizing the veiled threats as she headed for the stairs.

"I know. Just be sure to keep her out of my flower beds."

"We will," Tom responded. He patted her shoulder, then said to Kristen, who was already halfway up the steps, "Why don't you leave her up there? At least until Eliza leaves."

Kristen stopped and looked down at them. Maybe he was right. The dog was obviously nervous around guests—or at least this guest. Why else had she become so wild? Eliza was also upset. She wondered if the old woman was also afraid of dogs.

Slowly, one deliberate step at a time, she descended the stairs. She watched Eliza, whose attention was focused on the second floor. She didn't look frightened, only angry. Kristen prayed Amber never got into the old lady's flowers, for her own sake. She felt afraid for her pup and resolved to buy a strong leash.

Reluctantly, Kristen went back into the kitchen and put on a pot of coffee. Tom and Eliza sat at the table like two old friends. Eliza's mouth never quit. She babbled on and on about her travels around the country and Europe and Egypt.

Kristen listened. Some of her stories weren't bad, but after a while her voice became a blur once again. She caught herself yawning. Just when she was about to excuse herself to go upstairs to find Amber, Eliza looked at her and said, "May I use your little girl's room? This coffee is going right through me."

Kristen nodded. "Maybe I better go with you since Amber is up there."

"Oh, don't be silly. I'm not afraid of a squirt like that," Eliza said, scurrying out of the kitchen.

It wasn't Eliza she was concerned about; it was Amber. The old woman had one hell of an effect on the pup.

A few minutes later, Kristen heard Amber bark, then whimper. When she stood up to go for the dog, Tom grabbed her arm.

"Don't spoil the animal. She can take care of herself. Besides, Eliza won't hurt her," he said.

She wasn't so sure about that. From the way Eliza reacted to Amber . . . Suddenly she smiled. In another six months, Amber wouldn't be running from Eliza; it would be the other way around.

She sat back down and waited for the old woman to return. She crossed her arms over her chest and sighed. Almost the entire afternoon had passed, and she wondered how much longer Eliza would stay. Sooner or later, the goofy old bitch had to go home.

As Eliza Noman stepped into the small bathroom, Amber barked, then snapped at her legs. Again Eliza glared down at the dog and hissed. She laughed as it scampered out of the room. She closed the door behind her.

The bathroom was decorated in shades of pink and mauve that contrasted sharply with the white porcelain fixtures. On the tile floor she saw a puddle of urine. Tom was right—the dog was a Pisshead.

Her eyes scanned the .gold-speckled vanity top. There were bottles of hand cream, face cream and mouthwash. She turned to the lacy white shelves behind her and smiled. It didn't take long to find what she needed.

The pink hairbrush had Kristen's auburn hair tangled in its bristles. With the tips of her fingers, she pulled out the hair and rolled it into a ball. She stuck it in her pocket, flushed the toilet and opened the door. Smiling, she descended the steps and headed back to the kitchen.

By the time Eliza had decided to go home, Kristen felt exhausted and irritable. The old woman had stayed until 5:00 and hadn't stopped talking for a minute.

Soon after her departure, Tom retreated to his study, the small back bedroom, to prepare an exam. While Kristen cleaned the mess Amber had made in the bedroom and the bathroom, she heard him whistling that same odd tune. She had the urge to scream at him to stop but went downstairs instead.

After reading a copy of *Psychology Today*, she settled down to watch the news about the fires in Yellowstone National Park. She also worked on the crocheted doily that Rose was helping her with.

At 9:00 Tom came out of the study, poured himself a large glass of Eliza's homemade liqueur and went to sit on the porch. His mood was worse than this morning. He was sullen and withdrawn, and she decided to keep to herself.

An hour later, she still struggled with the doily, ripping out stitches, doing them over, then ripping them out again. She was having a terrible time of it.

Suddenly she heard Tom stir. Repeatedly, the lawn chair scraped against the wooden boards, the aluminum screeching like an owl and causing shivers to course up and down her spine. She heard him moan softly, then increasing in volume and intensity.

Alarmed, she threw down her work and ran to the porch. "Tom, are you okay?" She dropped to her knees beside him and shook him gently. "Tom, please tell me what's wrong."

Without warning, his eyes popped open, and he sat bolt upright in the chair. Sweat poured from his face.

"Tom, what's wrong?" she asked with growing alarm.

"Wh-what?" he answered between gasping breaths.

"Are you sick?"

"No, I'm okay. Just a dream." He flashed her an angry look, then leaned back and closed his eyes.

Kristen watched him with curiosity. She noticed that even his arms and legs were drenched with perspiration. Then her eyes saw it.

Beneath his crisp, white cotton shorts, she

saw he had an erection. A wet spot formed next to the zipper on his pants.

Oh, my God! She reached for him, hoping to hold him close.

"Leave me alone," he snarled. His lips curled up and exposed his teeth.

But she didn't leave him alone. She wanted to hold him. Even though his dream may have been erotic and he had no control over his dreams, she still felt a pang of jealousy.

"I said, 'leave me alone!'" he bellowed and shoved her away.

She kept her balance as he got up and stormed inside. "What the hell is wrong with you?" she screamed after him. Why was he so angry? Was he embarrassed? Wasn't he too old to be having wet dreams?

In all their years together, he had never experienced such dreams. So what was causing them? Who was he dreaming about? Not her—of that she was certain.

She stood up and stared out into the blackness. Not a single light shone. She felt a shiver. She felt cold despite the sultry night.

She looked up at the Noman house. A light burned in an upstairs window. Above the house, as if impaled on one of the tall spires, was a silvery moon. It was surrounded by an eerie, icy haze. She shivered again.

Her eyes focused on Eliza's window, and she wondered if Eliza played a part in his dreams as she had in hers. The thought brought a smile. Eliza was old enough to be his grandmother, and to have her as a participant in an erotic dream was ridiculous.

But something inside her cried out against that assumption. She suspected Eliza had more to do with Tom's strange behavior than she was ready to admit.

With that thought in mind, she moved away from the screen and went inside. Her hand shook as she bolted the door. She felt spooked but didn't know why.

She hurried to the living room, gathered her crocheting and tucked it into her basket. She closed the windows, then checked their locks. She double-checked the doors, then headed up to bed. She didn't want to be alone. Even if Tom wasn't himself, she wanted to be near him. It made her feel safe.

As she ran up the steps to the bedroom, she thought about Alan Kaspar and was glad they had a lunch date. Tomorrow could prove more interesting and informative than she imagined. Maybe Tom didn't care for his colleague, but she did.

By the time she reached the top of the stairs, she had an uncanny feeling that her association with Alan was going to play an integral part in finding answers to questions that had bothered her since her arrival in Burnwell.

TWENTY-THREE

UPSTAIRS, TOM GRABBED HIS PAJAMAS, AN OLD pair of red jogging shorts, and rushed into the bathroom. He stripped, depositing his white cotton shorts and his white underwear into the bathroom sink. They were a mess. Yellowish semen had soaked through and stained the material. He looked down at himself and saw some of the residue of his dream.

He smirked. What did it matter now? He had other things to worry about, one of which was his darling wife. He didn't want her to see the come all over his pants. He had easily hidden it from her in the past, but this time it was too late.

He recalled the look on her face when she saw the bulge in his pants. Nothing he could say would wipe the shock from her face. Goddamn her! So why try to hide it now?

Smiling to himself, he took a wad of toilet paper and cleaned the jizzum from his belly. He then filled the sink with warm, sudsy water and soaked his clothes. No sense in ruining a good pair of shorts, he mumbled, by letting it dry. When the stain lightened, he was satisfied.

He looked up into the mirror above the sink. He looked tired and worn, but satisfied. He raked his fingers through his hair. The dream was something else—great, terrific, but disturbing. What the hell was happening? He hadn't had a wet dream since he was a kid and dreamt about Judy Shelley from his ninth grade class. Judy had let almost every boy, including him, bury his head between those soft mountainous breasts. Just the memory started to give him an erection, and he turned his mind off. He was tired, too tired. All he wanted at the moment was a shower and some sleep.

But wasn't he too old for something like this to be happening? Wasn't he supposed to have passed that stage of his life? Shit, he didn't have to dream about sex; he could have it any time. If not with Kristen, then with the dozens of college girls who flirted with him every day, but he didn't want Kris or the other girls at the college. He wanted to be with the girl of his dream, the one who came to him night after night.

Unfortunately, he didn't even know the woman he was dreaming about, but God, how he wanted to!

She was beautiful and blond and perfect. Her breasts were plump and round, high and firm.

Her ass was tight, and the tuft of hair below her navel was softer than down. He thought about her eyes, round brilliant emeralds.

The erection began again. He tried to push her from his mind but couldn't. Who the hell was she? Damn, he had to know.

He turned on the shower, making sure the water was cool to douse his mounting tumescence, and stepped inside. He stood beneath the pulsating shower head, and the water rushed over him and ran in rivulets down his skin. He felt the heat leave his body.

He felt good—damn good.

Under the stream of cold spray, his testicles pulled up almost into his belly. He no longer felt horny. He no longer felt the urgent need to seek out and pop the woman of his dreams. After another minute, he soaped himself, making sure to scrub the sticky goo from his skin.

Kris came to mind once again. Damn her, she had seen. What the hell was he going to tell her? How the hell could he face her?

It wasn't like he was cheating on her. It was only a dream. She'd understand that; she was an intelligent woman. What he couldn't tell her was how much he enjoyed the dream, how much he lusted for the woman, how much he wanted to find her and really screw her brains out. No, they were the parts he would leave out. He also wouldn't tell her how real the dreams felt. It was almost as if the blond Aphrodite was actually touching him. God, he could still feel her satin skin beneath his fingertips. He could still smell the spicy aroma of her hair. It reminded him of the cologne Eliza had given him. And he could still feel the softness of her lips, her tongue circling his own.

At that instant, he made a decision, a decision that would affect both him and his wife, a decision that would possibly destroy them.

He said it aloud, beneath the rushing water. "Damn the bitch. If she doesn't like my dreams, she can go to hell. Who the hell needs her?"

TWENTY-FOUR

ELIZA NOMAN PULLED THE HEAVY VELVET DRAPES away from the attic window and stared down at the Roberts' home. She smiled. Tonight would be a night to remember for Kristen Roberts.

She saw the flash of lightning on the western horizon. Thunder rumbled in the distance. An expected cold front promised relief from the stifling heat by morning.

She closed the drapes and moved to the middle of the room. Her attention focused on the small scrolled brass box that lay upon the altar. She lifted the lid, then reached inside and withdrew the miniature object. It fit neatly in the palm of her hand.

The object resembled a human form, a woman with auburn hair—Kristen's hair. She had glued the ball of hair that she had taken from

Kristen's brush to the top of the mandrake root and created a doll.

She closed her fingers around it and thought about the foolish girl next door. Kristen left her little choice. She didn't drink the strawberry liqueur or use the toiletries. Now she was forced to try another method. The mandrake root and the doll would suffice. It was better than physically destroying her outright. If she did, there would be questions and suspicions as there had been with Simpson.

This afternoon she had invited Kristen to lunch, but the fool refused. She had an excuse for every day of the week—lunch with a friend, applying for a job, Rose Howard and on and on. There was no way to get the herbs into her system.

She thought about the Howards. She hated them. She had complained about them often to Thomas who said he wouldn't bother with them, but it wasn't him she worried about. It was his damn wife. If the Howards in any way interfered with her plans . . .

But Kristen also had another friend, the person she was having lunch with tomorrow. Who was it? Could this friend pose a threat? She doubted it, but she couldn't leave anything to chance. She would find out the new friend's name from Thomas.

She looked back at the mandrake and smiled. It would replace the nightshade and cause the physical illness. But what would replace the cubina and cause the madness? She would keep trying.

She pressed the root to her breast and anointed it. "This is Kristen Roberts. It can be no other. My lord, prince of the night, keeper of all that is unholy, I beckon thee to entwine Kristen Roberts and this as one. May they never be separated, as long as we both shall live."

She bowed her head and became silent.

A clap of thunder shook the windows. A bright flash of light shone through the velvet drapes.

Eliza closed her eyes and chanted:

Pain and sorrow engulf thee.
Sickness and infirmity plague thee.
From this day forward, Kristen Roberts,
your body and your spirit shall belong to me.

A feeling of power and victory rushed through her as she gently placed the doll inside the brass box and surrounded it with the five small, withered objects inside. The objects belonged to her children.

The anointing oil for her ceremony had been prepared precisely. The main ingredient had been pure—the essence of innocence, the hearts of virgins. Her victims had not succumbed to the loose values of society and had not despoiled their purity.

The microwave had made her task of drying the five human hearts easier. She had been able to remove the required amount from each, pulverize it into powder and mix it with the herb oil. Only one more was needed. Six was his desired number.

Then the final ceremony to restore her youth

could be performed as it had been many times before, but this time there would be an added bonus—Thomas. He would sign the pact as she once had. They would become one. Then they would leave Burnwell and begin a new life elsewhere. They would age naturally, then repeat the ceremony again, as she had done since the mid-1600's.

She closed the lid and locked the box with a miniature key that dangled from the gold chain around her neck. She tucked the key and chain inside her dress, where it hung safely against her breast.

Leaving the box and its precious contents on top of the altar, she turned and headed down the attic steps. She felt satisfied, content and confident that all would go as planned.

Kristen lay in bed listening to the patter of rain on the roof. Outside, the thunder rumbled. Streaks of lightning illuminated the room. But as the storm moved farther and farther way and the rain became heavier, she drifted off to sleep. She entered into a horrifying dream world from which she could not break free.

TWENTY-FIVE

WHEN KRISTEN WOKE UP, IT WAS AFTER 9:00, AND she felt awful. Her head ached, her stomach hurt, and her arms and legs felt like wood. As soon as she got out of bed, she found the need to steady her trembling body on the bureau before she could hobble over to the window.

Outside the day was sunny, the sky a cloudless blue. A chilly breeze whipped into the room through the open window, which she quickly shut. The air was cool, a brisk 50 degrees, unusual for the month of August. Since last night's storm, the temperature had dropped 40 degrees. The expected high for the day was in the mid-60's. The cooler temperature was more than welcome.

Up at the Noman residence, she could see Eliza stooping over a freshly dug flower bed.

This time she planted something yellow. Kristen shook her head. The old woman really was obsessed with her flowers or rather her plantings, as she so often referred to them. She needed another flower bed as much as a desert needed more sand.

She noticed the new bed was much smaller than the others. It appeared to be only two feet in diameter. In contrast to the others, the new addition was insignificant. Why would the woman bother with such a trivial patch?

Turning to look at the clock, she was stunned to see it was already 9:30. Damn! She had a noon meeting with Alan Kaspar and would now have to hurry. Her legs ached as she tried to make the bed. As she struggled with the sheet, she realized Tom had left for work without saying goodbye, but after what she had witnessed last night, she wasn't sure she really wanted to see him. Hell, what would she say? "I'm disappointed you came in your pants? Thanks a lot for cheating on me in your dreams?" Needless to say, when she did see him, it was going to be awkward. She decided the best thing to do was to pretend that she hadn't seen a thing.

As she tripped over to the closet looking for something to wear, her stomach quivered and her head pounded so fiercely that she was tempted to stay home, to call Alan and tell him she couldn't make it.

But she had to go, no matter how poorly she felt, even if Tom didn't approve. It was as if she were drawn to Alan. Of course, she couldn't explain her feeling of kinship to the man, considering they had just met, but there was definitely a magnetism between them. If she was coming down with a virus . . . well, she would just have to suffer with it. Today was important.

She put the small brush that was laying on the sink into the medicine cabinet before washing her face. She had used it last night to scrub the remaining stains of semen out of Tom's shorts. She noticed they were not hanging on the shower bar where she had put them to dry. Tom must have taken them to the laundry room and thrown them in the washer before he left, she reasoned. Good. She was glad she didn't have to see the shorts, let alone touch them until Wednesday, the regular washday—not because of what happened, but because of the way he had treated her afterwards.

Was his experience a tip-off of something? Had a young, nubile student caught his attention, and was it surfacing in his sleep? She hoped and prayed that if that was the case the lust was limited to his dreams.

Unfortunately, she was plagued by her own dreams, dreams hardly as pleasant, dreams that were not easy to forget or ignore. They haunted her day after day, and sometimes, for no apparent reason, she would burst into tears. She remembered the concern on Rose Howard's face and the sympathy in her voice when she asked, "What's wrong, dear? Are you feeling okay? You look upset."

"I'm fine, thank you," she answered. "I guess I'm just a little melancholy today."

"Want to talk about it?"

"Not really. I'll be fine." She had forced a smile, but she wasn't fine. She would never be fine. She was haunted by Scott Benson, coming to her room and leading her into the woods to see the mutilated infant. Each time she thought about it, she died inside, bit by agonizing bit.

She turned the shower on and stepped beneath the pulsating spray. It was then the memory came back to her. It was vague at first; then piece by piece, it crystallized. It explained her soreness. She tried to concentrate on something else—Alan, her mother, her sister, Amber, anything—but it was useless. Last night's dream was the worst.

It wasn't like the others. Scott wasn't present, but it was vivid and lifelike, almost too real. It was terrifying.

She had been running through a cornfield, the tall stalks bending and dipping beneath her weight. She could feel them bounce, the long coarse leaves slapping her arms, her legs and her face as she passed. The air was hot, thick and humid. Her right side ached. She tried to draw a breath but couldn't. She wanted to stop, to lay down between the rows of corn and rest.

From behind, she could hear the panting of a huge beast gaining on her. She had to run faster.

In the distance, she saw the warm glow of her home, a light in each window. Tom stood on the porch and waved to her, smiling. She opened her mouth to scream to him for help, but no sound came out. She reached the edge of the cornfield, coming to the boundary of her own property, when she got a whiff of rotting, rancid meat. She started to gag and choke, her stomach wrenching. She saw Tom coming to meet her, arms outstretched, laughing. She slowed down, and that was when it hit her. A searing pain crossed her back from shoulder to shoulder.

And then she woke up.

The dream made her shiver under the warm stream of water. It was only a dream, she told herself, only a dream, but her mind wouldn't listen. She wanted to remember more. She had to know how it turned out. She had to know if she got away. She wouldn't be showering if she hadn't. She laughed nervously as she forced the dream from her thoughts. Once again, she was making too much over something that was beyond her control.

She thought of her date with Alan Kaspar and wondered if the reason they were so friendly, the reason they were drawn together, was because they were both mad. She giggled and continued to laugh at herself, rinsing the mounds of lather from her hair, eager for the meeting.

The college campus had two places to eat lunch. One was the large cafeteria in the Student Union building; the other was the smaller, more intimate cafeteria in the building that housed the faculty lounge. The food was the same in each with no difference in quality, taste or variety, but there was a tremendous difference in atmosphere. Unlike the Student Union, the faculty building was more subdued and quiet. Few students, except for those intent on studying or those trying to catch up on their work, frequented the place.

Kristen and Alan Kaspar sat at a small, circular wooden table. Alan hungrily devoured an enormous, foot-long steak with mushrooms, while she nibbled at a chef's salad. Between bites they talked about the party and about Burnwell, which Alan praised as a terrific place to live—no crime and no pollution to ruin the tons of fresh, country air. He sounded like a rerun of Tom.

Kristen listened intently, but not once did she tell him that she didn't find it an attractive way of life. Other than the quaint, restored buildings that lined both sides of Main Street, the place had little else to offer.

But according to Alan, it was the nicest place he had ever lived, and he had lived in a lot of places—San Francisco, Washington, D.C., New York. The list went on and on. She was impressed and wondered how a man so accustomed to the thrill of the big city could settle for this place. "Old age," he answered, and they both laughed.

To Kristen, the last person on earth to be considered old was Alan Kaspar. Sure, his chronological age was up there, but he didn't act old. He didn't even look like a man ready for retirement.

After lunch they took a leisurely stroll to the Psychology building and immediately headed for the labs on the bottom floor. Walking through the corridors, she felt a pang of guilt that she hadn't visited Tom. She didn't intend to, either. For one thing, she knew he wouldn't be too happy to see her. It was far better to allow last night's incident to wear off.

The heels of her sandals clicked toward the west end of the building along with the squish of Alan's gummy soled shoes. They sounded like quite an odd pair in the silence of the lower level.

For one precious moment, she found herself wishing that she knew him better. She then would be able to talk about Tom or maybe even discuss her own dreams. God, how she wished to have someone to talk to.

"Yes?" Alan asked suddenly turning to her. "What is it you want to talk about?"

She flashed him a startled look.

"Is there something you want to discuss?"

She shook her head, almost too quickly. How on earth did he know? He frightened her, and she felt the urge to run. It wasn't natural to have someone read your thoughts, not natural at all.

Alan gave her a warm smile.

She was overreacting. She liked him and had no reason to fear him, and if he could tune into her, maybe it would be nice. It might be spooky, yes, but also comforting. It certainly would assure her of never having to worry about not having anyone near. But what if she had a negative thought about him? She doubted that she would, but just for argument's sake, what if she did? That could prove embarrassing.

He caught her eye and smiled again.

Somehow she doubted that she could ever think poorly of him. After today, she felt even more comfortable with him than she ever dreamed possible.

He stopped before a frosted glass door, dug into his pocket and pulled out a large slender key. He unlocked the door and gently touched her elbow to guide her inside. This slight touch from him sent a tingly sensation up her arm that felt good and warm and comforting, so unlike the touch of Eliza Noman.

Inside, the room was filled with about a dozen rectangular tables. Four wooden chairs flanked each table on either side. On her left was a battered brown and orange couch; an old brass pole lamp with amber globe lights stood beside it.

Across the room was a huge wooden desk covered with nicks and scratches and some graffiti. It read, "Ann loves Rick." A seven-inch penis was also carved into the side of the desk. Flower Power was scratched beneath it. It gave her some idea of how long the desk had been around and how many students had had the pleasure of its company.

Behind the desk was a large blackboard that ran the entire length of the wall. It had been erased clean. In front of the oversized desk were the student desks, small and cramped-looking, with their own brand of graffiti which she did not read.

She wondered what a class would be like in this room. What did they discuss? What type of experiments did they conduct?

She surveyed the remainder of the room.

Situated at the very back were a series of

padded, electric blue, vinyl mats, lying side by side, in an evenly spaced row. They took up an area approximately eight-by-ten.

She thought about her own college days when there had been rumors of such classes— experiments with ESP, hypnotism, telekinesis, relaxation therapy and searches for the aura. Back then, she had wanted to take a course in parapsychology but never had been able to fit it into her hectic schedule. Of course, she didn't always believe in it, having never experienced a truly psychic phenomenon. She didn't totally discount its existence, either. However, the experiments were probably fascinating and a lot of fun.

"It is fun, Kristen, but it's also a lot of work, just like any other branch of psychology."

He had done it again!

This time her eyes narrowed when she looked at him. "How do you always seem to know what I'm thinking?" she asked.

His eyes were bright with amusement.

"Do you do this sort of thing with everyone, or are my thoughts so transparent?"

Alan laughed and squeezed her shoulder gently. "Hardly everyone. With you it's easy." He paused. "You see, I noticed the connection the first time we met at the party. It is quite rare for two strangers to be so in tune with each other. That's the reason I asked you to come here. I'm certain you have a paranormal gift, a very strong one at that. To be honest with you, I've only been able to do this sort of thing with such accuracy with one other person. That was my mother when I was still a boy. She had the gift and undoubtedly passed it on to me. We could communicate without saying a word. It used to drive my father nuts."

She eyed him with suspicion. "I don't understand why you think I have a gift. I've never noticed it. I'm no different than anyone else."

"Oh, yes, you are," he said emphatically. "Most people have some sort of ability like feelings of déjà vu, playing hunches, premonitions, superstitions. But your ability to transmit thought is extremely refined. I suspect it's the same with reception, but you dismiss everything as coincidence, which of course it isn't. Your gift needs to be focused."

"How can you be so sure?" The cynicism was evident in her voice, but she noticed Alan didn't seem to mind. He appeared more amused than anything. She wasn't sure if she should be angry or not. If he was making a royal ass out of her, she would be furious.

"Well, how about giving me a chance to find out, or better still, to prove that you are special. Are you willing to take a few simple tests?"

She hesitated before answering. Tests? Were they safe? Sure they were. A feeling of well-being still lingered. She looked at him and nodded her head. There, she was committed. If things got out of hand, she would quit. She would simply walk out on him. What harm could a few little tests do?

"I'm glad you said yes. Oh, one other thing . . ."

Here comes the catch, she thought.

"There's no catch. If these tests prove me right, would you also be willing to develop your gift?"

"I suppose," she said, uneasiness rising in her voice. "But why?"

"Because it can be useful, to you, to me and to many others."

"Useful in what way?"

Alan took a deep breath, then closed his mouth in a formless line. Slowly, he let out his breath. "Well, first let's see what you've got, then we'll discuss the uses. Okay?"

She hoped that she hadn't made a serious mistake by agreeing to his tests without first finding out what they were. This is the same man that everyone refers to as a kook. "Okay," she answered. What the heck. What's life without a little risk? She would open her mind for what she hoped was a new and interesting experience.

"How about if we begin with a written test? We can go on from there." He glided to the oversized desk, withdrew a manila folder from its top drawer and handed it to her. "This shouldn't take too long. Just promise me that you'll be honest with your answers. Please." He looked at her with pleading eyes. "Please don't tell me what you think I want to hear."

"I won't. I promise."

He seemed to study her face for a moment as if to see if she was lying. "Make yourself comfortable. You can use my desk." He pulled out the chair and motioned for her to sit down. "I have to leave for awhile. I should be back in about a half hour. Then we can discuss your answers."

"Okay." She smiled, sat down behind the desk and opened the folder. Inside were three type-written sheets containing the questions.

She lifted her eyes to Alan who gave her an approving look before sauntering out of the room. After she was certain he had gone and the steady mush of his soft-soled shoes no longer reached her ears, she began:

1) Have you ever known who was calling you on the phone before picking it up to answer it?

She answered yes. That was coincidence. It happened to everyone. There was a direct rela-tionship to the time of day, or the day of the week, or how long it had been since hearing from a specific person.

2) Have you ever known who was at the door before you answered it?

Yes. Same reasons as the first question.

Smiling wryly, she continued, going through the first pages quickly.

On most of the questions, she had answered yes because they referred to things that hap-pened to people everyday of their lives, such as thinking about someone you haven't seen for a long time and they suddenly visit you. The test was ridiculous.

When she came to the next question, she burst out laughing. It read:

18) Have you ever wished to win something like a prize, a raffle, a lottery, and won?

If she could do that, she certainly wouldn't be living in Burnwell. She'd be traipsing across

Europe and be worth millions.

She read on, until she came to:

23) Have you ever been visited by the dead?

Scott Benson flashed inside her head, but since there was no proof the kid was dead . . . Of course, she dreamed about the dead like her Aunt Mary or her Aunt Katerine. She answered maybe.

27) Have you ever sensed danger for someone you loved, and then that danger existed?

Danger? Not really, but something similar.

A few years ago, when Tom accompanied his father to Laredo on a business trip, Tom was bitten by fire ants that had gotten into his bed during the night.

At 3:00 in the morning, the same night, she felt a sting and jumped out of bed.

When Tom returned home, he told her about the ants. Then she told him about her experience. They took into account the two hour time difference and realized it happened to them at exactly the same time.

She answered maybe.

The chances of her being psychic seemed slim, but for Alan's sake, she moved on.

29) Have you ever caused an object to move with your mind?

No.

30) Have you ever lost something and envisaged where it could be found with your mind?

Sure. Her wedding band. While searching for it, a picture of it sitting in the crook of the pipe beneath the kitchen sink flashed before her eyes. Tom opened the pipe, and it was there.

She closed the folder and pushed it away from her, then leaned back in the chair. Proving someone was psychic was difficult. Even the Amazing Randy, who had offered $10,000 to anyone who could prove their psychic ability to him, had no takers.

She heard the gummy squish of shoes in the hall and swiveled to face the door. A few seconds later, Alan Kaspar sauntered into the room.

"Finished?" he asked with a smile.

She nodded.

"Good. Let me have a look."

She watched him scan the pages. With a grim smile, he replaced them into the folder. On the outside of the manila folder he scribbled her name, then walked over to the gray file cabinet and tucked it inside.

"Want to talk about anything?" he asked as he perched on the edge of the desk.

She shrugged, then mentioned the incident about the fire ants, then the one about her wedding band. There was no point in mentioning Scott Benson and visits from the dead since they had been dreams.

They talked until three o'clock, and by the time she was ready to leave, she agreed to come back on Wednesday for another test.

The thought of having psychic ability, or second sight as Alan referred to it, frightened her, and yet it also intrigued her.

Alan seemed hellbent on proving she was psychic, but as she got into her blue Honda and started to drive home, her mind rambled with old adages. What you don't know won't hurt you. Ignorance is bliss. Were they true, or was it better to know what was going to happen before hand? Then, at least, she could prevent it from happening.

For the entire drive, she argued both points in her mind, and by the time she pulled up to her mailbox and slid across the seat, she had decided to see Alan's tests through to the end, regardless of the outcome. She shuffled through the mail. There were catalogs, offers for the lucky winner of a three-day excursion to Bermuda, the phone bill and finally something of interest, a letter from her sister. The gummed flap of the envelope was opened.

She threw the mail onto the car seat and drove up to the house. Eliza puttered around her flower beds near the front of the Victorian. Kristen averted her eyes and pretended not to see her. She hit the button on the sun visor for the automatic garage door opener and drove inside. She hurried up to the laundry room to release Amber, then plopped down by the kitchen table and began to devour the letter. She shook her head over the mutilated envelope.

Dear Kris,

Glad you're coming next week. Mom's got herself in a tizzy. She's worried about you, and I can't calm her down. She won't listen to my assurances that you're okay.

When you get here and she see's how good you look, I'm sure she'll settle down.

She's also talking about Dad again. She said he's worried about you, too. God, I hope she's not getting sick again.

Sorry I have to write and tell you about this, but I feel it's best to prepare you. Maybe you can help. Anyway, besides the bad news about Mom, I'm looking forward to seeing you. It's been too long. Maybe we can . . .

Kristen placed the letter on the table then and said a silent prayer that her mother wasn't becoming sick again. She and Tom were all right. Well, maybe not at their best, but still . . .

One question from the test flashed in front of her eyes. Did you ever sense danger for someone you loved?

Did her mother sense danger? Did she have psychic ability?

Kristen shook her head. She was getting as ridiculous as Alan. Maybe he was a kook like Tom had said, and now he was about to draw her into his private society. Before long, they'd be taking her away to the Enchanted Kingdom.

She picked up the letter. As she began to read it again, a brown spot, a smudge at the bottom of the page, caught her eye. She looked more closely.

It was a thumbprint. She could see the lines and ridges clearly. She brought the page to her nose and sniffed. Fresh dirt?

But her sister hated gardening. Her mother tended the garden. It was like therapy for her. Unless her mother had read the letter. She hoped she hadn't. She didn't want her to know that she and her sister were discussing her.

Then it hit her like a ten pound sack of

potatoes. It came into her mind and stuck. At first she wondered if she were going mad, if paranoia was taking over and she, too, was losing her mind, but when she calmed down, she knew. It was as if she was reading it off a huge slate.

She had opened the letter. The words flashed on and off like a neon light. No. Impossible. Her mind clung to reason, but only for an instant before the flashing sign came on again.

She did read it. It was her thumbprint. Eliza's. She was sure it would match the one on her hand.

Everything started to make sense. The gummed flap had been open.

Her sister always sealed everything, and if it didn't seal, she taped it shut. And another thing, why else would the smell of dirt be so fresh? It even had a moist feel to it. It wasn't her sister's print or her mother's, because it would have dried.

It made sense.

The only thing that didn't make sense was why Eliza would bother to read her mail. There was nothing left to find out about her or Tom. The old bitch knew it all.

She took a deep breath and let it out with an exasperated sigh before turning back to the letter. After finishing it, she tucked it behind the floral canister set on the countertop, then she started dinner.

She couldn't help but think about Eliza reading her mail. Damn, if the old bitch was, it was a blatant invasion of privacy. Somehow she doubted she would ever come across the likes of Eliza Noman again in her life.

And if she was not only shuffling through her mail but reading the letters too, then it was her job to prove it. She would face the old lady. But how could she get the proof? She doubted that Eliza would be foolish enough to get caught.

Somehow, someway, she vowed to catch the goofy bitch in the act. Maybe it would take a while, but damn it, she would.

TWENTY-SIX

THE NEXT MORNING, KRISTEN'S RESOLVE RE-
mained strong. She hadn't mentioned her suspicions to Tom, not because she felt he would
become angry, but because she felt he wouldn't
have cared. Since Sunday night, after his wet
dream, he had become even more distant. He
barely looked at her and spent most of his time,
when he wasn't entertaining Eliza, in his study.
Even when she tried to talk with him, to simply
inquire about his day at the college, he simply
grunted and avoided her eyes.

His lousy mood was taking its toll. If it wasn't
for Rose Howard, she was sure she would have
spent the day at home, brooding, but Rose and
George with their optimistic outlook had a way
of bringing out the best in her.

After cleaning the house, she scurried up the

road to pay them a visit. The day was sunny with wisps of clouds across the powder blue sky; a light breeze kept the air comfortable. Bees and birds and butterflies buzzed and flitted and chirped around her. The smell of fragrant wild-flowers danced through the air, making her forget her anger and her mounting hatred of the old woman.

By the time she reached the Howard farm-house, she felt revived and cheerful and care-free.

"This is just lovely," Rose chirped as she adjusted her wire-framed glasses on her nose. "You're doing fine. You've tightened your stitch enough to make it neat." She paused and lifted a finger in warning. "Now remember, dear, don't tighten it too much or it'll pucker. You want your crochet to lay flat." Rose turned the round doily over and over in her hands, examining it as a jeweler would examine a fine gem. "Once you finish this set, I'll give you a lovely old pattern for placemats." She lowered her glasses onto the tip of her nose and looked up at Kristen. A smile formed on her lips. "Would you like that?" she asked, nodding at the same time as if to convince her prodigy that she would.

"Yes, I really enjoy crocheting. It fulfills my need to create." It also took her mind off Tom.

"Good." Rose giggled. "I'm glad. By week's end, you should be finished. Maybe next week you can start the placemats. They're real pretty. Nice and lacy."

"Oh, I forgot. I won't be here next week. We're going home to visit."

"That's wonderful. I bet you both miss your families, and they you. When you get back then, dear."

Kristen nodded. Even though she was glad to be going home, she knew she'd miss Rose. She had been visiting three times a week since the first day they met and had grown to love and depend on her for her wisdom and advice.

"And I think this trip would be good for Tom. At least, he won't be hanging around Eliza," Kristen said. "I wish you'd tell me more about her."

"Oh, she's just an awful woman," Rose said. "George and I won't go near her. I suppose he knows more about her than I do since he lived near her all his life." She paused. "Just stay away from her, dear." She released an exasperated sigh. "I guess that's difficult for you and Tom since she lives so close, but do try."

"Believe me, I do, but she's such a pest. Sometimes I wonder if she has anything to do with Tom's mood."

Rose nodded. "I'm sure the trip home will cheer him up. And when you get back, we'll have you both over for dinner. George said he wants to talk to Tom." She frowned. "I haven't met your husband, but George tells me he's a nice young man."

Nice? If George saw him now, he'd never believe he was the same man he had met at the Farmer's Market.

"We'd love to come," Kristen said, even though the chances of Tom coming for dinner at the Howards were slim. For some reason, he wasn't pleased that she and Rose and George had become good friends. She didn't understand how he could prefer Eliza to people like them.

"Let's set a dinner date for two weeks from this coming Sunday," Rose said, excited.

Kristen nodded, then smiled. She hoped the trip home really would change Tom's hostile disposition. She also hoped he would agree to dinner with the Howards, but she didn't count on it.

After spending another hour with Rose, she returned home and went directly to the laundry room for Amber. The dog lifted her already good spirits by a big welcome. Amber could hardly control herself, jumping and yelping and licking her hand. Kristen had never seen the puppy so exuberant.

The dog was getting bigger and bigger and becoming more and more attached to her. She loved the animal. She was her best friend, always there and waiting, no matter what her mood.

She gave Amber the attention she so rightly deserved, then started dinner, Chicken Parmesan. Even though grumpy Tom would enjoy it, he would gulp it down silently. Then he would hurry off to his study with a bottle of Eliza's banana liqueur, or go up to Eliza's, leaving her to fend for herself. Grateful she had Amber? You had to be kidding.

It was nearly 4:00, and in an hour he'd be home, ravenous and, as usual, miserable. If only she could reach him and understand what was wrong, she'd do her best to help him. But he remained close-mouthed, and with each passing day, he seemed to be pulling further and further away.

As she cleaned and sliced the fresh beans, she wondered how a good, solid marriage such as their own could sour so quickly. More than anything in the entire world, she wanted their relationship to be as it had been before Burnwell, but as each day passed, she felt she was asking for the impossible.

What was happening? What the hell could she do to stop it?

Damn, she'd do anything at all to save her crumbling marriage.

With tears trickling down her cheeks, she continued to prepare dinner, hoping for a miracle.

But when Tom arrived home, he was more irritable and quiet than usual. She didn't pry. She had had herself a good cry and felt drained, almost immune to his mood. They ate their dinner in silence, and as she cleared the table, the phone rang. Tom bolted to answer it.

"Hello?" His voice was gruff.

She strained to listen, to try and identify the caller by the nature of his responses.

"Sure. No." Tom said in a more pleasant tone. "I don't mind at all." His voice became soft and syrupy. "I'll be right there." He hung up the phone gently and sauntered toward the back door.

"Where are you going?" she asked. She knew

perfectly well where he was going, but she wanted him to say it.

"I'll be right back." Once again his voice sounded cold and distant, as if he were talking to a stranger, to someone he disliked. Kristen turned her back to him. She didn't want him to go, but realized nothing she said would matter. They would only argue, and he would go anyway.

From the corner of her eye, she saw him slip out the door. For a moment, he stood on the porch whistling that same monotonous tune. As she heard him go down the steps, she moved to the sink, pretending to fill it with soapy water. She watched as he headed toward the Noman house, a definite bounce in his step.

Whatever was going on between those two was strange. If she didn't know better, if it wasn't for the old woman's age, she would swear they were having an affair.

The thought of Eliza and Tom writhing in bed flashed before her eyes and caused her stomach to turn.

Before she allowed herself to get sick, she pushed the thought from her mind and concentrated on tomorrow's meeting with Alan. She wondered what kind of tests he had in store for her. She thought about having a psychic gift, about how convenient it would be to be able to read her husband's mind, or Eliza's for that matter. And she started to laugh. What fun it would be to know what they were thinking and doing up in that rambling old house. What fun it would be that they wouldn't know she knew. Even though she doubted that Alan was right about her, there was no harm in dreaming, was there?

TWENTY-SEVEN

THEY SAT OPPOSITE EACH OTHER AT THE SMALL card table. Imprinted on each of the five-by-seven cards was a number. The cards were white, the numbers black. There were 24 cards in the deck. Out of the two dozen cards that he held up to her to identify, Kristen got 22 correct answers.

"That was good. Hell, it was terrific. The best test results I've ever seen." He laughed heartily, like a kid who just figured out the complexities of a new toy. "Now, how about humoring me a little bit longer." There was a definite twinkle in his eye that put her at ease.

She agreed and followed him to an area at the back of the room where there were no windows. A long rectangular table flanked the wall. Two wooden folding chairs had been positioned in front of the table. Sitting on top of the table was a twelve-by-twelve black mirror.

Alan told her to be seated as he pulled out one of the chairs. She watched him with curiosity as he flicked on the tape recorder that sat on a shelf a few feet above her. The sound emitted from the machine reminded her of radio static. The only thing missing was the crackle that went along with it. When she mentioned it to him, he laughed and told her it was supposed to be the sound of ocean waves. "At least that's what the brochure says it's supposed to be." He smiled kindly, then told her to relax.

As he dimmed the overhead lights and sat in the chair beside her, she realized that if she used her imagination the static did sound like the ocean moving in and out over the sand, lulling her into a hypnotic trance.

Once more Alan instructed her. "Listen to the waves . . . keep your eyes closed . . . listen to the sound of the waves. Breathe deeply. Block out all sounds and thoughts except the waves and my voice. Concentrate on your breathing. Relax. Soon you will feel like you want to sleep, but when I tell you to open your eyes, you will look into the black mirror." He paused and breathed along with her. She could feel her entire body becoming limp. The sound of the waves were soothing and reverberated inside her head, over and over. His voice was becoming a drone; it sounded distant, as if she were in a tunnel, or he was. Nothing else mattered. She was aware that her breathing had become shallow, like she wasn't breathing at all.

"At first, when you look into the mirror, you may see nothing, but keep looking. Soon you may see a series of flashing lights. Don't be alarmed by them. Don't avert your eyes. Keep looking. Then, soon after, you may see a picture. If possible, describe it to me. If you are unable to speak, don't worry, just remember what you saw and tell me later."

Kristen continued to do as he instructed. She knew that he was hypnotizing her, and she was surprised how easily and quickly it could be done. She always thought it would take longer, if it would happen at all. His voice, smooth and rhythmical, filled her head and she didn't resist. Closer and closer, she was being lulled to sleep.

"Tell yourself to relax. Breath from your diaphragm. You're doing great. Keep it up."

For a moment she felt her mind and body begin to rebel. A flash of white fear crossed through her like a streak of lightning. Her heart leapt inside her chest. But Alan was a friend, one of the good guys, she told herself. And if she wanted out of the situation, she would remain in control of her own mind. Hell, she wasn't about to jump around like a chicken. Stuff like that only happened on television.

She concentrated on his voice. "Relax, relax, relax."

The distant waves pounded on the unknown shore, rushing in and out, in and out. Her breathing followed the rhythm.

Her arms felt heavy, her hands resting in her lap like two wooden blocks. It was the same with her legs. His voice drifted past her through the tunnel and was gone. She wanted to open her eyes, but how? She was paralyzed. But she had to look into the black mirror. Something was there for her to see.

Her eyes popped open.

The mirror was no longer black. It was filled with brilliant points of light. Automatically her eyes squinted, trying to adjust. From one corner, at the top of the mirror, a smoky haze oozed out and crawled across the surface, covering the starlike lights. The whites turned to blues, a soothing relief to her own stinging eyes. Then the haze began to lift. It was almost as if it had been a window shade that was being pulled up slowly.

Little by little, millimeter by millimeter, it rose, exposing the true picture in the glass. It was a projection she didn't want to see.

Scott Benson rode his bike, moving fast on the narrow road. The air whipped through his hair, his shirt billowing out behind him. The scene was rolling by quickly, much faster than in her dreams. It appeared as one of those old silent films, except this one had been done in color.

Then she heard his squeals of delight as he descended the steep hill. The smell of fresh pine wafted in the air. She could see the perspiration on his forehead and smell it's salty aroma. His legs pumped faster and faster. She could almost hear the rush of blood inside his veins.

She heard the cry, the same chilling scream that she had heard dozens of times in her dreams.

Intently she watched, following his journey in muted horror.

He was struggling up the second hill now. He topped the hill. As he began to descend, his face twisted with fear.

There was the clickety-clack of bone and claw against macadam. She saw the massive front paw reach out for him, strike him, rip his shirt and shred the skin on his slender back. She watched as he went tumbling onto the road, unable to stop, rolling into the deep ditch. The boy fell unconscious.

But when he opened his eyes, the beast came. It moved toward him with stealth and cunning. It moved with deliberate purpose, with an intelligence she was not aware animals possessed. It seemed to be smiling when it knocked him back into his makeshift grave. It seemed to be laughing when it ripped open his throat and then his chest.

That was when she screamed. She screamed for herself, for the boy, for all those who would come in contact with this demon. "No. Stop. Please. God, save him. Save him, or he'll be damned."

Something touched her shoulder. Something pressed lightly on her arm. She pushed away hard, and then she began to fall into a bottomless pit—falling, falling, falling, as if in slow motion. She closed her eyes and softly hit bottom. Had she reached the eternal fires of hell? She didn't dare open her eyes to look. She was sure the beast would be there, because it had come from hell.

A distant, nebulous voice gently called her name, the sound echoing all around her.

"Kristen, Kristen."

She felt the solid tile floor beneath her, its coolness pressing against her right arm and shoulder. She opened her eyes. Hot tears stung and glazed her vision. She had no idea where she was.

The voice seemed to be coming closer. Should she try to run? No. The soft nurturing inflection in his voice comforted her.

Her vision cleared. She could see the vague blur leaning over her. The figure touched the top of her forehead, stroked her hair and repeated her name.

Slowly, she focused on his face, and their eyes met.

"Oh, thank God you're all right. You are, aren't you?"

It was difficult to speak. It was even more difficult to move, but she nodded her head.

"Can you get up? Let me help you."

Alan lifted the old wooden chair off her legs and placed it upright beside the table. She grunted and moaned as he grasped her from behind, beneath her arms, and lifted her to her feet.

It was difficult to stand, and she plopped into the chair. She felt weak, tired and disoriented. She couldn't remember what had happened. She was sitting, being hypnotized . . .

Her eyes followed Alan as he reached for the recorder and clicked it off. Then he snapped on the overhead lights.

Squinting, she shielded her eyes from the brightness.

"I shouldn't have done this," he was saying. "If I hurt you I'll never forgive myself. I should have known. I should have known your gift is too powerful, maybe too powerful for an old bungler like me."

She looked at him and saw his eyes were filled with tears. She tried to speak. Her mouth felt dry and sandy, and she tried to build up saliva. Her lips trembled when the words formed. "I-I-I . . ." She stopped. The sound of her own voice startled her. She swallowed hard, then tried again, "It's not y-your fault." She stopped again. What was wrong with her? It felt as if her brain was unable to make the right connection. She had to regain her composure and tell him about herself. She had to confide in him about her dreams.

Suddenly, the entire scene that she had experienced under hypnosis flooded into her mind, and she shuddered.

Yes, she had to talk to someone about Scott Benson and the beast that stalked her night after night. And she had to talk to him about Tom's dream, or what little she knew of it. Something strange was happening to them, something that neither one of them could explain.

After a few minutes, she began again, this time sounding more like herself. The words came easily although her voice still remained shaky.

"Dr. Kaspar . . ."

"Alan, please."

She nodded and gave him a small smile. "Alan, don't blame yourself. It's not your fault. I didn't tell you about my dreams." She paused and looked down at her arm. The scrape was almost gone. "I didn't tell you about my arm." She held out her arm to show him the faint scar running down her forearm. In some places, a brown crusty scab still remained. "I got this in one of my dreams."

Gently, he examined her arm. With eyes wide and brimming with tears, he looked at her sorrowfully and barely mumbled, "What? That can't be. I've never heard of such a thing." He lowered his head and wiped at his eyes with the back of his hand. "I have hurt you. My God, forgive me."

"You haven't."

"Then you sleepwalk and don't know it."

She shook her head.

"Kris, you must."

She smiled. Then she began her story. She told him of Scott Benson and of their adventures together. She told him of her beast from hell, or wherever it was from. She told him of her morning exhaustion, of being psychically ill, of her terror. And finally she told of Tom's erotic dream, blushing as she spoke, avoiding his eyes.

He sat staring at her, appearing numbed by her tales. "Why didn't you tell me before?" he said. "I could have helped you. I should have known before we did this experiment."

"I was afraid you'd think me crazy." She looked away from him, remembering Tom's reaction. "I did tell my husband, but he didn't take anything I said seriously. 'It's a manifestation of your anxiety,' " she said, trying to imitate Tom's voice. "I thought he was right until I saw the boy in your mirror."

Alan started to speak, but she lifted her hand to quiet him.

"The only difference between that vision and my dreams is that now I saw the boy die."

"Die? Who killed him?"

"An animal. At least I think it was an animal. It had these huge orange eyes and three-inch fangs. And claws. My God, the claws were so long. And . . . and they ripped open his throat, then dug into his chest and pulled something out." She paused for a moment. "No. That was in the dream, or was it? I'm getting things confused. Wait." She thought about the dreams and about the episode in the mirror. Did the creature take his heart? She didn't know. "Scott Benson came to me with a horrible hole in his chest. He didn't have a heart. I don't know for sure what happened, but I do know that the baby in the woods didn't have one either. God, that's disgusting." Just thinking about it made her want to throw up. "Is someone sacrificing children? I mean, could they be using them for some kind of ritual? There are so many damned kooks out there, so many cults and devil worshippers. Are they hurting kids?"

Alan shrugged. She could see that he, too, was upset. She was certain that he had also heard stories about crazy groups who wanted to make sacrifices. But that was barbaric.

She was beginning to get too upset. She had to

maintain her rationale. Of course, there were people out there who did such things, but if they were in Burnwell, wouldn't the police already know about them? Wouldn't they be keeping a watchful eye on them? Yes, they would. And if a child disappeared, they would be the first suspects.

"When you were looking into the mirror, I heard you yelling 'no' over and over again."

Kristen brushed at the stray tear that rolled down her cheek. "I had to try and stop the murder, but I couldn't." She reached into her purse for a tissue.

Alan scrubbed his hand over his forehead. He mumbled to himself, "A beast . . . from hell. It killed the boy and now it's after you. But why? Where did it come from? Maybe someone conjured it up. Maybe there *is* a hell . . . a Satan."

He hesitated for a moment. She noticed the fear in his eyes as he stared at the wall above her. "Good God, who could have such powers?" He shuddered. "Maybe it was all just a dream. Maybe."

Kristen sensed that he understood and half-believed. At least he hadn't laughed. She felt grateful for that. She leaned over toward him, touching his arm with her fingertips.

"Alan, if it is possible, I think I know who."

His eyes darted toward her. "Who?"

Taking a deep breath and letting it out very, very slowly, she said, "This may sound weird and crazy, but I think it's Eliza Noman, my neighbor." She watched his reaction. There was none as he continued to look into her eyes. "You see, what I didn't tell you was that when Scott took me into the woods, she was there, and so were the others who were visiting her. They were a strange bunch. I'll tell you about them later. Anyway, they were all naked and wrapped in flowing black robes."

Alan appeared to be deep in thought, focusing again on the wall behind her. Finally, he looked at her and said, "How many?"

"Six."

"Six. A coven is supposed to have thirteen. They're not witches, at least not in the conventional sense. Besides, the witches of today are given a bum rap. Most are just a group of people who are attuned with nature. They don't cast spells, fly past the moon on brooms, wear pointy hats or scare children on Halloween. They're basically harmless." He stared at the wall. "If it was a Satanic cult, they would be caught. Too many kids have disappeared. Mostly they perform animal sacrifices, when they can get away with it, but it's very risky. And if there are any humans involved, it's just a sexual thing. You know, willing participants." He continued to stare past her. "But you said a beast from hell. How do you know it's from hell?"

"I don't know. It may be just an expression. It seemed a proper description."

"Are you sure? You must be sure. If it isn't a dream, then we have to do something about it. Fight it."

"Fight it? How? How do you fight something like that."

"I don't know, but the boy came to you for a

reason." He paused and drew in a long breath, letting it out slowly through pursed lips. "Do you believe in an afterlife? If so, then maybe there is a specific reason he visits."

To Kristen, this all sounded farfetched. Even though she was trying to remain objective and keep an open mind, it was difficult. She didn't want to insult Alan. She thought that maybe he was a little off with his thinking. However, she did believe in an afterlife, and maybe, just maybe, . . . "Yes, I do believe in an afterlife, and the boy did say I could help." She thought about Scott's words.

"Exactly what did he say?"

"He said there were others. Alan, he said I could help."

"How many are there?"

She shrugged and raked her hand through her hair. How could she help? What the hell could she possibly do to help someone who was dead? Somehow she always thought they were the ones to help those here on earth. After all, they were the ones who transcended to the other side.

Fighting back the urge to cry, she got up and walked toward the front of the room. Sure, she'd help. She'd do anything to help a child, but right now she wanted to go home. She wanted to forget about the entire scenario for a while.

"Alan, I don't feel well. I think I just want to go home. I felt bad this morning, but I feel even worse thinking about this stuff." She turned to face him, grimacing. "I've always been healthy, that is, until Burnwell came into my life. When

Tom accepted this position, I got nauseated and dizzy for a week. My doctor said he could find nothing wrong with me. The morning we moved, I got the same way. When we pulled up to the house, I had to run inside and throw up. The following morning, I was looking out the window watching Eliza plant a flower bed, and I got so damn dizzy I thought I was going to faint. I dismissed it as a panic attack. There were other times, too, but since the doctor I saw before we moved said I was as healthy as a horse, I guess I'm okay physically. But mentally, I'm turning into a basket case."

"Kris, don't—"

"No, I must. I have these awful dreams, my marriage is suddenly falling apart, and it seems my entire life is turning into one big nightmare. But why? I don't have the slightest idea." She turned from his gaze. "My mother had a breakdown after my father died. Maybe that's happening to me."

He took her into his arms and held her tight, so tight, in fact, she thought her lungs would burst. "Let me help you," he said. "Together we'll look into the dreams and conquer them." He released her and held her at arm's length. Tears misted his eyes.

"You are an important person. You may have a gift, but first we have to conquer whatever is worming its way into your life."

"How?"

"Come tomorrow. Next week. We'll find a way."

"I can't. We're leaving for home on Friday. My

mom's expecting me. My sister said she's worried about me.''

"Your mom?''

"She always seems to know when I'm not feeling well. Maybe she, too, has a gift.'' This time there was sarcasm in her voice. She watched as he winced, as if she had slapped him. "I'm sorry. I didn't mean to . . .''

He waved her apology away with his hand. "What do you mean she always knows when you're sick?''

"Intuition, I guess.''

"Tell me a little about your mom's breakdown.''

Kristen hesitated. She really didn't want to talk about it to anyone—it was too painful—but she knew he would understand. "She used to say that my dad was visiting her after he died. I guess she couldn't accept his death. We had to put her into the hospital. That's about the sum of it.''

"Maybe he was. That is possible.''

She thought about what he had just said. Now she wondered if her mother was special since she always suspected things would happen before they did. She even knew if someone was about to die. Kristen felt a wave of guilt wash over her.

"Alan, what if she did see my father? What if we put her in the hospital for no reason? My God, how can I ever forgive myself?''

She felt her body tremble. Could she have done that to her mother?

"Stop it, Kris. You're getting hysterical. Just keep in mind this talk about ESP is speculation. We have no proof."

No proof. That word bounced around inside her head. Was there ever any proof? Real proof? She remembered her mother's face and the look of betrayal and hurt in her eyes.

"Stop it, Kris!"

He grabbed her shoulders and squeezed hard. It took a moment for her to regain some composure. He was right. She had to remain calm. Her mother still needed her, and she needed all her faculties, not to mention the strength she needed to conquer whatever was happening to her. And what if Scott needed her?

She had to be strong, but to back down would be so much easier. To run and hide would be very easy indeed.

She looked into Alan's kind eyes and lowered her own. She was embarrassed. "I'm sorry. I have to pull myself together. I can't let this stuff get to me. Right now, I just don't know what I'm fighting."

"But you will. Once you get back, we'll both know. I'll do anything and everything to help."

"Thanks, but I'm not sure you want to get involved. Be careful about the promises you make." She hesitated, not sure she should say what was on her mind, but she did anyway. "I have a powerful foreboding, a strange feeling, that something is coming. Whatever it is, it's going to be bad—real bad."

"Then we'll fight it together."

Kristen was grateful for his support, but deep down she felt fear for him, more fear than she felt for herself.

After spending another hour talking to him and discussing the possibilities, both rational and irrational, she finally felt calm enough to drive home, innocent to what was waiting for her there.

TWENTY-EIGHT

"WHERE THE HELL HAVE YOU BEEN? THIS GOD-damned dog's been yapping ever since I came home," he yelled as she walked into the kitchen. His eyes were red with anger. "I can't believe you left her locked up all day. You should see the laundry room."

Kristen avoided his eyes and moved nimbly around him. She certainly didn't feel like getting into a shouting match with him, especially after what had happened that afternoon with Alan. She opened the refrigerator to get a package of ground beef. Hamburgers would be tonight's dinner. That was all she had the strength to make.

"I asked you where you were. Don't pretend I'm not here," he screamed, but still she didn't answer. "Don't ignore me!" His voice had risen another octave.

From the corner of her eye, she saw him approach, and before she had a chance to move, he grabbed her arm and swung her toward him. She stumbled away from the refrigerator, the door closing silently behind her.

With one swift jerk, she wrenched free and moved swiftly to the opposite side of the room. "Don't you dare touch me like that again," she screamed back at him. "Not ever!" She rubbed the upper part of her arm where his fingers had left five red welts.

"Just tell me where you were all day."

"None of your business."

"Oh, it's my business, especially when you're haunting the campus with some lunatic. I saw you. I saw you with Kaspar." The anger in his voice, in his eyes, in the way his mouth twisted when he said Alan's name, terrified her, but still she would not give in to his tantrum.

"What the hell did you two do today? Wait. Don't tell me. The old goat's banging you." He let out a laugh, shrill and almost inhuman.

Kristen bolted across the room and slapped his face hard. Stunned, he took a step back. She watched as his fingers on both hands balled up into fists.

"Don't you ever insinuate something like that again. Alan and I are friends. How dare you?" She had the urge to hit him again, but she stopped and whirled around and stomped in the direction of the living room. Something about him scared her, something she had never seen before. She sensed a fury, an uncontrollable anger, a possession that was almost inhuman. Never in their entire married life had he spoken to her like that. Never had he looked at her with such hate in his eyes. And it frightened her. God, how he frightened her, but she held onto her fear, keeping it in check, because the worst fear, the thing she feared the most, was that any sign of weakness on her part would send him over the edge. Then he would come after her, and God only knew what he'd do.

At the doorway leading into the kitchen, she stopped and turned to face him. "Maybe that's what you and Eliza are up to, huh?" Now it was her turn for sarcasm. "Maybe that's why you're up there so much. Maybe that's why you're accusing me."

He glared at her. She had said enough. His arms hung at his sides, his hands still curled into tight fists. He opened his mouth to speak, his voice shaky and unsteady. "That's sick, you know, real sick."

"No kidding." It *was* sick, she had to admit. She turned to leave, but before she took her first step, he called out to her.

"Forget about visiting your mother. I'm not making any trips."

"Fine. I don't need you anyway."

"If you go, don't come back." His voice had reached the highest pitch she had ever imagined it could, until he said, "I mean it."

At that moment, she knew he did mean it, but suddenly she didn't care. Enough was enough. After weeks of wondering how to save her marriage, it didn't matter anymore. Let it crumble, she thought. Let it fall into a billion pieces, because she wasn't about to beg or worry or put herself out again, not for the bastard who stood glaring at her, foaming at the mouth.

"I didn't intend to. I thought I'd leave you to your neighbor. Forever." This time he didn't have a comeback. She stomped out of the room and headed upstairs.

Before she reached the top of the stairs, she heard the kitchen door close with a bang. She ran the remainder of the way into the bedroom. When she reached the window, she saw Tom stalking toward Eliza's.

"Damn you both!" she screamed. Tomorrow she'd be far enough away not to care. Nothing could please her more. Nothing at all. She hurried to the closet and pulled out a suitcase, the largest one, and began to pack. Hot, bitter tears streamed down her cheeks.

TWENTY-NINE

AT 30 SECOND INTERVALS, SHE GLANCED OVER HER shoulder to make sure no one was up and about, watching. She moved toward the forest hurriedly, pulling the dark cloak tight around her, trying to block the stiff westerly breeze that made the August night seem more like October.

As she stepped into the forest behind her house, Eliza sighed in frustration. Everything was going slower than she had anticipated. First, she had to wait to get her last sacrifice because of the uproar over the missing kids. The police made it difficult with their constant patrols. Second, Kristen proved tougher than she expected.

Kristen leaving town put another halt to her plans. She wanted to get rid of the fool, but in her own way. She didn't want her to suddenly come back for Thomas. If she did, she'd be forced to destroy the girl outright, and that could lead to more delays. She wanted to use the cubina, the nightshade, and the mandrake, but the little bitch wouldn't cooperate.

It was frustrating and becoming more and more impossible. Because of the distance created by Kristen's trip, the effects of the mandrake would lessen. She was losing precious time. She couldn't wait much longer for the final ceremony; the oil had to be used soon, or it would lose its potency. And she couldn't wait much longer for Thomas, her desire was too great.

How unfortunate Thomas couldn't prevent Kristen from leaving. She had hoped he would have been more forceful. But no matter, she loved him enough to understand and forgive his weakness. She would make sure, with his help, that Kristen returned, and then, since Thomas confided in her regularly, getting rid of the girl would be child's play.

She moved swiftly along the narrow path. The trees rustled in the wind, the branches reaching out and snagging at her cloak and hair. She ducked repeatedly beneath the foliage, so much so that she stumbled to her knees, scraping one on a protruding rock. The polished brass chamberpot tumbled from her hands, rolling down the bumpy path. Its contents, a single sheet of yellowed paper, fluttered beneath the trees, catching on the low boughs of a tremendous fir.

Cursing to herself and rubbing her bruised, skinned and bleeding knee, she staggered to her feet and hobbled after both. She retrieved the parchment first.

With one hand, she held it firmly as she picked up the pot and wrapped her cloak tight around her nakedness, shielding her shivering body from the cold. She scuttled through the twisted path, beneath the gnarled trees and on into the deepest part of the woods.

Soon, the path began to angle sharply to the left. She stopped and stepped around a group of pine branches onto another path, an adjoining trail very few were aware of.

Oh, her previous neighbor had found it, but that turned out to be more his problem than hers.

She turned to check that all the pine boughs were in place, just in case anyone had decided to follow. Then she shuffled deeper into the already pitch-black forest. The trees were so thick and the foliage so dense that not even the sliver of a moon nor the billion stars above were visible.

But her eyes saw quite well, better than any animal in the forest, and as she moved more hurriedly, she could hear the small creatures darting beneath her feet and hiding in the brush. She passed a twisted oak and saw an owl in the upper branches. He ceased his hooting. Crickets stopped their melodic chirp, and frogs stopped their throaty croak. They recognized her evil.

Among the trees, the fireflies, resembling a mobile string of Christmas lights, danced. But as she approached, they, too, scattered, leaving only blackness, the blackness that she loved.

As soon as she reached the clearing, she moved up to the stone altar, still stained from the fluids of the last and most important sacrifice—a baby, so young and tender, so without mind to resist. Upon the altar she placed the brass pot, the aged sheet tucked neatly inside. For a moment she looked at its contents, and the signature of Agatha Crenshaw looked back at her.

There was a tear, small and insignificant, forming in the corner of her eye and rolling down the side of her nose. She didn't want this. If only there could be another way . . .

She shook her head, fighting back the remaining tears. She smothered any feeling of love that rose inside her. She took long deep breaths, then released them with a whistle.

There was no other way. She had to protect herself and the others. She didn't dare forget the others. If she didn't protect them, then she herself would become their target.

They had argued bitterly when they visited—she not wanting to destroy but only to teach a lesson; they not wanting anything but total and utter destruction. But they were right to call for Agatha's demise, right because she was dangerous. What was it Darwin had said? Survival of the fittest? Well, that applied. So they had agreed that Agatha was a threat to their security, then elected Eliza to perform the ritual.

"Why? Why Agatha have you forced my hand? Oh, how I love you," she cried out loud. The tears once again formed. "But I have no choice. I must. You have left me no choice." She paused and wiped at the tears on both cheeks. She lowered her head over the brass pot and broke into sobs.

It was impossible to do this. Agatha had been a part of her for so long. Someone else should have taken up the task, one who had little attachment to the foolish woman. The Kacher sisters would have been her choice.

She continued to sob, knowing that if she would have asked them, they might have considered her weak.

Then she would have risked her own fall from favor, her loss of standing. But worse, she would have risked her own life.

She had to do this alone, no matter the hurt, the pain or the agony that crept into her being. Agatha had brought it upon herself. Time after time Eliza had pleaded with her to be more careful, but the woman never heeded her. And now it had come to this.

From the inside pouch of her cloak, she pulled a small box of wooden matches, then struck one against the rough stone altar. She shielded the flame from the swirl of wind with the edge of her satiny cloak.

She touched the flame to the corner of the page. Dry and brittle, it caught quickly, and a blue-orange flame licked its way to the signature at the bottom.

She stepped back to watch. The pot glowed in the darkness, the flame dancing wildly in the wind. "Good-bye, my dear." She choked back a sob. "Please understand that I had no choice. I do love you."

As the flames consumed the page, leaving only its charred remnants in the pot, she repeated her farewell.

Agatha Crenshaw lay awake beneath the champagne-colored, satin sheets, mourning her lost love, Alyssa.

It had been more than a month, and still she missed the girl and the warmth her body had brought to fend off the cold and loneliness of the night. Agatha had always feared the night and the darkness. She feared death and its finality, which was why she eagerly joined Eliza. She sacrificed a great deal to remain alive past her time. She sacrificed her immortal soul.

But now that Alyssa was gone, she wondered if it had been worth it. During the past century, she watched other loves—Laura, Jennifer, Mary and many others—be destroyed by Eliza while she lived on. Yes, she feared death, but she feared the isolation of her life, because there was no one to share it with.

Eliza and the others never did understand. They found her habit, her quirk, humorous. She resented them for their constant ridicule, but she didn't dare confront them.

They were the strong ones. She, on the other hand, was weak. And for that reason alone, she needed a companion, a strong-willed one at that. Unfortunately, finding one that the others would accept was impossible.

Tomorrow she would have better luck. There

were countless women-children out there. They traversed the streets by day and by night, some as hookers, others as the lost children of the world. They were on the streets, waiting for a kind word, waiting for someone to love them and take them home. She, of course, was doing them a favor by bringing them with her. She was their salvation. Otherwise they would only perish in the harshness of the cruel world. Better that they perish with her. Better still, one of them could prove worthy and join her forever.

With that in mind, she began to drift asleep. Her eyes were heavy as she watched the sheer lace curtain billow before the window.

Soon her lids closed, her lips fell apart, and her mind's eye produced the doll-like face of Alyssa—the crystal blue eyes, the porcelain skin, the small pout of her mouth, and her hair, as beautiful as a raven's feathers, a shimmering blue-black that cascaded past her shoulders and danced across her nipples.

She felt a tear trickle from her eye, and she heard her lips speak the girl's name. "Alyssa."

Then her body began to warm, a flush covering her skin, but it wasn't the warmth of sexual arousal. It continued to grow in intensity with each passing second.

She threw back the covers. The heat stirred inside her belly, and she felt as if she was being cooked from the inside out.

Her skin glistened with perspiration, her eyes opened wide, and her hands clenched into fists.

"No," she cried at the top of her lungs. "Eliza, please don't. Put it out. Put it out." The sight of the brass chamberpot flashed before her on the altar where she had joined Eliza and the others in sacrifice so many times, where she was now being sacrificed. She saw the flaming parchment, her name scrawled across the bottom. She screamed and pleaded, but to no avail. She tried to get up from the bed, hoping to make it into the shower where she could drench her body with ice cold water. But before she was able to move even an inch, her entire body burst into flames.

There was a brief flash of light, as if someone had just taken a picture. Within seconds, Agatha Crenshaw was a mound of gray ash upon the satin sheets. Immediately the flames extinguished, not touching another object in the entire room.

A gust of wind blew in through the open window and scattered her ashes throughout the room. Another gust, stronger and colder, spread them around the entire apartment, leaving a fine film over the mahogany tables and white velvet furniture.

When the cleaning woman would arrive the next morning, she would shake her head and wonder how the Crenshaw woman's home became so dusty.

She would enter the bedroom to see the faint imprint of Agatha on the sheets, then without any knowledge of the previous night, she would replace the sheets with bright yellow ones and continue with her chores, erasing all traces of her employer from the luxurious apartment.

Agatha Crenshaw was unpredictable and often left town for days at a time, but usually there was some kind of note or instructions.

Finally, after a week, when the milk had gone sour and the bed hadn't been slept in or the notes that she left each day went unanswered, the maid would suspect that her employer was missing. She would not suspect that she was dead for a very long time.

THIRTY

WHILE ELIZA NOMAN RID HERSELF OF AGATHA
Crenshaw and while Kristen and Tom slept
dreamless for the first time in a week, Alan
Kaspar paced his tiny living room.

The room was dimly lit by a small three-way
brass lamp that stood on an old rickety end table
beside the worn plaid couch. Ominous shadows
danced around the room, ominous and threatening, but Alan barely noticed. He was busy, his
mind reeling like a motion picture from the
stories that she had told him. He wanted to call
her to discuss them, but realized it was too late.
She was probably in bed sound asleep, he
hoped.

Chilled by her tales and the unusual August
cold, he crossed to the window and slammed it
shut. He peered into the darkened street below.

It was quiet, not a single human being passing below. The arc lights cast a bright, fluorescent glow in the clear cloudless night, a night he knew to be haunted by those who could find no rest.

Across the street stood Good Shepherd Roman Catholic Church. He longed to go inside to find the peace and solace that he so desperately needed, and he could only find it there. But to risk waking Father Leonard Sloan would be cruel. The parish priest needed his rest. He worked hard, constantly battling to save the most unsalvable souls.

And why would he wake him? To tell him of Kristen and her dreams. But what if it was fantasy, the workings of an overactive imagination?

He thought about Father Sloan, young, compassionate and understanding. He liked the priest, the pastor of the church to which he and his wife had belonged, and it felt good and safe and reassuring to have him sleeping beneath him, occupying the bottom floors of the huge, old stately house.

The Victorian had once been used solely as a rectory, but after Sloan arrived, two years ago, he built a one bedroom apartment in the third floor attic to help defray the costs of upkeep for the too large home—costs that a dwindling congregation was unable to absorb.

Alan, a long time member of that congregation, had sold the home that he and his wife Mary shared and moved into the apartment before the finishing touches on the place were made. He had to get away from Margaret's house. The memories, the guilt he carried with him, the blame he forced himself to live with had been too much to swallow while he traversed the hallowed halls of her domain. As soon as he moved into the parish apartment, the guilt eased though never disappeared, but with the help of Father Sloan, it lessened more and more with each passing day.

At this moment in his life, Father Sloan was his best friend. The priest never laughed or ridiculed him when he talked about contacting Margaret. Instead, he would smile thinly and nod. Maybe he didn't agree with his attempts, but he never, not even once, discouraged him.

Sometimes Alan felt Sloan knew something that he wasn't telling. When they played chess on Saturday nights, he would always sense a certain mystery hanging or hovering around the priest like a dense fog. At times it seemed as if he knew, or had, some dark, frightening secret, but if he did, he never spoke of it, at least not to Alan.

Maybe he should wake him, he thought. Maybe he would understand. He would know more about heaven and hell, about inherent evil, than anyone else. After all, he was a priest who specialized in such matters.

He glanced at the school clock on the wall— 3:30. Hardly an hour to disturb even the best of friends, except for an emergency. Was it? Was this an emergency?

No, he would disturb no one. He would think this thing out on his own. Then if he was convinced she was telling the truth, if what she said was reality, he would talk to Sloan.

He thought of Kristen. She *was* psychic. There was no doubt about it. Powerful, too. But was she also a woman with a vivid imagination? Could she also be interpreting her dreams the wrong way?

He remembered when he had met her for lunch. She had looked awful—lackluster eyes, black rings beneath them, pale complexion, jittery.

And after the experiment, which he never should have done in the first place, she was even worse. He was terrified he had done harm to her. He contemplated what she had said.

Was Scott Benson murdered? And by Eliza Noman? But how? She was an old woman.

So how the hell could she be a murderer?

Maybe Kristen was losing her mind. She admitted her mother had problems. Did she have the same tendencies under stress? Was the stress of moving to Burnwell the cause?

Absolutely not. He couldn't believe that. She seemed too stable and she had the ability to analyze her own behavior.

Then what the hell was the problem?

He lay back onto the battered couch, then tucked a pillow under his balding head. He folded his arms across his chest and closed his eyes.

He thought about the sacrificial baby she had spoken of and the six women. Even the thought of sacrifice or ritual was horrifying. But surely, if an infant had been missing, the news would have been ablaze with it. He would never have missed such a story. Somehow he would have heard about the incident.

But what if the women had brought the child with them? If that was the case and it came from the west coast, he wouldn't have heard anything. The local news wouldn't carry it, and if it was mentioned on the national news, it would have been a small item.

He rubbed his temples and felt a massive, blinding headache coming on.

Damn! How did he get involved?

If he was wrong, if Kristen was wrong, he'd make an ass out of himself—and possibly, no, probably, lose his job. If any of this was mentioned to the wrong person . . .

It was best to tell no one, not even Sloan. He would investigate himself, and if nothing became of his inquiries, no harm would be done.

But from somewhere deep inside he knew, he sensed, that she was right. She had seen something in that mirror, and it had terrified her—and him. Besides, he had promised to help her. Maybe he shouldn't have, but he had.

The link, the feeling of oneness he experienced whenever they were together, prevented him from turning her away.

He would help her. God, he would, no matter what the consequences to himself. She needed his help. She needed him, and he needed her.

THIRTY-ONE

"KRIS, IT'S GOOD TO SEE YOU," LINDA RIPA SAID AS she opened the door to greet her sister. "You look tired. Maybe a little undernourished, but good nonetheless."

Kristen smiled. She was tired from the trip and from not sleeping the night before because of her argument with Tom. And yes, she had lost weight.

She opened the door and let Amber in ahead of her. The puppy jumped and yelped and frolicked around Linda's feet.

"Cute pooch. Where'd you get him?"

"It's a her. Tom brought her home as a gift." With the mention of Tom, she could hold in her feelings no longer and burst into tears.

Her sister hugged her and helped her to the

kitchen table where she sat down in the nearest chair. She hadn't meant to cry; she had intended to be strong. She really didn't want to burden her sister or her mother with her problems, but now it was too late. Now she had to tell all—and so she did. She told Linda about Tom and Burnwell and Eliza Noman and Alan Kaspar and the Howards. She told her about her dreams.

Linda sat across from her holding her hand and comforting her. She was the same old Linda, a bit overweight, a bit dowdy and a bit too old for her age of 39. But Linda had gone through her own private hell, and Kristen, the baby sister, had witnessed it but was too young at the time to understand.

Jim, Linda's husband, had been in Vietnam and never returned. He was still listed as an MIA, and the many years of not knowing, the years of grief, had taken their toll.

Kristen felt a pang of guilt. To greet her sister with uncontrollable sobbing was wrong. "Sorry about the tears," she said. "Guess I've been holding it in, and it just came out all at once."

"No problem. That's what sisters are for. Want a cup of coffee?"

Kristen nodded. After driving nearly three hours, she needed one. Besides it would give her and Linda a chance to catch up on their news, and it would help her get in better shape to see her mother.

"Afterwards, when you feel better, you can go up to see Mom. You don't know how upset she's been about you. She's constantly praying for you. Has me doing it, too. I don't know what's bugging her, but if she saw you in this condition, it would kill her."

Kristen felt her spine stiffen. Could her mother have a psychic gift as Alan suspected she had? And if she did, how much did she sense about Kris and Tom?

She watched Linda pour coffee into a red ceramic mug, then fill a plate with chocolate chip cookies. After she placed them on the table, Linda sat down.

"Now, tell me more about your dreams. They do sound strange. Awful! And that Kaspar character thinks there may be something to them?"

Kristen looked at her sister with blurred eyes. "He thinks we should try to find out if there is. I don't know if we should."

"What does Tom think?"

"He thinks they're dreams and nothing more. And he despises Alan. Thinks he's a kook."

"Why?"

Kristen told her about Alan, about him losing his wife in a car crash and about how the faculty regarded him. "So they feel he's turned into lunatic. Tom doesn't want me bothering with him."

"I see." Linda paused, then smiled. "What do you want to do? Do what you want, not what Tom tells you to do. Now, tell me more about Scott Benson and Eliza Noman. She sounds like one real dizzy broad."

Kristen laughed and told her sister all she knew about Eliza. She told about Scott Benson and the other missing children, and by the time she finished, it was nearly 6:00 o'clock, and she felt ready to see her mother.

Kristen stood in the doorway of her mother's bedroom. She felt saddened. The woman appeared more frail and aged than the last time Kristen had visited. She had lost a considerable amount of weight, and deep furrows creased her face. Her hair was almost all silver, except for a few strands of dark brown.

Wrapped around her hand was a rosary, and her fingers moved nimbly over the beads. She faced the window, looking downward, probably at the rose garden below.

Beatrice Weaver turned from the window. "Kristen!" she cried. "My Kristen's come home."

Immediately, Kristen knelt beside her and scooped her into her arms. "Mom, I've missed you. How have you been?"

"Now that you're here, I'm fine." Her mother pushed her to arm's length and smiled. A tear rolled down her cheek. "You've lost weight, but Linda will fix that." She looked at her eldest daughter for confirmation.

"Right, Mom," Linda said. "Now, if you'll both excuse me, I'll head to the store and pick up a few extras for dinner."

Kristen turned to Linda and nodded. Amber squirmed in her sister's arms. Linda nuzzled the pup and placed her on the floor before leaving. Amber rushed to Kristen's mother and jumped all over her, wagging her tail and lapping at her hands, until Beatrice giggled.

"Who's this little one?"

"Amber."

"Hello, Amber." Beatrice rubbed the pup's head.

Amber nuzzled against her hand, then took off to explore the room.

"Where's Tom?"

Kristen sighed. "He couldn't make it. He had to work." She hated lying, but she didn't want to tell her mother about the argument. She swallowed hard and forced back her tears.

Her mother nodded. "Well, we'll have to make do without him." She watched Amber pull magazines from the wicker basket beside the nightstand. A smile formed on her lips. "I'm glad you have a dog. You need a dog for company—and for protection."

"Protection?" Kristen asked as she stood up and put the magazines and the basket on top of the bed. She didn't feel like spending an hour cleaning up shredded paper. She waited for an answer, but none came. She wondered what her mother sensed.

"Tell me about your new home."

Kristen told her about how she intended to furnish some of the rooms and how she planned to plant mums in the fall. She told her about George and Rose, but she didn't mention Eliza or Alan.

"And how about your other neighbor?"

Kristen bristled. "What other neighbor?"

"Don't you have a neighbor on the other side, too?"

"Yes, I do, but . . ."

"Well?"

Kristen hesitated. She didn't want to talk about Eliza for fear of upsetting her mother, but then, she knew she had little choice; her mother would keep probing. She decided to keep it on a superficial level, so she told of Eliza's snooping and how it got on her nerves.

"She's the one you have to watch," her mother said, matter-of-factly.

The hair on her arms stood straight up. "What do you mean by that, Mom?" Kristen's curiosity had been peaked. She couldn't understand how her mother knew Eliza needed to be watched. When her mother didn't answer, she asked again. "Well? What do you mean I have to watch her?"

"You know what I mean. I don't have to explain."

Her mother was groping. She couldn't know about the dreams or about what she and Alan discussed or about Eliza, unless she overheard her talking to Linda, or . . .

"Come on, Mom. Explain."

"I can't. If I do . . . Well, you know what can happen." Her eyes misted as she turned to look out the window. "I've forgiven you and your sister for putting me in that psychiatric ward after your father died, but I won't let it happen again."

Kristen moved to her mother and knelt beside her again. She felt uncomfortable. "Talk to me, Mom."

Her mother continued to face the window, then took a deep breath and let it out slowly before speaking, "If I talk, will you lock me away?"

"No."

Her mother studied her for a long time, then said, "When your father died, I was upset because he was gone from me, but I was also relieved. I no longer had to watch him lie in that hospital bed, writhing and moaning and crying in pain. His death gave him peace, but because I missed him so much, he returned to me. He came to visit me. Here. In this room. You and your sister thought I was crazy, and probably still do."

"Mom, don't—"

"So I take this drug they gave me in the hospital, but Joseph still comes. He tells me he's worried about you and that you're in danger."

"Mom, please." Kristen took hold of her mother's hand and squeezed it gently. It was impossible for her to be sure if this psychic ability Alan thought she possessed was also in her mother, or if her mother's dosage needed to be increased. If it wasn't for Alan, she would choose the latter. "Go on, Mom, I want to know more."

Her mother looked down at her and smiled. "If you and Tom would come home, all would be well."

"We can't. Tom needs this job."

Tears flowed from her mother's eyes. "You must be careful, darling. Someone wants to hurt you. Tom, too."

"Mom, that's nonsense! Don't get yourself worked up over nothing."

"It's not nonsense. You must be careful! You must pray that God helps you. Promise me you'll pray."

"I promise."

Silence hung in the room as her mother dug into the pocket of her pink floral housecoat. She pulled out a glittering chain, a small gold cross dangling from it. "Wear this. Always," her mother said, then handed it to her. "It was a gift from your Aunt Dorothy. It's been blessed by the Pope. It will help protect you."

"Thank you, Mom. It's beautiful." She fastened it around her neck and allowed the cross to fall between her small breasts. She leaned over and kissed her mother.

Her mother smiled, then said, "Tell me about your other friends."

Kristen had no intention of talking about what happened in the lab, but she decided to talk about Alan. "One is Alan Kaspar. He works at the college with Tom."

Her mother smiled and looked into her eyes. "Stick with him. Soon there will be another. He, too, will help."

"How do you know that? Did Daddy tell you? Please, tell me."

Her mother put an index finger to her lips and hushed her. She shook her head, refusing to say more.

If the situation in Burnwell wasn't so bad, she wouldn't take a word of her mother's warning seriously, but now she suspected her mother had a gift. And she wondered if it was a family trait.

She decided not to ask any more questions. Enough had been said. A warning had been given.

She fingered the tiny gold cross. For some strange reason, it felt comforting to have it around her neck. Maybe it was the power of suggestion, or maybe the cross was like a talisman that would protect her. Either way, it didn't matter. What mattered was that she was home, and she intended to enjoy her stay.

THIRTY-TWO

THE WEEK AT HOME WENT FAST. SHE HAD SPENT most of her time with her mother and sister, then briefly visited relatives and close friends. Tom had called every night and pleaded with her to come home, which she finally did.

As she pulled into her driveway in Burnwell, she was pleased to see him sitting on the front steps, waiting. When she got out of the car, she hurried to him, then threw her arms around his neck and kissed him. Even though he hugged and kissed her in return, he did it without enthusiasm. She was baffled. On the phone, he had acted like he couldn't wait for her to come back, but now . . .

"I've missed you," she said, pulling away. The spicy aroma of Eliza's cologne stung her nose.

He said nothing.

She forced a smile. At least, they weren't arguing. "How about some dinner? I'm starved."

He nodded.

Leaving her suitcases in the car, she headed inside. Regardless of his behavior, she had no intention of saying anything to disturb him. She went directly to the kitchen and started to cook spaghetti.

Tom sat at the table listening to her talk about her visit home. Amber stayed at her heels, following her from one end of the kitchen to the other.

After dinner they relaxed in the living room. She treated herself to some white wine, while Tom drank a large glass of Eliza's banana liqueur. She continued to tell him about her visit home and about their old friends.

"Kathy had a baby girl, and Jennifer Higgins is pregnant, and Theresa Woods is getting a divorce."

He nodded and acted disinterested.

She mentioned his family and her call to his mother, who was upset that they hadn't visited, but Tom didn't seem to care. She, on the other hand, did.

His father was furious about the way Tom had spoken to his mother, but there was little Kristen could do to patch up the rift between father and son. Both possessed the same stubbornness, and it would be best for the anger and the hurt to wear off before attempting to restore peace.

Besides, she had a lot more to worry about—

the warning from her mother, making things right between herself and Tom and, most importantly, finding out what was wrong with him.

Even though he was sitting with her and listening to her, he seemed to drift off and stare vacantly while she talked. From the dark circles beneath his eyes, she knew something was wrong. She had to help him, regardless of the cost.

That night, Tom lay awake while Kristen remained locked in a deep sleep. He had another dream, the same recurring dream of the voluptuous blonde.

Whoever she was, she was driving him crazy. Never had he known anyone like her. She was so damned beautiful—her golden hair, her luminous green eyes, and a body that looked like it belonged in a magazine centerfold.

But actually he did know someone. He had met her during the summer in his Psychology 101 class and, coincidentally, she was also in his Psychology 102 class right now.

For months he had seen her and admired her and been attracted to her, even drooled over her, but he had always suppressed the attraction.

Was that suppression surfacing in his dreams? Was it Aimee Clark that he dreamed of night after night? But the girl in his dreams had green eyes, and Aimee's were blue. It hardly mattered.

She, too, was gorgeous with long golden hair and a body that wouldn't quit. Damn, she was beautiful!

He knew the girl was interested in him. He could tell by the way she smiled at him, and since he had an interest in her, too . . . He sighed. Just thinking about her gave him an erection.

Slowly, silently, he crawled out of bed and tiptoed to the bathroom. He went to the sink and splashed cold water on his face, as if to wash her from his mind, but it didn't work.

He wanted her, needed her, to satisfy his desires. His sex life with Kristen had taken a turn for the worst. He no longer found the same excitement with her and just went through the motions. She couldn't compare to the girl in his dreams or with Aimee Clark.

It didn't matter if he cheated on Kris. Their marriage was over. Sometimes just the sight of her upset him, and he had no idea why. He just couldn't stand being near her.

As for Aimee, he surmised she was looking for an A in the course. She was probably bright enough to get it on her own, but he might be able to guarantee it, as long as she was willing to play his game.

With that thought in mind, he went back to bed, sleeping on the very edge of the bed to get as far away from his wife as possible.

THIRTY-THREE

ON TUESDAY AFTERNOON, KRISTEN SAT IN ALAN Kaspar's office, eagerly awaiting the end of his class. She had spent the morning with Rose and George Howard, telling them about her visit home, about Tom's refusal to go with her, then about his calls and pleas for her to return. She confided her concerns about his worn-out appearance and his obvious preoccupation with something. She also told them that she hadn't seen Eliza since she came back and surprisingly neither had Tom.

George and Rose listened intently, then tried to ease her concerns. Before she left, George reminded her about their upcoming dinner. He said he needed to talk to Tom. He didn't elaborate, and when Kristen pushed, he just patted her shoulder and smiled.

After her visit with the Howards, she stopped at Tom's office, then took him to lunch at the faculty cafeteria. Even though he wasn't in a nasty mood, he appeared distant. His face was tired and drawn, his cheeks hollow, his eyes listless. She suggested he see a doctor, but he smiled and shook his head.

When the bell outside Alan's door chimed twice, signaling the end of the 1:00 o'clock class, she was thrilled. She couldn't wait to see him.

As Alan strutted into the room, she jumped up and, to her own surprise, hugged him tightly.

"Well, that's a nice greeting. Wish someone would do that all the time." Alan laughed. "So tell me, how are you feeling? You look much better. Rested."

"I am." She laughed. "The farther away I got from Burnwell, the better I felt. And I had a wonderful time, too. I enjoyed being with my mother and my sister and my friends."

"Good. How is your mother?"

"Fine. Except she said that I'm in danger. She said my father came to her and told her. If it wasn't for you, I would have thought she was getting sick again, but . . ."

"Hmm, I wonder if she knows more than she's saying." He dropped the books he was carrying onto the desk, then gave her a serious look. "Want to try another experiment?"

"Yes. But after the last time, I'm a little scared."

"Don't be. I'll be there. Besides, what could possibly happen to you in my classroom? Trust me."

"My mom says I should."

"Smart lady."

Kristen giggled. She followed Alan downstairs to the lab.

He held an eight-by-ten inch piece of glass in front of her. It looked as if it had been taken from a picture frame. They sat at the card table across from each other.

"Okay, let's get started."

"What should I do?"

"Just look into the glass and tell me what you see."

"I see the card table beneath the glass, and . . . and . . . something else. My God, it looks like . . . fingerprints."

"Smart ass. Stare at it and concentrate. This time think about colors. I'll give you a name and you tell me if you see any color associated with that person."

"Okay."

"Let's see, who should we start with? How about your husband? Yes, think about Tom."

Kristen looked into the glass and thought about Tom, his loving ways, his handsome smile, his blue eyes. She thought about his moods. At one time, the most adoring husband anyone could ever want, and now, distant, sullen and withdrawn.

It took a few minutes, maybe three, before the glass became smoky. Another minute, and it began to take on a different hue. Then she saw a definite color.

"Gray. I see gray. What does it mean?" She looked up at Alan.

He shrugged. "I'm not sure gray means anything. I suppose it could mean undefined. You know, when something is in the gray area."

"Is that supposed to be a joke?"

"Not at all. Look, you and Tom have been going through a rough time. Right? So your relationship isn't what it used to be. Instead of blue or pink or some other happy color, you're getting something bland. Maybe when you both straighten everything out or when Tom quits being such a jerk, you'll see something else." Alan smiled. He rubbed his hands over the bald spot on the top of his head.

"How about another?" she said. "Let's try . . . um . . . you."

Once more Kristen looked into the glass. She concentrated on Alan, his kindness, his gentleness, his willingness to help her.

"I see red. Red? What the hell does red mean?"

"What type of red?"

"Dark red. The color of blood."

"Oh, God."

"What's it supposed to mean?"

Alan became serious. "It means I'm in for some trouble. Possibly death. Well, I am getting old and I guess I have to go sometime. But blood red . . . Well, that could mean violence."

Kristen gasped. Violence! She rolled the word over and over in her head. "Why violence?" she finally asked. "You mean you're going to die a violent death?"

"Something like that—that is if there's any truth to the colors. I sure hope not. Personally,

I'd like to go quietly, like in my sleep."

Kristen thought for a moment. She wondered how valid a stupid experiment such as this could be. "If this is real, can we change it?"

"Who knows? Like I said, it may not be worth a damn. Let's try another. How about Kristen Roberts?"

This time when she looked into the glass, she barely had to think. The color flashed before her eyes within seconds.

"I see blood red."

"Jesus, are you sure that's not left over from me? Do it again."

She did, and once more the color flashed a dark, dark red. "Blood red."

"Looks like you're in for it, the same as me."

"Want to try another?"

"Yes. Eliza Noman."

"Really? Why her?"

"Curious. Just curious."

Kristen concentrated on Eliza. There wasn't much about her that she liked, and she didn't feel like thinking about all her negative qualities. She barely thought about the woman before the glass turned.

"Black."

"Black means death. Always has and always will. Maybe the old girl is going to kick the bucket."

"Maybe she already has."

"Why do you say that?" He studied her. "Huh? What makes you think she's dead?"

"I don't know. It just popped into my head."

"Well, since she's walking around, she couldn't be."

"Unless she's a vampire." She giggled.

"Vampires don't exist."

"I know. Just making conversation. But why should I see black for her?"

"It's possible she's going to die soon. No surprise. How old did you say she was? Eighty?"

Alan picked up the glass and headed for his desk. He placed the glass inside one of the drawers. "That's enough for today. Want to come back tomorrow?"

Kristen shook her head. "Maybe another day. Soon."

"Call me and we'll have lunch."

When she left, she stopped at the grocery store for a couple of steaks. From the way Tom looked, he needed all the nourishment he could get, and after her week away she was eager to please him.

As she drove, she thought about the colors. They disturbed her. Alan had tried to downplay their importance, but his eyes showed concern. He had looked upset, especially when he heard they were both blood red.

As she pulled into the drive, she wondered if violence really was in their future, and if so, why. She had no enemies, and as far as she knew, neither did he. Why would anyone want to hurt such a lovely man.

Tom's car was already inside the garage. Damn! She had wanted to surprise him with a special dinner.

When she got inside, he was sitting at the kitchen table with a fork in his right hand and an apple pie in front of him.

"Where'd the pie come from?" She really didn't have to ask. She knew.

"Eliza. Why?" he growled with a full mouth.

His mood had changed since lunch. It was going to be another one of those nights.

Once Alan felt certain she had gone, he took the glass from the drawer and laid it on the desk. He felt uneasy, even scared, but he still wanted to try it himself.

He cradled his head in his hands and stared into the glass. He concentrated on the same people he had mentioned to Kristen, and he saw what she did. Tom was gray, he and Kristen were blood red, and Eliza Noman was black.

A shudder ran through him, then lodged in his chest. The anxiety he experienced was almost paralyzing. He had told her not to worry, but how could *he* not worry? The colors were real and frightening.

He and Kris would encounter violence, maybe die a violent death. But the black wasn't there for either of them, because if it appeared, it was time to bid the world farewell.

Tom's color was nothing to get excited about, but the Noman woman's was scary. Either she was dying, or she would be dead soon. He wondered if she knew. He wondered if she had a terminal illness. If not, then the black stood for something else—evil!

If Kris's dreams had any validity to them, then

Eliza Noman was evil. God, how that terrified him. How did one deal with that type of evil?

He didn't want to think about it anymore. He wanted to go to Jake's Tavern and have a few beers, watch a little baseball, then go home and fall into bed.

Kris is slowly killing me, he thought, as he shuffled out the door. She was powerful. She could see too much, and that scared the hell out of him.

THIRTY-FOUR

DURING THE NEXT FEW WEEKS, KRISTEN SAW Alan often. They had lunch, he showed her around the campus, and he helped her apply for a job at the student counseling center. At the present time there were no openings, but since one of the girls, a pretty girl named Wendy Bowers, was pregnant, there would be an opening after Christmas.

Today Alan and Kristen had hamburgers at the faculty lounge. Afterwards they went back to the lab, but instead of conducting experiments, they sat and discussed Eliza Noman.

"Asked around about her," Alan said. "Found out she's been living in this area all her life. None of the old timers at Jake's know much about her. She mostly keeps to herself; no one ever sees her."

"Well, I sure as hell see her," Kristen said, "and so does Tom. He's been going over there every night again. Sits out on the back porch with her and then comes home and goes to bed. I'm his wife, but I stay home alone."

"Other than that, how are things between you two?"

"About the same. He's as distant as he ever was. Worse, in fact. If I didn't know better, I'd say he no longer loves me."

"Don't you think that's a little harsh?"

"Not really. When he's with Eliza, he's just fine, happy, jolly, not-a-care-in-the-world-Tom." She paused, trying to remember something she wanted to tell Alan. It took a few seconds before it came to her. "Oh, one night Eliza sent him home with another box full of toiletries. She said a friend of hers makes them. I hate the stuff. It's made from cucumbers and God knows what else. It has a strange odor and makes me sick, but Tom loves it. I guess he doesn't mind the underlying odor."

"What kind of odor?"

"Like nuts or something. It really stinks. I guess I'll end up throwing it away, unless you want it. And she's always sending things over—pies, cakes, cookies, muffins. I throw them out. You would think that she would have learned to bake, considering her age. Everything has that same offensive nutty smell and taste to them. Tom says he doesn't taste anything unusual. Says it's my imagination, fueled by my dislike of the woman. I suspect she may have run out of ideas on how to use all those herbs she grows."

"Herbs? She grows herbs?"

"Yes. Her kitchen is crammed with bottles and jars of the stuff. She's obsessed with them, with all types of plants."

"Well, I sure hope she knows what she's doing. Some of those herbs can make you sick, even kill you, if you don't know what you're doing."

"I didn't know that."

"Sure. Herbs are like mushrooms. Most types are edible, but others are deadly. If I were you and Tom, I wouldn't eat anything else until you find out what your neighbor is putting in her recipes. Tell Tom to stay away from the toiletries, too. Plant toxins can be absorbed through the skin. That may be an explanation for his behavior. Dangerous stuff to fool with. People who grew up or live in the big cities think that everything in the country is good for you, that everything is health food."

"I'll remember that," Kristen said. Another reason to be watchful of Eliza, she thought. Hell, the old woman could end up poisoning or even killing Tom since he used and ate her concoctions. That wouldn't make sense. She liked Tom. Kill *her* maybe, but never him.

"How are the dreams?"

"I haven't had one in a while, at least not since I've been back. Actually, I'm feeling better, too. Healthy." She fingered the crucifix around her neck. "I guess I was just upset about the Benson boy. It's strange that the police don't know any more than they did the night he disappeared. Gone without a clue, without a trace."

"Well, if the dreams start again, let me know." Alan paused.

"I have something else to tell you. I've concluded the results of the experiments, and I'm convinced you have definite psychic abilities. If you'll stick with me, we can develop them. We can work with the cards and try to hone your telepathy skills, although I don't think it's really necessary. Trust in yourself and your gut instincts, and it'll surface all by itself when you need it."

Kristen nodded and smiled. She wasn't sure she wanted to develop any of it, but there was a certain excitement associated with it all. If it pleased Alan, she would cooperate with him. And maybe some evening, when Eliza and Tom were together, she'd be able to tune into their conversation and finally know what was going on between them. Maybe she'd even be able to read Tom's mind and find out what the hell was bothering him.

THIRTY-FIVE

WHEN THE FRONT DOORBELL RANG AT 8:00 IN THE morning, Kristen dropped her dish towel and scurried to answer it. She couldn't imagine who would visit so early. At first, she thought it was the pest, Eliza, but when she opened the door and saw a police officer, her breath caught inside her throat.

"Good morning," he said. "I'm Chief Walters. Burnwell police. I'd like to ask you a few questions."

He was a stout, gruff-looking man with piercing hazel eyes and a large nose that had a bump in the middle.

Kristen forced a smile, then stepped aside and allowed him to enter.

They sat down opposite each other.

"What kind of questions?" she asked.

He took a small photo from his pocket and handed it to her. "Her name's Louise Faulkner. She vanished last night after leaving The Dove, the ice cream parlor on Main Street. I know it's a long shot, but we're checking with all the residents in the area, hoping for leads."

She studied the photo. The girl was about 16 with red frizzy hair, large, round blue eyes and a delicate, heart-shaped face.

"I'm sorry, but I can't help you." She took a deep breath and released it slowly. "This is the fifth child who disappeared since March."

"Tell me about it." Chief Walters said. "I wish we had some leads about these kids, but no one knows anything. They vanish without a trace."

She felt her temples throb and her stomach quiver. "But you have to have something. I mean, kids just don't vanish into thin air," she said in a slowly rising, irritated voice.

"We know that, but we can't find any evidence."

"Well, maybe you should try harder. This can't keep happening. What if these kids are being murdered? You have to find out who's doing this."

"We're doing our best." He got up to leave. "Unfortunately we don't have much to go on, but maybe we'll get lucky."

She sighed, then handed him the picture of Louise Faulkner and walked him to the door.

After he had gone, she sat down on the edge of the couch and buried her face in her hands. The thought of five missing children made her mind reel. She had hoped Scott Benson was the last.

Since July and August had been uneventful, the monthly pattern had been broken. Now it started again.

She thought about the Benson boy and the chilling dreams, and goosebumps covered her arms. Would she dream of Louise Faulkner? She prayed she wouldn't.

Jumping up from the couch, she ran to the kitchen to call Alan. She had to try the test with the colors on Scott Benson and Louise Faulkner. After she dialed, she glanced through the kitchen window and saw Eliza kneeling beside a new flower bed. Suddenly the goosebumps returned. She hoped Alan would answer his phone.

The following morning, Kristen hurried to the lab. When she walked in, Alan was waiting, his nose buried in the newspaper. The photo of the missing 16-year-old took up half the front page. The picture sent a surge of fear through her body. She traced her finger over the outline of the girl's face and, once again, as with Scott Benson, she knew something dreadful had happened. She had to find out more. They agreed to use the colors.

The mystery surrounding the missing children gnawed at her, and if her dreams of Scott had any truth to them, she was willing to do her best to help.

They seated themselves at the small card table once again. Alan held the square piece of glass, while Kristen concentrated on the boy. It took only a few seconds for the color to surface.

"Alan, I see red. Blood red. No wait. It's turning . . . it's getting darker. It's black." She drew in a deep, gasping breath. "My God, does that mean he's dead?"

"Possibly. Now do the girl."

She glanced at the photograph, and once the girl's image was fixed in her mind, she looked into the mirror. "Blood red. Turning black. Are they both dead? It can't be."

"Maybe not. But maybe they are, Kris. If your powers are as strong as I think they are, then we can assume that they're dead."

"It can't be. How am I supposed to help them if they're dead? What's the point?"

"That's something we have to figure out. Let's go over what we know. The Benson boy has constantly been part of your dreams. He's shown you what happened and who did it. The results of this particular test would indicate that he is dead and the events in your dreams are accurate. What are we—excuse me, you— supposed to do next?" He paused and looked at her with cold, serious eyes and put his hand softly on her shoulder. "Kristen, I think you're faced with a very difficult decision. Obviously, you're the key, but are you willing to help them and do whatever is necessary, regardless of the cost?"

She stared at him for a moment. Would she be willing to risk herself, her own life, to help an innocent child? Yes. She felt certain she would. The madness had to stop. For the sake of the children and her own peace of mind, she had to do whatever she could. She knew there would be danger. Her life was in jeopardy as it had been since she came to Burnwell.

"Yes, I'll help," she finally answered. "I don't think I have a choice. I've been haunted by this for some time and I guess its time I found out what's going on." She hesitated before she said what else was bothering her. "You know, I told you before I suspected Eliza Noman was a part of all this, but I didn't have proof, just a gut feeling. And that feeling tells me she's involved or responsible.

"I saw her this morning in her garden digging another flower bed. She's been doing that ever since I got here. She must have fifty beds, maybe more. They're all shapes and sizes and scattered throughout the lawn, but still she plants more. Now I wonder if there is more to this flower thing than just a love of plants."

"Why do you say that?"

"There seems to be a pattern. Scott Benson disappears, and she's planting. I have that dream about the baby, and she's planting. This girl, Louise Faulkner, vanishes, and again she's planting. It sure is an odd coincidence."

"Now don't jump to conclusions. It probably is a coincidence. The woman's old and lonely. She needs a hobby."

"It's more than a hobby. It's an obsession."

"That's Eliza Noman's problem, but I can see where you're heading. You seem to think that she's directly connected somehow to this girl's disappearance, as well as the others. But is that really a possibility? She's old and frail. How on earth could she overpower a teenager? Keep in mind that the police didn't find any evidence of a struggle."

"I guess you're right, but she is a lot stronger than she looks. One night Tom and I were going for a walk in the woods and she stopped us. She came after me and pulled my arm with such force that my feet left the ground."

"No kidding."

"Her grip was like a vise."

"That's unusual for someone her age, but it still doesn't mean she had anything to do with those kids."

"I suppose not. But is it possible to overpower and control someone without using force?"

"What do you mean?"

"I mean, she has a hold on Tom. It's like he's in her control. He goes to her house every night and comes back moody, usually belligerent. I can't get near him, and I certainly can't say anything against her in front of him. He gets furious."

"Odd. I would think he'd be more concerned about you and your feelings. Are you sure he didn't find a substitute grandmother and you're jealous? You know, she is a model citizen." Alan laughed. "She plants a garden, bakes cookies and gives you and Tom presents. Is that the description of a dangerous person?"

"It's probably just an act. She bothers me, and her relationship with Tom is more than just friendship. I'm not a jealous person, and I believe she's in my dreams with Scott Benson for a reason. She knows something about those kids."

"I don't discount your feelings. You could very well be right. But what about the baby? There's no mention of a missing infant. Don't overreact. There's nothing we can do without proof."

"Proof? How do we get it?"

"Well, I guess we start by finding out all we can about her."

"I thought you tried that. No one seems to know anything."

"I guess we could check the courthouse for records, deeds, birth certificates, stuff like that." A sly smile creased his lips. "We could also break into her house and ransack the place."

"It would be easy. Eliza's going away. I overheard her tell Tom." She felt a surge of adrenaline. "And wait until you see the stuff in that house. It's like a museum. Beautiful." She paused, remembering. "I forgot to tell you about the book I found on her desk. It was handwritten in a strange language, one I've never seen before. It looked like an address book, but it had no order to it. There were two special pages, one signed at the bottom by an Agnes or Agatha Crenshaw, I don't remember which, and the other by Eliza Noman. I tried to decipher them but couldn't. Like I said, it was the strangest language I ever saw. At first I thought it might be Latin, but it wasn't." She felt herself getting excited, her pulse quickening along with her heartbeat. "But that's not all. When Eliza suspected that I saw it, she went totally nuts. She was furious."

"Maybe she didn't like your snooping."

"That's what I thought at first, but then she locked the book in a drawer. I wonder why it was so important. If we could get our hands on it . . ."

"Well, we could get it and try to decipher it—or a friend of mine, Father Sloan, might be able to. He's great with languages. But breaking and entering is against the law. Don't even think about it."

"But there's more to that book than just addresses. I'm positive."

"Forget it. That's as bad as stealing her mail."

"How about her going through my mail and reading my sister's letter? That's a crime, too."

Alan smiled and patted her hand. "Look, you have no proof of that either. You didn't catch her."

Kristen pulled her hand away from his. "Why are you defending her?"

"I'm not defending her. I want you to be reasonable and consider all the possibilities."

"It's difficult to be reasonable when I know she hates me. She probably thinks I'm trying to ruin her relationship with Tom. He's the one who gets the pie, not me."

"How was it?"

"Huh?"

"The pie. How was it?"

"Okay. I just had a bite. It had that undertaste. Nutty, bittersweet. Come to think of it, every time I ate any of her food, I got a bad stomach and had one of those horrible dreams that night." Kristen's eyes widened. "Do you think she's putting something in the food? Something to make me sick?"

"I doubt it. She doesn't make anything for you. Apparently it's for Tom, and he doesn't notice anything unusual. He's not sick. And she would have to be an extremely good chemist to mix something in to affect you and not him, especially herbs. Most likely she's just a lousy cook or you have a sensitive stomach."

"I don't know. Coincidence maybe. But the dreams were always more vivid. Either Scott Benson appeared, or an animal had me pinned down and was ready to devour me."

"What kind of animal?"

"A big cat. It had these orange eyes and huge fangs." She shuddered. "I don't really want to talk about it. I dreamed about it chasing me before, but that was the first time it caught me."

"It could be a manifestation of something else. By any chance, do you feel trapped?"

"Funny you should ask. Yes, I do. I feel trapped in Burnwell."

"That's interesting. We'll get into that later. Right now, I have class."

Kristen nodded. She had to be going, too. She would have liked to stay longer. Alan was comforting and made her feel confident.

They said their good-byes and she hurried home, concerned about the Faulkner girl, the Benson boy and all the other missing children. There had to be proof. She was certain Eliza Noman knew something.

THIRTY-SIX

AFTER HIS 3:00 CLASS, HIS LAST ONE OF THE DAY, Tom headed to Willow Park. He had a meeting with someone very, very special. He was eager to fulfill his fantasy.

He pulled the car into a shady, secluded area and turned off the engine. He looked into the mirror above the visor and smoothed his hair with the palms of his hands. He took off his brown sportcoat and placed it across the seat. Then he sat back, tried to relax and waited.

A few minutes later, a white Volkswagon Golf came slowly up the road. Tom licked his lips, popped a breath mint into his mouth and quickly got out of the car.

He watched as she parked the car and came to him. It had been easier than he thought it could be. Earlier, Aimee Clark had come to his office to talk about the exam he had just given to the class and career opportunities in the field of psychology. They talked, she flirted, and he took advantage of the situation. He put his arm around her shoulders, and when there was no protest, he slowly slid his hand to her breast. Still there was no protest. He asked her to meet him after his classes to discuss the exam at length. When she suggested the place, he didn't protest.

Tom watched her as she strolled up the small dirt road. She was dressed in a short skirt and a pretty sheer floral blouse. She wore no bra. She looked seductive, enticing and voluptuous. He couldn't wait and licked his lips again.

"Good afternoon," she said in a deep, sultry voice. She smiled a full smile.

"Good afternoon," he replied, smiling, and opened the door of the New Yorker for her.

Immediately, she pushed the driver's seat forward and crawled into the back seat. Tom followed, closing the door behind him.

Neither spoke again. In a matter of seconds, they were in each other's arms. Moments later, her clothes lay strewn on the floor. His soon followed. And then he took her with all the excitement and hunger he had experienced in every dream.

And when they were finished, he decided Aimee Clark deserved an A.

It moved silently through the woods until it finally saw the white New Yorker and the two lovers inside. It sat on a small incline and watched. Somehow it knew this would happen. It knew Tom was ripe for an affair. The dreams had been too frequent, too real, too disturbing for him not to want another woman. This was all her fault. She had miscalculated.

Jealous and filled with fury, it watched until it was over, then stole back into the deepest parts of the forest. It would handle this new development the way it knew it had to.

The anger and rage subsided. Soon his love would belong only to her. There would be no other.

THIRTY-SEVEN

BEFORE KRISTEN EVEN WALKED INTO THE Howards' kitchen, the odor of roast beef touched her nose. Even though it smelled delicious, she had no appetite. The walk to the farm had helped calm her down a little, but not enough. The argument with Tom was comparable to the one she had the day before she went home to visit her mother and her sister.

The man was impossible. He had refused to come to the Howards for dinner, because Eliza told him they were weird people.

He had stormed upstairs with a bottle of her liqueur, leaving Kristen with the embarrassing task of making excuses for his absence to George and Rose.

As she stepped onto the screened porch,

George called out, "Don't bother knocking you two. Just come right in."

Kristen obeyed and walked into the kitchen. She tried to fake a smile, but it didn't work.

"Is anything wrong, dear?" Rose asked, crossing the room in her wheelchair to greet her.

"No," Kristen lied. She couldn't say that she and Tom argued about them.

George put down his carving knife and spun around. "Hope you like roast beef. Rosy makes the best." He looked behind her. "Where's your hubby?"

Kristen shrugged. "He couldn't make it. He didn't feel well. Guess you're stuck with me."

For a moment George and Rose stared at each other, then Rose said, "Well, there's no one else we'd rather be stuck with. Now, have a seat. Dinner's about to be served."

"Is there anything I can do to help?"

"Not a thing," George said, then turned and continued to carve the roast.

"Is Tom very sick?" Rose asked.

"Well . . ."

"He's with that old witch, Rosy. I wanted to talk to him about—"

"George! Hush up."

"No. I wanted to talk to him about her. Wanted to tell him a story so he would stay away. Now I won't get the chance." He placed the platter of meat in the middle of the table, then added the mashed potatoes, the peas, the salad and a gravy boat. He sat down. "But I can tell Kristen."

"No, George, you'll scare her."

"She needs scarin'. She's got to know what she lives next door to. She's got to keep her man away from the witch."

"I don't really understand," Kristen said. "Why do you keep calling Eliza a witch?"

"Some people," George said, "those of us who've been around a while, refer to Eliza as a crone, a witch." He eyed her, before he scooped the mashed potatoes onto his plate.

"Please, go on. I'd like to hear more about Eliza."

"Hmmph. It may scare the hell out of you, if you believe—and you should, because it's true." He put down the bowl of mashed potatoes, folded his hands over his plate and began his story.

"When I was a boy, oh, no more than nine or ten, I saw what I thought was a mountain lion in the cornfields. Me and my daddy were headin' into the barn that night. I yelled to him and told him, but he pushed me into the barn.

"Suddenly, there was a loud cry. I got real scared. And when it came a second and a third time, I started to cry. It was the most godawful sound, inhuman.

"My daddy told me to be quiet so she wouldn't hear me. I asked him who it was that shouldn't hear me, but he just told me to ignore the cry and she'd go away. I kept asking who, until he got mad.

" 'Eliza,' he yelled. 'She's no good. She comes at night to steal my crops. Comes and looks for what damage she can do. She's a demon.'

" 'How do you know?' I asked.

" 'I've seen her, boy. Seen her with my own eyes. A demon.'

"I didn't understand. We were brought up as Christians. We didn't believe bad about others, and here my father was telling me bad about our neighbor."

" 'Stay away from her. She's no good. She can do you harm.' he said.

"We sat for a long time, then finally I asked him to tell me more. He hesitated, then he told me.

" 'Georgie, one night when I was young, I was walking Willow Road. The moon was full and bright, and the stars cluttered the sky like diamonds. I was passing the Noman house when I saw her come out and climb onto the roof above her front porch. I didn't know what she was doing, but I hid in the trees and watched. She stood and stared at the moon, singing some sort of song. Then she took off her clothes and threw them down. She laid down. I couldn't see her anymore so I got up to leave. But just as I took a step, I heard a shriek, like a wildcat calling into the night. I looked back to the roof and saw it all glittery and shimmery in the moonlight. The cat was huge, with silver fur and eyes the size of silver dollars. It pranced back and forth, then leaped to the ground. I was scared stiff. I crouched beneath the pines all night. When the sun came up, I ran home as fast as I could and never went that way again after dark.

"So when the cry came again that night when we were in the barn, my father got up and started for the door. I was scared, damn scared, and I called him back, but he kept going.

"He threw open the barn door, and screamed, 'Get thee behind me, Satan! Get thee behind me!'

"Suddenly, the animal's wail ceased. I ran to the door to be next to my dad. And what did I see? Well, I saw Eliza Noman. Her eyes blazed like hot coals. She raised her fist to my father, then ran into the cornfield and disappeared."

George took a drink of water and set the glass down gently on the table. "You see, I saw her with my own eyes. I may have been a little boy, but I never forgot. I stay away from that demon and her property."

Kristen stared at George. Somehow, even though his story sounded farfetched, it chilled her. She reminded herself that all old people had stories of witches and ghosts that they truly believed, but in today's high-tech society . . . She thought about Alan.

She looked across the table. Rose had stopped eating. Fear covered the woman's face. She knew Rose didn't doubt a word of George's tale.

The mood in the room turned solemn, and as Kristen ate her dinner, she thought about her dreams of being chased through the corn by a huge cat. She thought about the walk home and wished she would have taken her car.

THIRTY-EIGHT

IN THE DARK, SHE STOOD INSIDE THE BARN, waiting. She knew he'd come soon. Kristen had gone home. It was only a matter of time before he checked on his lousy chickens.

Their frantic squawks echoed in the barn. The musty smell of hay filled the air. Her impatience grew.

She had heard George Howard tell his story to Kristen. For the second time—and the last time—he had angered her. She had suspected he filled Simpson's head with his stories and caused the man to follow her into the woods, leaving her little choice but to kill him after he had seen the altar and her transformation.

But when Thomas told her about tonight's dinner, she had to hear what George would say about her. It was vital to know her enemies. She didn't want George or Rose helping Kristen or taking Thomas from her. She had come too far, worked too hard, to tolerate their interference.

But what was keeping him? She wanted to get this over with quickly.

Her legs ached from standing and waiting. She plopped down on one of the bales of hay and released an exasperated sigh. She heard footsteps. Her head bobbed up; her ears perked up.

Within moments, he shuffled into the barn and flicked on the light that hung from the ceiling. She peeked between the slats of the wooden stall and saw him standing in the middle of the floor, massaging his forehead. Then he moved to the barn wall and grabbed a rake. He headed in her direction. He stopped and looked at his damn white hens, then continued toward the back of the barn, turning into the stall directly in front of her. He started to rake the dirt floor.

She stood up. "Hello, Georgie," she said in a singsong voice.

George Howard turned on his heel and faced her. His left hand flew to his chest, his right hand tightening around the handle of the rake. "Get off my property, demon!"

She laughed. "Not yet, Georgie. We have some business."

"I got no business with you. Get out!" His eyes blazed with anger. Both hands gripped the rake.

"I heard your story tonight. But that's not the first time you told it, is it?"

"You've got no business coming here and

snooping. What I say in my house is my business."

"What you say in your house is *my* business. When you try to interfere, it's my business," she growled.

His eyes narrowed. "Interfere with what?"

"My future."

"You have no future. You're an old witch. You'll die soon, and go to hell where you belong," he yelled.

She laughed again. "No, Georgie, I'll never die. Soon I'll be a young woman again, like I was when you were a boy. Remember how beautiful I was?"

"You were never beautiful. You were always ugly and evil."

She continued to taunt him. "And when I am young again, I'm going to take Thomas Roberts for my own and get rid of that little bitch of a wife."

George's face twisted and contorted in anger. He picked up the rake as if ready to hit her. "Leave those kids alone!"

She enjoyed his anger, watching his face turn red and his eyes bulge. "What are you going to do if I don't?"

"I'm going to do what my father should've done, what I should've done years ago."

"Kill me?" She laughed. "No, I'm going to kill you like *I* should've done a long time ago." She waited for his response. When there was none, she continued, "I never knew until tonight that your father saw me change. If I would've known, I would've killed you and him that night in the barn." She glared at him, and the transformation began.

She saw his eyes fill with fear and heard his breathing quicken. He swung the rake and caught her left shoulder. Pain coursed through her as she dropped to the barn's dirt floor.

"Devil!" he screamed. "Devil!"

She heard him move out of the stall toward her. She scrambled to her feet and faced him. Shock, terror and horror covered his face.

She ran her tongue over the long, pointed teeth, then swiped at him with the claws that extended from her fingertips. She released a howling screech.

He swung the rake, and she ducked. It hit the wall of the barn. He swung again. This time she grabbed it and wrenched it from his hands. She threw the rake behind her as he ran toward the front of the barn.

But with the partial transformation, she was faster and stronger. Before he reached the door, she grabbed him and threw him to the floor. He rolled onto his back, his eyes wide with fear as his legs pushed him away.

He scrambled to his feet and lunged for the pitchfork. He grabbed it and kept her at bay. "Get thee behind me, Satan!" He jabbed at her with the sharp tines.

She moved swiftly from side to side, avoiding injury. She saw his red face, his sweat-stained shirt, his trembling hands. He was tiring fast.

His stabbing efforts with the pitchfork slowed. She lunged for it, then screamed in agony as the tines grazed her right side near her ribs. She felt the trickle of her own blood beneath her blouse.

"I'm going to kill you, demon!" he screamed as he ran toward her, ready to impale her.

She jumped out of the way, then clamped her clawed hand onto the handle of the pitchfork. She tried to wrench it free from his hands, but he held on tight. The pain in her side worsened, the blood flowing more freely.

He yanked at the pitchfork with both hands. She screamed an ear-piercing cry, then snapped at him with her feral teeth. He pulled again, hard.

She released her grip.

George Howard flew backward and crashed into the wall of the barn. His eyes widened, then closed. The pitchfork fell from his hands.

She pounced on him and pressed her clawed hand to his chest, then recited, "Master of darkness, lord of the night, I beseech thee to enter this man and destroy him." She removed her hand.

George's eyes popped open, and he gasped for breath. His hands grabbed at his chest. Rivers of perspiration rolled down his face. Blue tinged his lips and his fingernails. He writhed on the barn floor, agonizing moans escaping from his lips.

His eyes focused on hers. She glared down at him with fiery eyes that burned into his soul. He shuddered. His hands tore at his chest, his fingers ripping at the buttons on his shirt. He took in a ragged breath, then released a gurgling gasp. His heart attack was fatal.

She knelt beside him, staring into his glazed,

lifeless eyes. The battle was won, but the flow of blood continued from her side. She had to go. Getting to her feet and wincing from the pain, she picked up the pitchfork and wiped her blood from the tines. She placed it against the wall. Her eyes scanned the barn. She had left no trace, no blood.

Satisfied, she headed outside and into the cornfield toward home. She walked slowly, her hand pressed against her wound. She needed a poultice, a concoction of herbs and mud, to relieve the pain and to heal her. Since she had been partially transformed when the pitchfork grazed her, she would heal quickly, by morning, and then she would continue as planned.

The pain had subsided. The pitchfork had hit the lower rib on her right side preventing the tines from penetrating too deep. She had smeared the poultice over her entire side and covered it with gauze, fastened to her skin with adhesive tape.

George Howard's fight had surprised her, she didn't think he had it in him. She had expected him to crumble sooner. But the important thing was that he was gone and could no longer help Kristen.

Smiling, she leaned forward in the rocker she had placed by the attic window and looked down at Thomas' house.

In her hand was the mandrake root, the image of Kristen. She stroked it with her fingertips, willing the girl to be ill. She pierced the stomach and then the head with two pearl-topped hat-pins.

She watched and waited for a light to come on at the house below. None did. She heaved a sigh.

She had to work harder to rid herself of the girl. Kristen was getting stronger. She felt the girl's power grow.

The man Kaspar was helping her. Thomas had told her about him and his work with the supernatural. If necessary, she would deal with him, too.

THIRTY-NINE

AS SOON AS GEORGE'S FUNERAL ENDED, KRISTEN hurried home. She felt tired and drained. She needed to rest and put his death out of her mind. Seeing Rose crunched up in her wheelchair crying had been gut-wrenching. Knowing George was gone left her numb. Tom not attending the funeral was embarrassing. She needed to be alone.

When she got home, she headed for the laundry room and found that Amber wasn't there. She checked the house. The dog was gone.

Puzzled, she headed for the back door. Her eyes opened wide. The latch on the door was broken.

She stepped out onto the porch. Still, no Amber. She went down into the yard and called her, but the dog was nowhere in sight.

She glanced up at Eliza's, remembering the day when she had been outside pulling weeds and had heard Eliza's frantic screams. That day the dog had gotten into Eliza's flower beds, and the old lady had dragged her home by her collar, causing the poor animal to gag.

But Amber didn't break the latch on the door and get out by herself. She had help.

With a feeling of unease, she headed for Eliza's and found the old lady leaning over a new flower bed. "Eliza," Kristen said, "have you seen Amber? She's gone."

The old woman sat back and flashed her an angry look. "I haven't seen her, but I did warn you about dogs. They're trouble. You better hope she doesn't end up in my beds."

Kristen stepped closer. Eliza was planting gold mums in a small oval bed. The sight of it gave her an awful feeling. Her heart skipped a beat, and her breathing quickened.

"Is there something else?" Eliza snapped.

"Huh?" She couldn't take her eyes off the flower bed.

"What else do you want?"

"Oh, did you see anyone around the house? The latch on my back door is broken."

"I haven't seen anyone. People around here don't break into each other's homes."

"I just thought—"

"I have seen nothing. No one broke into your house. And I don't know where your dog is." She placed the last bush of gold mums into the dirt, then pushed the loose soil around the roots of the plant and patted it down with her hands.

A surge of anger rushed through Kristen. Eliza was impossible. Someone had broken the damn latch and, for all she knew, it could have been Eliza.

When the old woman stood up, she flashed her an angry look. "Anything else?"

Kristen shook her head.

"Good. I'm too tired to chat. Putting in that new bed wore me out." She turned and started to walk away.

Kristen eyed her with suspicion, then whirled on her heel and headed home. It was bad enough that George was gone and that Rose was leaving for Harrisburg to live with her daughter, but to lose Amber on top of everything was unbearable.

She continued to search, until she finally gave up. She stalked into the house and dropped into a chair, then leaned over the kitchen table and cradled her head in her hands.

Did Eliza break in and take Amber? If so, why? It didn't make sense. The old lady hated dogs, hated Amber—and Amber hated her. But the feeling that she had took hold, and she shuddered.

Suddenly she burst into tears.

She was losing everyone around her, and Tom was more distant than ever. He came home from work later and later every night. Then after a silent dinner, he headed for Eliza's.

Her whole life was falling apart, and she didn't know how to stop it.

FORTY

ALAN KASPAR FILLED THE BLUE CERAMIC MUG with coffee, then went to the window. He looked down into the street at Good Shepherd Roman Catholic church, where Father Sloan was pastor.

Behind him, Sloan puzzled over his next chess move. Tonight, just like every Saturday, was their night for chess, but Alan wasn't interested. He had someone on his mind—Kristen Roberts.

Yesterday she had told him George Howard's story about Eliza Noman, had cried to him about the missing dog and had anguished over her fading marriage. She talked about the missing kids and insisted Eliza Noman was the root of all the trouble.

He turned from the window and watched

Father Sloan. The priest sat on the edge of the worn, brown plaid couch, leaning over the coffee table and the chessboard. He was a tall athletic man and had a face that seemed carved of stone with a deep cleft cut into his chin.

When Sloan arrived in Burnwell two years ago, he converted the huge Victorian that had been used solely as a rectory into two units. The two bottom floors housed the priest; the top floor, the attic, housed Alan. It was a cozy, stamp-sized apartment, a welcome escape from the house that he and Margaret had shared.

He got along well with the priest. They were best friends, and when Alan talked about contacting Margaret, Sloan never laughed or ridiculed him. Instead, he nodded and smiled. Maybe he didn't agree with his attempts, but he didn't discourage him.

Father Sloan cleared his throat. "Alan, if you don't want to play tonight, what do you want to do?"

"I was waiting for you to make your move."

"I did that a while ago." The priest's hazel eyes searched his face. "What's the problem? You seem preoccupied. Want to talk about it?"

Alan nodded, then sat in the chair opposite Sloan. "I want to talk about . . . evil." He hesitated before continuing. "Let's discuss people who are evil, and how far they would go with their evil." He nervously fingered his coffee mug, then placed it on the table.

"Interesting subject," Father Sloan said. "Where should we begin?"

Alan grunted. "At the beginning."

He told the priest about Kristen Roberts and her dreams of Scott Benson and the sacrificial baby. He told him about the tests he had done with her in the lab. He mentioned George Howard and talked about Eliza Noman.

Father Sloan listened quietly, nodding his head, then shaking it at other times.

When Alan finished, Sloan said, "Are you positive this girl doesn't need help? I mean, this all sounds a little farfetched. There is evil, but the type of evil you're talking about may not exist, may not be possible."

"I'm certain Kristen knows what she's talking about. If you met her, you'd believe her, too."

"Maybe." Sloan paused and studied Alan's face. He sighed. "I suppose if you believe her . . ." He took a sip of coffee. "One thing you must keep in mind is that you need proof—lots of it. Now, if I had that page, I might be able to get you some kind of proof."

"But how could I get it? I'd have to break in. If I get caught, I'd go to jail."

"Exactly. It looks as if it'll all remain as conjecture. Without proof, you can't do a thing. If you went to the police with such a story, they'd think you were crazy. Looks like you're stuck between a rock and a hard place."

"Maybe not . . . maybe not."

"Please don't do anything you'll regret," Father Sloan said, looking deep into Alan's eyes.

But it was too late to reason with Alan Kaspar. A plan had formed in his mind, and one way or another, he would see it through.

* * *

"I'm glad you could come," Alan said to Kristen as he hugged her shoulders gently.

"I wouldn't miss this for anything. You've piqued my curiosity, and I'm ready whenever you are."

"It's just an experiment. I don't expect too much to come of it, but it's worth a try."

Kristen felt jittery. She was curious, but she was also frightened. What if something happened? What if she made a fool out of herself? But even worse, what if nothing happened at all? Then she'd be disappointed.

"Come over to the couch and lie down. I'll sit beside you. I'll put you under, and we'll see if we can make heads or tails out of the situation. Good enough?"

She nodded.

She positioned herself comfortably on the couch, lying on her back, her hands folded across her stomach. Alan sat in a straight-backed chair. In his hands he held an octagonal pendant. It was two inches wide and made of shimmering crystal. He held it before her and began to sway it back and forth.

"Now, relax. Watch the crystal pendulum swing back and forth, back and forth. It should make you sleepy, and when you are, just close your eyes. I'll be talking to you, asking questions, and you'll answer me. Okay?"

Once again she nodded. She watched the crystal swing. After a few minutes, she felt her body begin to relax. Her lids became heavy, and she closed her eyes. She had a feeling of weightlessness, a feeling that she was floating and drifting.

"Kris, listen to me. I want you to think about Scott Benson. I want you to tell me what you see."

Immediately, the boy's face flashed into her mind's eye. She saw Scott riding his bike on Willow Road. Once again the whole scenario played itself over in her mind, and once again she told the story of his bike ride and of his pursuer.

"All right. Now think about Louise Faulkner and tell me what you see."

Her body tensed. She could see the newspaper photograph of the missing girl. She didn't want to know anymore about the girl, but it seemed she had no choice.

"I see her walking away from the ice cream parlor. It's dark, and she's turning down one of the side streets. She has an ice cream cone in her hand. Raspberry. She's hurrying because she thinks someone is following her. She cuts down an alley. No, don't go that way! She starts to run. Faster. Faster. It's too late. It's already too close.

"Louise keeps turning her head looking for her pursuer. It's the . . . my God, it's almost on her. Run. Run. It grabs her. It pins her down on the ground. I see a huge claw taking a swipe at her throat.

"Oh, my God. No." Kristen began to hyperventilate. Her body twisted and turned as if she was going into convulsions. "Please, save her!"

"Save her from what? Tell me what got to her."

"It's too late." Tears streamed from beneath her closed lids. "She's dead."

"Kris, calm down. Relax. Relax."

Her body went limp as she settled back into the couch. Alan wiped the tears from her cheeks with a tissue.

"Can you go on? Do you feel strong enough to continue? Would you rather we stop now?"

"We can't stop. I feel better. The Faulkner girl is dead. Dead by the same hand that killed Scott Benson."

"Whose hand is that? Tell me, I must know."

"It was a beast. A wild beast."

"Can you see the beast?"

"Oh . . . my . . . God."

"What do you see, Kris?" Alan said.

"I see a huge cat, bigger than any I've ever seen. The size of a tiger—no, larger. It has silver fur. It has long, long claws. Its teeth are like spikes. And its eyes, God, its eyes are big and round and fiery. I've got to run. I've got to get away. It wants to kill me, too."

"Before you go, tell me what you know about the cat. Where is it from? Who does it belong to? Tell me anything you can."

"It's from hell, I think. And it belongs to . . . to . . ." Kris paused, as if she was too terrified to continue, then said, "It belongs to Eliza. No. Behind the eyes is another creature, another being."

"What is it? Concentrate."

"I can't," Kris said desperately. "I have to escape before it traps me."

"Please tell me what is behind the eyes," Alan said. "I have to know. Then you can run. Who is it?"

"It's . . . it's Eliza Noman."

FORTY-ONE

THE AIR WAS COOL, THE SKY WAS CLEAR, AND STARS twinkled above. A silver moon hung recklessly above the Noman house.

On Willow Road headlights flickered between the pines, then disappeared. A few moments later a lone figure walked up the drive. Zipping up her hooded gray sweatshirt, she moved from the side of the garage.

As Alan approached, she saw the grim look on his face. "I told you earlier, you're not going in. It may be dangerous."

"She's not here," Kristen reassured him. "So I'm going with you."

Yesterday they had decided to go in and find the page and take it to Father Sloan. They also hoped to find evidence to link Eliza with the missing children.

"Kris, listen, if we get caught, we're both going to jail. I'd rather if only I got locked up."

"No, *you* listen! I'm the one Scott Benson came to, and I've been inside the house. I know my way around. I know where she keeps the book. Besides, who's going to catch us? She's out of town."

Alan gave her a worried look. "I know, but I have a bad feeling." He sighed. "All right. I can't stop you, but I don't like it. Come on, let's be quick about it."

They hurried toward the Noman house. Even though Kristen wanted proof, she was still scared but not of the police. The police would be easier to deal with than Eliza. Only God knew how the old lady would react if she found out they had broken in. And if she was a demon, like George had said, she'd kill them.

They circled the house, trying the basement windows. Not only were they locked, but, when Alan shone his flashlight through them, they saw steel bars on the inside.

Once again they went around the house, hoping for an open window on the first floor. All were locked. Kristen suggested breaking the glass on the back door, but Alan disagreed.

"For God's sake, Kris, that's one way to make sure she knows someone got in while she was away."

"So what? She'd never guess it was me."

Alan shook his head and rolled his eyes. "If she's what we think she is, she'd know. Chances are she may already know someone's here."

The thought of Eliza showing up while they

rooted around inside her home made her shiver.
But Eliza was somewhere in New York, or so
Tom had grumbled when she had asked. They
had nothing to worry about.

The trip to Coventry, New York, was tiresome.
She had left Burnwell yesterday afternoon,
stayed overnight in Binghamton, then spent
today with Joan Miller from Century 21. It had
taken all morning and most of the afternoon to
find something suitable. She had almost given
up, until she saw the old Victorian home outside
of town.

The house wasn't as large or as modern as her
home in Burnwell. It needed work. She would
have to remodel the kitchen and the bathroom
and have some of the rooms wallpapered. Of
course, the entire exterior would need paint.
The ghastly yellow had to go.

By the time she finished, it would rival her
present home. It would be perfect for her and
Thomas. With his help, she would redo the
landscaping and rip out the tacky, overgrown
shrubs. She would plant a garden on the skimpy
two acres. It would be their love nest.

She had given the Miller woman a sizeable
sum with instructions to have a cleaning crew
come in this week. She told the real estate agent
the home was for her grandaughter and her new
husband. Joan Miller complimented her gene-
rosity.

Eliza smiled to herself. Before September
ended, she and Thomas would be out of

Burnwell, while Kristen would be . . .

Suddenly, a feeling of impending doom coursed through her. A tightness formed in her chest, and her breathing quickened. She stepped down on the accelerator of her Mercedes. She had to get home.

As she zoomed past the Harrisburg/Allentown Interchange on Interstate 81, the feeling of doom increased. Something was wrong. Someone was trying to . . .

She brought the car up to 80. She had to stop them.

After circling the house and checking all the windows on the second floor, Kristen and Alan looked at each other and shook their heads. The place was like a sealed vault.

"She told me that people from the country don't break into each others' homes, but she sure as hell locks up tight." Kristen sighed. "Now what?"

"We'll check again. Maybe I missed something."

Alan walked along the side of the house, shining the light up at all the windows. Not one was open. He moved toward the back of the house. Kristen followed in silence. He directed the light toward the windows above the porch roof.

"Looks like we're not getting in," he said, glumly.

"Why don't we just break a window. It's the only way." She paused and watched him back up. The beam of light traced the window frames. "Alan, we're wasting time. We could have been in and out by now."

"Sssh. We can't break . . . Hold it, I think I found one."

Kristen followed the beam of light that shone on a second floor window. The window was open. It was located about a foot away from the edge of the porch roof. It was also smaller than the other windows.

"Great. How are we supposed to get up there? Because of evolution, I'm no longer—"

"I'll do it," he said and tucked the flashlight into his pants pocket. He hurried to the side of the porch.

"How? First, we have to get up onto the roof, and then, if we're lucky . . ."

"Piece of cake."

She watched him climb the latticework banister of the porch and balance himself by placing the palm of his right hand against the side of the house. With his left hand, he reached upward. His fingertips grazed the edge of the roof.

"Wish I had a damn ladder," he griped.

"Yeah, well, if I get one out of the garage, I'll wake Tom."

"Obviously," he said, then turned back to the house.

The small window of Eliza's pantry was to his right, directly beneath the upstairs window. She watched Alan twist his body, then raise his right leg and place the tip of his sneaker on the outside ledge. He pushed up.

"Alan, you're going to kill yourself."

He didn't answer. With one swift movement, he hoisted himself up onto the roof. The upper half of his body fell flat against it, while his legs dangled in midair. It took a few seconds before he was able to crawl on top of the roof completely. Then he stood, looking down at her.

"Looks like I'm not that old and decrepit yet." He laughed. "Still spry."

Kristen sighed. "Well, if *you* can do it, I guess I can, too."

"Maybe you'd better stay where you are. I don't want you to get hurt."

"Hey, I may be small, but I'm feisty."

She hurried to the porch and followed Alan's movements. Because she was shorter and didn't have the reach, it took her longer. But with his help, she made it.

They stood side by side, calculating the distance and the acrobatics needed to reach the small window. Alan moved to the edge of the roof and leaned over, grabbing the window sill. Then he pulled the top half of his body inside. Slowly, his legs disappeared. A few seconds later, he poked his head through the window.

Kristen went to the edge of the roof and leaned toward the window. Once again she repeated his movements and, with his hands clasped firmly on her arms, he pulled her into the bathroom. As soon as she stood up, she felt a shudder pass through her.

"Alan, I have a bad feeling. Something's wrong. We'd better hurry." She wasn't sure if the feeling came from being inside Eliza's house or from Eliza herself.

Alan pulled out the flashlight and turned it on. She hurried out of the bathroom. He followed at her heels, shining the light ahead of her. She ran past the polished mahogany doors that lined the hall.

By the time she reached the stairs, the feeling worsened. "I don't know where Eliza is, but I think she knows someone's in her house. It's as if I can feel her anger." Goosebumps rose on her arms as she ran down the steep, shadowy steps to the living room.

She headed for the small den, then went directly to the desk drawer where she saw Eliza stash the book. She held her breath as she pulled on the ornate handle.

The drawer opened easily, but the book was gone. She let out a frustrated sigh. "She moved it." Frantically, she tried all the drawers on the right side of the desk, while Alan searched the opposite side. "Nothing. Now what?"

"Think, Kris. Concentrate on the book. But hurry. If I stay in here much longer, I'm going to wet myself."

Kristen nodded. She, too, felt it. Eliza was getting closer. The old woman's anger surrounded her. If Eliza walked in and found them . . .

She closed her eyes and tried to picture the gold-trimmed leather book in her mind, but all she could see was Eliza's face. She shook her head, trying to concentrate on the book. It was useless.

She saw Eliza driving, speeding down a highway. She saw the old woman's face twisted in anger, her eyes blazing with rage. She saw her stomp down on the accelerator, zooming past cars on her right as if they were standing still. And then she saw the Mechanicsburg exit as a blur. Eliza was almost home.

One of them was Kristen; the other she couldn't make out. They were inside, snooping.

Hatred for the girl overwhelmed her. She increased her speed. Her eyes scanned ahead, looking for State Troopers. The last thing she needed was to get pulled over. She couldn't be delayed. She had to stop them.

If they dared to break into her home, they knew too much. But did they suspect her involvement with the missing kids? Did they suspect her plans for Thomas and Kristen? How much did they know?

She heaved a ragged breath. Her shoulders knotted as her hands tightened around the steering wheel.

They were looking for proof, but they would find none. She had left no evidence to connect her with the kids. The six dried hearts were hidden safely beneath the loose floorboards in the attic. But if they made it to the attic . . .

At breakneck speed, she took the Middlesex exit. She had to stop them.

"For God's sake, Kris, concentrate," Alan urged.

"I can't. She's on her way." She wrung and twisted her hands. Her heart drummed inside her chest. She tried to focus on the book but couldn't. "Alan, help me. Can't you do it?"

"No. I've never seen the book." He grabbed her shoulders. "Look at me. Relax."

"I can't relax. If she walks in here—"

"Look, I'm scared, too, but since we've come this far, we have to get it. You must concentrate."

She sighed and closed her eyes. Eliza still dominated her thoughts. She had left the highway and was speeding down Route 34, heading for them.

She took a deep breath and released it slowly. Her mind saw the book, sitting on top of . . . Eliza's face flashed before her. She took another deep breath, released it and saw the book. It was in the house. But where? Once again, Eliza's twisted face appeared, and again she breathed deeply. The book flashed before her eyes. It was upstairs.

"Alan, we've got to hurry. Follow me." She ran out of the den and headed for the stairs.

He followed close on her heels. "Where is it, Kris?"

"Upstairs. Somewhere."

"Concentrate!"

By the time she hit the top of the steps, her vision of Eliza returned. She was much closer. Panic set in. "I can't focus. She's breaking into my mind."

Alan pulled her to him and hugged her against his chest. She heard the rapid beat of his heart. "Kris, if you can't zoom in on where it is, we have to get out."

"We can't. We must find it." She pictured the book in her mind. It was in one of the bedrooms. No. In the floor above them. The attic. "I found it. We have to go up to the attic."

"How? Where's the door, the stairs?"

She breathed deeply. "It's . . . at the other end of the house. In a bedroom. This way." She pulled away from him and ran down the hall. She flung open the bedroom door.

Alan ran behind her, shining the flashlight around the room. Two doors flanked one wall. She flew to the one on the right. A closet.

Her hand reached for the doorknob of the other one. She twisted. It was locked. "This is the way up."

He nodded and pushed her aside. He tried the door, then let out an exasperated sigh. He thrust the flashlight at her. "Hold this. I'll have to pry it open."

She took the flashlight and focused it on the lock, while Alan dug frantically inside his pockets. The yellow beam danced up and down the door.

"Hold it steady," he barked as he opened the three-inch blade and dug it between the doorjamb.

She watched the tiny wood chips fall to the floor. When Eliza saw the nicks, she'd know the lock had been broken, but she prayed she wouldn't suspect her or Alan.

Suddenly she heard the metal pop, and Alan reached for the doorknob. The door swung open.

* * *

She passed Carlisle Springs and Sterrets Gap and headed into Shermansdale. She angled off Route 34, taking the small road into Burnwell. Her fingers strangled the wheel as she sped recklessly on the winding road.

They had reached the attic door. She'd never make it in time to prevent them from going up. Once they saw what was up there, she'd be doomed. The plans she had made would be ruined.

She had to get to them before they left the house. She had to destroy them. If they found the pact and understood it and realized how to use it against her, she didn't have a chance.

But that was the key—understanding it and using it. The way it was written made it nearly impossible to decipher. If they did manage to leave the house before she got there, she'd get to them long before they figured it out. But still, she didn't want to wait. She wanted to stop them now.

For the first time in a long time, she felt fear. Not since her beloved Louis had lived had she sensed such danger. When he had refused to join her, then threatened to expose her, she had been torn between her love for him and her own survival. As always, her survival won out, and Louis lost.

She struggled to push her fear aside. Her rage surfaced once again. She was tired of playing with Kristen. The game had to end.

When they reached the top of the attic steps, Kristen scanned the room with Alan's flashlight.

Her breath caught inside her chest. Behind her, she heard Alan gasp.

Her hand searched the wall for a light switch, then clicked it on.

Alan spoke first, "Oh . . . my . . . God!"

Kristen said nothing. Chills coursed through her body.

Heavy black velvet drapes covered the windows. The walls were painted a bright red. A crucifix was nailed to the wall—upside down.

An altar fashioned from wood, with black velvet curtains hanging around its side, stood in the middle of the room.

She stepped closer.

The gold-sleeved leather book lay on top of the altar, surrounded by gold and silver chalices. Black candles in all shapes and sizes lined the edge of the altar. They had been recently burned. A crude doll-like figure lay beside the book.

Alan picked up the doll and examined it. He looked at Kristen and shook his head. "I think this is supposed to represent you. From the hatpins jabbed into the head and the stomach area, I'm sure it was the cause of some of the sickness you experienced."

"But I've been feeling better."

"Probably the cross you got from your mother prevented her spell from working." He paused. "Just to be sure, I'm taking it with me. Once it's out of her hands, it can't hurt you at all. Even if you take off the cross, the curse will be broken for good." He tucked it into his pocket.

Kristen nodded. She felt a flutter inside her

stomach. How far would Eliza go to hurt her? If Alan had the doll, what would Eliza resort to next? The thought made her shudder.

She turned her attention to the book, then opened it. The page with Agatha Crenshaw's signature was gone, but the one with Eliza's remained.

"Come on, Kris. Take it and let's get out of here," Alan urged.

Tears stung her eyes. She couldn't believe what Eliza housed in her attic. The dreams of Scott Benson and the dream about the sacrificial baby in the woods were probably not dreams at all.

"Kris!" Alan barked. "Let's go!"

"What is she?" she asked. "A Satanist?"

"Probably."

She shook her head and picked up the book.

"Just take the page with her signature. That's all we need for now," Alan said.

Obediently, she ripped the page from the book and tucked it inside her jacket against her chest.

He grabbed her arm and pulled her toward the door. His hand flicked the light switch before they headed down the steps. He pulled the attic door closed behind them, then they hurried out into the hall. Kristen headed for the bathroom, but he grabbed her arm.

"No point in killing ourselves going out that way. May as well use the door. When she gets back and sees the way I chewed up the attic door with my knife, she'll know for sure someone was here. Let's hope she doesn't know it was us."

They headed for the staircase. When they reached the bottom, Kristen stopped and flashed the light on the portrait above the fireplace. "Take a look at this," she said.

"We don't have—"

She watched his eyes widen. His mouth dropped open. "He looks like Tom."

"Creepy, huh?"

Alan shot her a worried look, then grabbed her hand and pulled her away from the portrait. He started toward the front door, but she pulled him back.

"We'd better go out through the kitchen. Any minute she's going to come flying up the drive. She's real close." She led the way, holding Alan's hand as he trailed behind her.

Within moments, they were outside and running toward her house, not stopping for a breath until they reached the front porch.

"Give me the page," Alan whispered.

She unzipped her jacket and handed it to him.

"In the morning I'm taking this to Father Sloan so he can decipher it. I'll let you know exactly what it says."

Kristen nodded, then watched Alan run down the driveway and disappear behind the pine trees. Her eyes kept watch on Willow Road. Her ears listened for the start of his engine.

Suddenly, she heard the sound of a car speeding in her direction. It was Eliza. She held her breath, hoping Alan was out of sight and safe inside his car. The flicker of Eliza's headlights appeared between the trees. Her tires squealed as she turned into her driveway and sped up to the house.

Kristen heard the start of Alan's engine, and she relaxed. He was okay. Hopefully, Eliza hadn't spotted him, but even if she did, she wouldn't know who he was. She hurried up the porch steps, slipped inside and headed for the kitchen. After what she had seen tonight and the implication of it, there was no point in trying to sleep. She was too damn wired.

Furious, Eliza got out of the car and slammed the door. They were gone. They had the pact.

The urge to go after them built inside her, but she had to remain calm. She had to do it right, or there would be cops and questions.

She knew who the fool was who had gotten into his car on the road. Thomas had told her about him, and given her a description. She would deal with the college's resident lunatic swiftly.

She stared down at the house next door, wanting to rip out the bitch's throat. She took a step forward, then stopped. She had to control her rage. She had time to take care of them. Before Kaspar deciphered the writing and realized how to destroy her, he would be gone, leaving Kristen to face her alone.

She stomped into the house, then up to the attic. She flicked on the light and moved to the altar. The book remained. The mandrake root in the image of Kristen was gone—but what of it? The game had ended.

She could no longer control her anger. She swept her hand across the altar, sending the book, candles and chalices crashing to the floor. She released a wild, tortured scream, then dropped to her knees.

Kaspar would die, painfully. Then she would deal with the bitch next door.

FORTY-TWO

"FATHER, I HAVE WHAT WE NEED. I THINK WE HAVE some proof," Alan Kaspar said as he burst into the rectory's kitchen.

Father Sloan sat at the table, nibbling a small bran muffin as he read the morning paper. He looked up, startled. "Proof of what?"

"Proof about Eliza Noman. Look at this root. It resembles a human figure. And I'm pretty sure that's Kristen's hair on it. And here's the page we took from the book. It's in some kind of language. I can't make it out, but maybe you can decipher it."

Father Sloan took the page. "It's certainly a language *I've* never seen." He studied it. "Wait. It resembles Latin, but not quite."

"What do you mean not quite?"

"The words don't make sense. Something's

wrong with them." He placed the page on the table. "How about if I study it later. I have a few things to do this morning, so I'll get to it this afternoon. We'll talk about it tonight."

He fingered the mandrake root that Alan had placed on the table. "What's this supposed to be? It looks like some sort of doll."

"Yes. The mandrake root grows in human form."

"Interesting. What's it used for, or shouldn't I ask?"

"I think Eliza has been using it in rituals. Maybe to put a curse on Kristen."

Father Sloan nodded. "Witchcraft?" He shrugged. "What's Kristen's last name again?"

"Roberts."

Father Sloan sighed. "I'll get to this later. You may have something here. It certainly seems odd." He paused and studied the root. "And you think this woman, Eliza . . ."

"Noman."

"You think she has something to do with the missing children?"

"Possibly. At least, that's what Kristen thinks."

The priest looked at him thoughtfully. "Alan, do you realize how bizarre this all sounds?"

"Yes. I've had many sleepless nights trying to put it into some kind of scientific perspective, but I believe the girl. And it does make sense. Ritualistic sacrifice has happened before." Alan sighed. "But theories are worthless without evidence."

"True." Father Sloan stood up. "Sorry to rush you, but I have to visit Mrs. Malone. She's still unable to get to Mass, so I have to take communion to her. We'll talk later."

"Good. Because I've got a lot more to tell you. The woman has an altar in her attic. There's a crucifix hanging on the wall—upside down. Unbelievable. Spooky." Alan headed for the door. "About what time can I expect you?"

"About ten."

Alan nodded. He saw the worried look on Sloan's face, but it made him feel good. At least someone was paying attention and not viewing him or Kristen as lunatics. If Sloan could make sense of the strange writing, it could lead to other clues or evidence that the police could use. As he ran down the steps, he smiled at the possibility of solving the mystery of the missing kids.

Trask's tavern was located on Route 34 about seven miles outside of Burnwell. It was a small place with old wooden clapboard shingles and a large front window where TRASK flashed on and off in a bright orange, fluorescent light.

Inside, the tavern was homey and rustic. A clutter of wooden tables filled the dining area, while a half-circle bar occupied the opposite side of the room. A huge stone fireplace covered the entire back wall. Stuffed deer heads and stuffed pheasants were strategically hung on the walls.

Alan sat near the fireplace finishing his dinner—a porterhouse steak with fries and cole slaw. He relaxed against the back of the chair and stared into the flames, sipping his third Michelob.

At ten he would see Father Sloan who, with luck, would have the page translated. Alan felt a flutter inside his stomach. From what he had seen in Eliza Noman's attic, he felt certain that Sloan would confirm that the old woman had been involved with the missing children. But then, they needed evidence—bodies.

He thought about digging up Eliza Noman's flower beds and shuddered. Who would have the stomach to face what lay beneath the earth? He pushed the thought from his mind and glanced at his watch. 9:30. He guzzled his beer, paid the check and hurried out the door.

Outside, it was damp and drizzly. He shivered as he slipped behind the wheel of his red Nova and started it. He switched on the heat and waited for the blast of hot air to remove the chill, before turning on the windshield wipers and headlights. As he headed down Route 34 toward Burnwell, the fluttering continued inside his stomach.

The rain-slicked country road twisted and turned. The effects of the beer reminded him of the awful night when he hadn't negotiated a turn and Margaret had died. But tonight she wasn't with him. He was alone and not drunk.

Margaret. How he wished he could contact her, tell her how sorry he was, how much he missed her, but . . .

Suddenly, a light appeared directly ahead. It hovered in the middle of the road, and he slowed to a crawl. The light grew brighter and larger. It stung his eyes.

He glanced in the rearview mirror, saw no one behind him and came to a complete stop. He sat motionless, staring at the approaching ball of white light. He shielded his eyes with his hand against its brilliance, then slowly eased the car to the side of the road.

The light moved with him, floating closer, until finally it stopped at the hood of the car.

Its brilliance faded, and what he saw in its center made him gasp. It couldn't be. His mind was playing tricks with him. He had tried for so many years without success, and now she came to him.

"Margaret," he cried. "Oh, Margaret."

"Alan," a soft voice whispered.

She was just as he remembered, exactly as the photograph above her obituary when she had died. She was plump, with rosy cheeks and short, curly brown hair. She was beautiful.

Her arms opened to him; her lips called his name. She smiled, then beckoned to him with her hand.

Without a second thought, he jumped out of the car and followed her she drifted back into the woods. His mind reeled with excitement, his heart raced, and his feet stumbled.

And then she stopped. The light around her faded, and her smile became a scowl.

"Oh, Margaret," he said, "please don't be angry. I didn't mean for you to die. I was a fool that night to drink so much. Forgive me." He sobbed as he stood before her. "It's been so lonely without you."

"Has it?" she asked, sarcastically.

Alan's breath hitched inside his chest. He felt his eyes widen. He backed up. Fear surged through him. How could he have been so stupid? He wanted so badly to see Margaret, so that was what he saw.

Eliza Noman now stood before him. She smiled, exposing a row of jagged fangs. Her eyes turned a glowing orange. Long claws extended from the tips of her fingers.

Her hand shot out and grabbed his wrist, the claws digging into his skin. He tried to pull free, but the claws dug deeper.

"Fool!" she screeched. "Did you think I didn't see you duck into your car? Did you think I wouldn't come for you?"

His lips parted, but the words caught in his throat. Eliza Noman was . . . what? A Satanist? No. More. A demon straight from hell.

"Return what you stole!"

"I stole nothing." He heard the quiver of his voice.

She laughed, wickedly. "Liar! You and that little bitch entered my home and took what belongs to me. Return it, and I may let you live."

The page flashed in his mind. "What was it that I took?"

She smiled again, then flicked her tongue over her lips. Her eyes glowed brighter. "Where is it?" she demanded.

"I no longer have it."

"Liar! Return it to me!"

"I destroyed it."

Her clawed hand flew at him and slashed across his face. He dropped to his knees, warm blood oozing from his cheek.

She released his wrist and howled.

On hands and knees he tried to crawl away from her, but her powerful claws ripped through his jacket and dug into the flesh on his back. His knees buckled. Pain wracked his body. As he rolled onto his side, his eye caught the thick fallen branch, and he wrapped his hand around it.

Screaming, she came at him with eyes that bubbled like molten lava. She moved swiftly and stealthily, like a cat.

"Where is it?" she screamed, as she perched above him. "Return it!"

"First tell me what it is, and why it's so important."

"Fool!" she screeched, then swiped at him.

He swung the thick branch and caught her on the side of her head, but he didn't stop swinging. He hit her again and again. He kept hitting, until she staggered. Then he got up and hit her once more and watched her drop to her knees. A dark liquid trickled down the side of her face.

He turned and ran toward the road. Blood gushed from the wounds on his back. He felt dizzy and disoriented as he staggered to his car. Behind him, he heard the cry of a wild, angry beast, but he didn't turn to look. He opened the car door, fell into the seat and locked the door.

He dropped his makeshift weapon on the seat

and slumped over the wheel. The throbbing pain in his back increased, and the side of his face felt shredded. He fought the urge to pass out. He had to get moving. He had to get to Sloan, and then to Kristen. He had to . . .

The car vibrated and rocked. He picked up his head. Through blurred eyes he saw her at the hood of the car, her face more bestial than before. The fangs had grown longer; the claws extended farther. Her eyes flamed, and her ears resembled those of a cat. She seemed to be transforming herself into an animal before his eyes.

He put the car in gear, but before he could press down on the accelerator and ram her, the car flipped. It rolled off the shoulder of the road and into the trees. He bounced and tumbled inside the car as shards of pain coursed through his back. His head slammed into the side window.

As the car crashed into a tree trunk, jarring his wounded body, he heard her shrill laugh. Then—*whoosh*! He opened his eyes. He saw the flames, then reached for the door handle. He pushed, but it wouldn't budge. Panicked, he pushed again and again and again. Finally, it opened. He swung his left leg out of the car. The smell of gas stung his nose. He heard her cackle above the crackling fire. Then the flames leaped out and grabbed him.

". . . Last night, Alan Kaspar, age sixty, died in a fiery car crash on Route 34. According to police, Kaspar was killed when he lost control of his car and struck a tree," the radio announcer said.

Kristen screamed. The coffeepot in her hand dropped to the floor. She fell into the nearest chair and started to cry.

Tom stood in the doorway, watching. He sauntered into the room, looked down at her and shook his head. He had heard the news report, but the loss of Alan Kaspar was nothing to get hysterical about. He picked up the coffeepot and placed it on the countertop.

"Tom," Kristen said between sobs, "Alan is dead. He was killed last night in a car crash."

"Yeah, I heard." He shrugged.

"Is that all you can say? Don't you care?"

"I didn't know him very well," he replied, then stepped over the puddle of coffee and headed for the refrigerator.

"How can you be so callous? What's wrong with you? The man is dead."

He poured himself a glass of orange juice that Eliza had squeezed herself and given him last night, then headed for the screened porch.

"Tom, say something. Alan's dead."

"Exactly what would you like me to say or do?" he snapped. "Accidents happen." He opened the door, went out to the porch, then dropped into the webbed lounge chair, and he gulped his juice as if nothing had happened.

FORTY-THREE

THE DAY WAS SUNNY, THE SKY A CRYSTALLINE blue, the temperature near 60. A stiff wind blew in from the northwest, and Kristen pulled the collar of her gray blazer tight around her neck. She stood by the gravesite at Holy Cross Cemetery with Tom and Dean Jensen.

She felt a tug on her elbow and turned.

A young man, tall and square-jawed, with a face as sharp as the chiseled granite headstones, stood behind her. He wore a black jacket and black pants and the collar of a priest.

"Kristen Roberts?" he asked in a whisper. "I'm Father Sloan, Alan's friend."

Kristen nodded. Alan had told her he intended to bring the page they took from Eliza's to Father Sloan, and from the serious look on the priest's face, she concluded that he had. "It's nice to meet you, Father."

He took hold of her elbow and led her away from Tom and Dean Jensen. "We need to talk. Soon." His smile was grim. "I know Alan's death has been a shock, and I'm sure you need time, but what I have to tell you can't wait. Will you come to the rectory as soon as you can?"

"Yes." A tightness formed in her chest. The priest must have translated the page.

"Good. Call me. Right away."

Nodding, she watched Father Sloan ascend the hill and disappear behind a clump of trees. Whatever he had discovered about Eliza seemed serious. She detected it in his voice, his facial expression and his sense of urgency.

"Who was he?"

Kristen jumped. Tom had come up behind her. She looked into his face. He seemed irritated, as usual. She sighed, then shrugged. "Just a friend of Alan's offering condolences," she lied, offering a weak smile. She had no intention of telling him about her midnight adventure at Eliza's or about the page. Not yet.

Tom heaved a sigh. "Let's go," he barked and started toward the car.

"Aren't we going to the brunch that Alan's nephew is having?"

"No."

She didn't feel like arguing. She knew the only reason he had attended the funeral was because he had to since Alan was a colleague. She followed him to the New Yorker.

In silence, they drove home. She paid little

attention to Tom's indifference about Alan's death. She had more to occupy her thoughts— Father Sloan's translation.

She went inside, then headed for the bedroom. She undressed, slipped into her pink robe, then stretched out on the bed.

She thought about Alan. Tears poured from her eyes. She sobbed uncontrollably until she felt drained, then she drifted off to sleep.

With a bottle of Eliza's banana liqueur, Tom reclined in the lounge chair on the screened porch. He was glad the funeral was over. He had had little use for Kaspar and attending his funeral made him feel like a hypocrite. But he had no choice—Alan was one of the team, a part of the Psychology department. If he hadn't gone, it would have looked bad in front of the Dean.

He leaned his head back and closed his eyes. Aimee Clark filled his thoughts. He wanted to call her and spend the rest of the day with her. The thought of being home with Kris disgusted him. He couldn't stand being near her. Aimee took her place and filled his needs. She was his dream girl.

Even though he met Aimee every day after classes at Willow Park, the erotic dreams continued. Each night, he woke up drenched with perspiration and covered with semen. It was impossible to understand, but he didn't fight it. The dreams made him want her more.

What puzzled him was that the gorgeous blonde he dreamed about had green eyes, not blue like Aimee's but green like Eliza's. He thought about Eliza's portrait that hung over her fireplace. She had been a beautiful woman. He wished he had known her when she was young.

He smiled and took a gulp of banana liqueur. He was doing all right. He was getting it from Aimee and getting it while he slept. He had nothing to complain about. No man in his right mind would complain.

He had nothing to worry about. His life couldn't be better. He had a good job and a sexy blonde to satisfy his needs. He drained the glass, sat up and looked up toward Eliza's. She, too, sat on her porch. He got up and headed for her house, whistling his favorite tune.

FORTY-FOUR

IT WAS MIDNIGHT, BUT STILL KRISTEN COULDN'T sleep. Father Sloan dominated her thoughts. She had wanted to call him earlier, but she had fallen asleep. When she woke up, Tom was around, and she didn't want him to overhear her conversation. But now Tom was fast asleep, and she wondered if it was too late to call the rectory.

As she walked into the kitchen, she saw the chocolate layer cake that Eliza had delivered. She dipped her finger into the creamy icing and tasted it. The same bitter aftertaste stung her tongue.

She picked up the cake, walked to the garbage and dumped it inside. She took the plate back to the sink and rinsed the remaining crumbs down the drain. She had enough of Eliza and her lousy goodies.

Exasperated, she went out to the screened porch. The air felt damp and chilly. She pulled the pink robe tight as her eyes focused on the six large moths that clung to the screen.

She moved closer, then backed away. Her heart fluttered inside her chest. She folded her arms around her waist, then moved forward again. A small cry escaped from between her lips. It wasn't her imagination. It was real.

The six moths had human faces. She saw the faces of Scott Benson and Louise Faulkner. She saw the face of an infant. The remaining three also had faces of children whom she didn't recognize.

Tears misted her eyes. They were all the missing children, and they were all dead because of Eliza Noman, as she suspected George and Alan and probably Amber were. She felt her anger build. She had to do something, but she needed proof that Eliza actually did kill the children and sacrifice them. She needed more than intuition.

She ran back into the house and looked up Father Sloan's number. She dialed quickly. The phone rang twice, then she heard the priest's husky voice.

"Hello?" he said.

"Father Sloan?"

"Yes."

"This is Kristen Roberts. I'm sorry to disturb you this late, but—"

"It's okay. I'm glad you called." A brief silence followed, then he sighed and continued. "Alan gave me the page you took from Eliza Noman. He also gave me the root, the doll. I think . . . Well, I'm not positive yet, but there could be a connection between the Noman woman and the missing kids. I'm still working on it. As soon as I decipher all of it, I'll call you."

"What do you think that page is?"

"Well, I hate to say this, but . . . I think it's a pact."

"A pact? With whom?"

He sighed. "Do you believe in the devil?"

"I guess."

"Well, that's probably who we're dealing with. Maybe not directly, but indirectly." He paused, then asked, "Are you a religious person? Do you go to church?"

"Yes and no, Father. I believe in God, but I haven't been to church in a long time." She felt embarrassed to admit that to a priest.

"What denomination?"

She sighed. "Catholic."

"Well, it might be a good idea for you to start going again. Regularly. I expect to see you at Mass, not only because you're Catholic and it's a requirement of our faith, but because if this is what I suspect, you're going to need all the help you can get."

Kristen felt her skin prickle. She fingered the tiny gold cross that hung around her neck as she agreed to attend Mass every Sunday.

After she hung up, she went back out to the

porch. The six moths had disappeared. She sighed and crossed her arms tightly over her robe.

Eliza had signed a pact with the devil. She had sacrificed the children to him. But for what purpose? What did he give her in return?

She shivered, then went inside. She heated a glass of milk in the microwave, then sat by the kitchen table. She hoped the warm milk would help her to relax. She needed to sleep and extinguish the horror for a few hours before she could formulate a plan to help the children.

Eliza Noman sat by her bedroom window. She watched Kristen pace the house a dozen times. She saw her go outside. She saw her on the phone and wondered if she had a new ally.

Kristen was up to something. She could feel the fool's anger directed toward her. Had she found out enough to destroy her? Did she know how she had used the innocence of the children? Did she know that they were caught in her web and could not escape as long as she remained alive? And could the fool prove any of it?

She wondered if Kristen had eaten any of the cake that she made especially for her. It was Thomas who had told her of Kristen's love of chocolate and had given her the opportunity for a final try.

She had laced the cake with cubina, enough to drive her insane almost instantly. The cubina was the preferred way to rid herself of Kristen. The fool would be institutionalized with little chance of recovery. And who would question the reason for her mental illness? She was already upset because of the deaths of Howard and Kaspar, and since it had happened to her mother. . . .

But why did the bitch make it so difficult by not eating or drinking anything she sent? Eliza sighed. The fool was impossible. She didn't want to destroy her like she had destroyed her friends. She wanted more. She wanted the bitch to suffer for her insolence.

Eat the cake! Eat the cake!

Angered, she got up from her rocker and headed for the attic. She lighted the candles on the altar, then placed another mandrake root in the center. She took a razor-sharp kitchen knife and placed it over the part that resembled the head.

"Kristen Roberts, I shall destroy you!"

She bowed her head, then mumbled a prayer to her god. She sang his praises, then begged for his help. When she pressed the knife into the root, it split in two.

She dropped to her knees, then collapsed on the floor.

Her potions were useless on the fool. Her spells didn't work. She had no choice but to kill her.

The church was dimly lit. To her right Kristen saw a statue of the Blessed Mother crushing a serpent's head beneath her foot. To her left stood a statue of the Sacred Heart of Jesus. Directly ahead, above the altar, was the Crucifixion. What they symbolized gave her comfort.

Kristen bowed her head and recited the Lord's Prayer in her mind. Father Sloan knelt beside her, his hands folded in front of him, his head bowed, his lips moving.

This afternoon he had called and asked her to meet him at the church. He had completed the translation, and now she waited to hear what he had found.

When she touched his arm, he turned to her, then slid back into the pew. She did the same. His face looked grim.

"Tell me, Father," she whispered, "is it as bad as I feared?"

He nodded, slowly. "It's definitely a pact. And you were right about the Noman woman's involvement with the missing children." He took in a deep breath, then blew it out. "The pact was written in Latin, but backwards. Part of it reads: 'Each time I will age naturally. Each time I will sacrifice six innocents. For the praise and glory of you, my father.'"

Kristen gasped. "Then Scott Benson really did come to me for help?"

"Probably. Their souls may be trapped in some kind of limbo."

"But what can I do to help them?"

He sighed. "Maybe you have to destroy her." He sighed again. "But that won't be easy. From the way it sounds, she's been around a long time. And, if things aren't bad enough, she has the power to transform into some type of beast."

The dreams of being chased through the cornfields by a huge beast flashed in her mind, as did George's story. "How can she do it? Why?"

"The power to transform was given to her by the devil. That much was stated in the pact. The reason for it is probably for strength and power."

"Oh, my God, if she can do that, how can she be destroyed?"

Father Sloan smiled. "I suspect by burning the pact."

"Then what are we waiting for? Let's burn it now."

"It's not that easy. It has to be done at her altar or near it. You see, that's where the sacrifices are made, and that's where the pact can be broken."

Kristen shook her head. "You mean, I have to get inside her house again? But she was away when Alan and I broke in. I don't think I can get in with her here."

"What about the sacrificial altar in the woods where you saw the baby?"

"Do you think it would work there?"

"Yes. I think the altar in the house is used only for casting spells, but the one in the woods . . ."

She nodded. Somehow she'd have to find her way back to it. If she was lucky, she wouldn't get lost. If she was luckier, Scott Benson would come for her again.

"Kristen, you must be careful. She probably knows you have the pact. She's probably too powerful not to know."

"Yes, I think so, too. I also think she killed

George and Alan and made it appear as a heart attack and an accident. It seems that everyone who gets involved with me dies." She paused. "Except Tom. She adores him. You know, he resembles this Louis that she loved. I wonder . . ."

"It's possible she wants to get rid of you, then initiate your husband, since the pact states she's supposed to regain her youth."

Finally, it all made sense. Tom was controlled by Eliza. But how? Spells? Herbs? She sighed. "What about that root with my hair on it? Could she hurt me or kill me with that?"

He nodded. His eyes dropped to the small cross that hung around her neck. "The cross will protect you from her spells. Just make sure she never sees it."

Kristen tucked the cross inside her blouse. "Father, when do you think she's going to become young again?"

"I don't know, but five children are missing, and you saw a sacrificial baby. I'd say it's going to be soon. And you must be careful. It might be a good idea for you to get away. I can find the altar and destroy the pact."

"I can't. What about Tom? He won't leave."

"He may be under some sort of spell."

Kristen nodded. She had no doubt about that. Now, all she had to do was break the spell, then destroy the pact, which would destroy Eliza and release the children. Some job!

"If you stay, you'd better take the pact and keep it with you at all times for your own protection, until we can get to the altar and burn it."

Kristen heaved a sigh. Somehow, she would do it. She had to do it for Tom and Alan and George and the children—and for herself.

FORTY-FIVE

THE WHITE VOLKSWAGEN PARKED BESIDE THE pine trees that bordered the road. The headlights went off. The blonde turned off the engine, then stepped out of the car and leaned against the hood.

Eliza stood between the trees, a smile forming on her lips. Getting Aimee Clark to come had been easy.

Earlier she had called the whore at her dorm and told her that she was Thomas's mother and that he wanted to see her. At first, the girl seemed confused that his mother knew about their affair, but Eliza explained Thomas had told her and also had told her he was leaving his wife.

The bitch became ecstatic. Then she told her that Thomas begged her to call because he was afraid Kristen might overhear if he did it himself. Since he wanted the divorce to go smoothly, without the complication of another woman, he wanted to be careful.

She told Aimee how much she disliked his wife and how pleased she was that her son had found someone who loved him. Aimee admitted her love. Then she told her to meet him at the edge of his property on Willow Road at 9:30. She also said he had a surprise, and Aimee agreed to come.

She watched the whore light a cigarette, then pace the side of the road. The tight jeans, the form-fitting turtleneck, the long, thick mane sent waves of anger through Eliza. She remembered the scene in Willow Park when Thomas made love to her. Filled with rage and jealousy and hate, she shrugged off her cloak and started the transformation.

She watched the claws sprout from her fingertips and felt her teeth grow long. She flicked her tongue between her fangs, then dropped to all fours. A shiver coursed through her as her hands turned into paws. Her back arched. Her eyes focused on the girl.

It stretched, then sat back on its haunches and howled.

Aimee Clark stopped pacing and stood perfectly still. Her head turned fearfully from side to side. She threw the cigarette onto the road, then started toward her car.

It moved swiftly and stealthily from between the pines, until it reached the girl's heels. It smelled the fear and the terror. It heard the beat of the girl's heart and the rush of blood through her veins. And then it howled.

The girl spun around. She screamed and backed away, stumbling, until the hood of the car prevented her from going any farther.

It followed silently, patiently, hungrily. Then it pounced and pinned her down with its left paw.

The girl screamed again.

It picked up its right paw, extended the claws and swiped at her face, her throat, her chest. The girl's body went limp. It licked the blood from its claws, then lapped the blood from the wounds until the flow ceased.

The girl's blood covered the hood of the white Volkswagen and dripped down the sides onto the road. She pushed the whore's body out of the way, then got into the car. The keys dangled from the ignition. She started it, then drove it into Thomas's driveway. It would be safe here until the ceremony was over, then she would get rid of the blood and the car. With her claws, she would turn the gravel alongside the road and hide the whore's blood as she had done with the Benson kid, so no trace of violence could be found.

She slid out of the car, walked back to the road, then grabbed the girl by her long blonde hair and dragged her to the back of the Victorian. She opened the cellar door, then threw the body inside. After slamming the door closed, she hurried into the house and grabbed the small purple ginger jar from a top shelf in the kitchen and headed for the attic.

She threw off her cloak and stood before the

altar, then bowed her head. She offered herself
to her father. She opened the ginger jar and with
her fingertips smoothed the oily liquid over her
skin.

The ceremony was about to begin. Before
night ended, she would be young again and
Thomas would be initiated. Before daybreak,
she would retrieve her pact and Kristen would
be dead. She and Thomas would bury Aimee
and Kristen near the altar in the woods. Then
they would be free to share an eternity.

Eliza glanced up at the starry sky and saw the
full moon. Excitement flowed through her. Finally, after months of preparation, she would
succeed.

Pulling the black satin cloak tightly around
her waist, she stepped onto Thomas's screened
porch and tapped lightly on the back door.
Within moments, he opened it. She smiled.

The large dose of Paris she had put into the
banana liqueur when he had stopped by to visit
at 6:00 had taken hold. His eyes appeared
glazed, and he smiled down at her with a
crooked smile.

"Eliza." His speech was slurred. "It's great to
see you." He leaned against the doorframe as if
in a drunken stupor.

"Thomas, I need you to come with me.
There's something we have to do."

He smiled again. "Sure, Eliza, anything for
you."

She took his hand and led him toward the
woods, pulling him along gently but swiftly.

The full moon illuminated their way as they hurried down the narrow path. Behind her, he tripped and stumbled over the jutting stones, but she took hold of his waist and became his crutch. When they reached the path that angled to the right, she quickly threw aside the branches and led him into the clearing and to the altar.

Placing her hands on the sides of his head, she pulled him to her lips. The kiss was long and passionate and loving. When she released him, she looked into his eyes. She saw no resistance.

Slowly, she unbuttoned his shirt and removed it. She kissed him again, and he returned her kiss. She stripped him of his clothes, then instructed him to lay upon the altar. She removed her cloak and took the ginger jar from an inside pocket. She massaged the clear liquid over his body, then she said, "Thomas, tonight I will become young again. Will you accept me? Will you pledge your love to me?"

He whispered, "Yes."

"Do you accept my god as your father? Do you offer him your soul in return for his gift?"

Again he whispered, "Yes."

"Will you sign the pact in your own blood? Then fulfill the terms of that pact?"

Smiling, he nodded.

She breathed deeply, then threw the empty jar to the ground. She circled the altar in a counter-clockwise motion. Her lips sang the chant. She circled faster. The ceremony had begun.

FORTY-SIX

WHEN KRISTEN TURNED OFF MAIN STREET ONTO Willow Road she felt it. A shudder traveled through her. A scene flashed before her eyes of Tom and Eliza at the altar in the woods. Something was happening to him. He was involved in some ritual.

She pressed down on the accelerator and negotiated the twisting turns of the road. Her heart drummed out of control; her body trembled.

She had to help him. She had to stop Eliza.

Her eyes flashed to the pact that lay beside her on the seat. Her hand touched her pocket and the lighter that Father Sloan had given her. If only she could pull over to the side of the road and burn it and destroy Eliza, but Father Sloan was certain it had to be done at the altar. She had to find her way into the woods. She had to get to Tom before it was too late.

She drove wildly, recklessly, carelessly. The car bounced and shuddered as she went up and down the hills. When the pine trees in front of her property came into view, she hit the brake hard. The tires screeched and screamed on the macadam. She made a hard right into the drive, as the back end of the car skidded. She turned the wheel again and drove between the trees.

A white Volkswagen was parked directly in her path. She slammed on the brakes. Her body stiffened, the wheels screamed, and she rammed the Volkswagen, pushing it up the drive. The Honda stalled. She leaned back in the seat and released her breath. For a moment, she closed her eyes.

She saw Eliza remove his shirt. She saw them embrace.

"You can't have him, bitch!" she screamed as she grabbed the pact and jumped out of the car. "You'll have to kill me first." She glanced at the Volkswagen. Blood. But whose?

She ran toward the woods, the pact firmly in her hand. When she reached the path, she ducked beneath a low branch and went on.

The path was narrow and rocky, the uneven ground making it difficult to hurry. Suddenly, she stumbled and fell to her knees. A sharp stone bit into her leg, penetrated her jeans and pierced her skin. Pain coursed up her leg as stinging tears rolled down her cheeks. She struggled to her feet. Warm blood trickled down her leg. Limping, she continued until she came to an area where the path broke in two.

She stopped. Confused, she looked at each path. One was wide, the other narrow. Both led deep into the forest, but which one led to Tom?

Closing her eyes, she tried to remember the night Scott Benson led her to the altar and the sacrificial baby. The baby lying on top of the altar appeared in her mind's eye, but when she tried to recall the direction, all she saw was Tom, lying naked on the altar, and Eliza applying a glistening fluid to his skin.

She opened her eyes and glanced from one path to the other. She had to choose the right way, or Tom would . . . Eliza flashed before her eyes. The old woman circled the altar.

"No!" she screamed and headed for the path on the left.

She went in only a few feet, then gasped.

Scott Benson appeared in the middle of the path. His blue eyes shone brightly in the moonlight. Once more the hole in his chest and the slashed throat horrified her. She turned from him and had the urge to vomit. She swallowed hard, then said, "My husband . . ."

Scott Benson smiled and exposed his tinseled teeth. He shook his head. His voice reached into her mind. "The wrong way."

"Oh, my God," she cried, then turned and ran toward the other path. As she glanced over her shoulder, she saw he had vanished, but she didn't want him to go. She wanted his help— needed it.

She stumbled forward. The gash on her leg

throbbed, and she gasped for breath. A stitch formed in her left side. She kept going, then burst into the clearing.

Horrified, she stopped and drew in a gasping breath. She tried to call his name, but the word caught in her throat.

Tom lay on his back, his skin glistening and shimmering in the moonlight. His eyes were closed, but he was alive. She could see the rise and fall of his chest.

Above him, circling the altar like a bird of prey, was Eliza. She, too, was covered with the strange oily liquid.

Kristen watched in awe. With each counter-clockwise revolution, Eliza grew younger. Her sagging skin pulled tight, and her breasts became firm. She developed the figure of a woman of 20. Her thin gray hair turned blonde and grew long and thick.

"Oh, God! Oh, God!" she cried, then dug into her pocket for the Zippo lighter and ran to the altar.

Her eyes focused on Tom. Was it too late? Had he joined with Eliza? Had he made his own pact? Her fingers fumbled with the lighter. Her thumb shook as she tried to light it—once, twice—and then the flame shot up. Her hands shook violently as she moved the flame to the bottom of the page.

Suddenly, her head was wrenched back. Her hair was being ripped out at the roots. A hand grabbed her throat, and she was thrown away from the altar. She landed on her back, stunned and dazed, clinging to the pact and the lighter.

Eliza came at her, young and beautiful, as she had been in the portrait. Her green eyes blazed with anger, her lips curled into a snarl.

Kristen scrambled to her knees, then tried to reignite the lighter. Her thumb barely rolled over the wheel. She tried again.

The powerful hand struck the side of her face, and the lighter flew from her hand. She fell on her side. The fiery sting on her cheek caused tears to form.

She heard Eliza laugh.

She rolled onto her back as Eliza came at her again. With one swift movement, she smashed her foot into Eliza's face. Eliza reeled and screamed, then bent in half. Kristen kicked her again, this time in the stomach. Eliza dropped to her knees. She scrambled away as Eliza screamed and howled.

As she groped for the lighter, she saw the claws spring out of Eliza's fingertips. "Oh, God!" she cried, grabbing the lighter and struggling to her feet.

She stumbled toward the altar. Behind her, Eliza released a shrill bestial cry. Kristen kept going, circling to the opposite side of the altar. Gasping for breath, she glanced at Tom. His eyes remained closed. She focused on the pact and rolled her thumb over the lighter's wheel. The flame shot up.

From the corner of her eye, she saw Eliza rush toward her. Instinctively, she backed up. And then, Eliza pounced on Tom. She raised her clawed hand over his chest, directly above his heart.

"Give me the pact," she growled, "or I'll kill him."

A small scream escaped from Kristen's mouth as she looked at Eliza's face. The woman's eyes bubbled orange like molten steel; her teeth resembled long, serrated fangs.

"Give it to me!"

She shook her head. "If I do, you'll go on living. You'll take him anyway."

Eliza dug the tips of her claws into Tom's chest, then stopped. "I'll rip out his heart right in front of you."

She saw the blood ooze from Tom's wound. Her tears came quickly. She couldn't stand to see him hurt. "Please, Eliza, leave us alone. He belongs to me. I love him."

"If you love him, you'll give me the pact." She dug the claws deeper.

"No!"

"The pact." She dug deeper.

Kristen felt her body go limp, and the lighter fell from her hands. She moved toward the altar. She had no choice. She had no doubt that Eliza would kill him.

Obediently, she handed the pact to her. Eliza took it from her hand, then pulled her claws out of Tom's chest. His blood flowed more freely.

"I love him, too, fool," she said. "And you *are* a little fool. Now, I'll kill *you*." She moved around the altar, the pact in her hand.

Kristen backed away. Eliza would be on her in seconds, ripping out her heart and her throat, as she did to Scott Benson.

At first, she came slowly, with the movements

of a cat. Then she moved swiftly and pounced. Kristen darted to the side.

Eliza howled angrily and whirled around. "You don't have a chance, bitch, so why fight? Let's get this over with quickly." Eliza lunged for her.

This time Kristen reached for the pact. She had to try. She couldn't go down without a fight. She caught the very edge and ripped it with her fingertips.

Eliza screamed as if in pain, then doubled over.

Kristen stared in horror, then satisfaction. A deep gash appeared on Eliza's leg. Blood flowed from it like a river. She lunged for the pact again and ripped half of it from Eliza's hands.

Eliza screamed again, as a gash coursed across her stomach. The blood dripped to the plush grass at her feet. The top half of the pact fell from Eliza's clawed hand. Kristen grabbed it and tore it in half. She watched the wound form in Eliza's cheek.

The woman dropped to her knees and clawed at the earth. "Help me, father!" she screamed. "Help me, father!"

Suddenly, the ground beneath their feet rolled. At the edge of the clearing, the earth cracked. A huge fissure opened and crawled toward the center of the clearing, toward the altar and Tom. A violent wind howled and tore through the trees. It whipped around Kristen, tearing at her.

Kristen stumbled back and stared at the fissure in horror. Smoke escaped from its center;

steamy lava, the color of Eliza's eyes, bubbled up. "Oh, God! Oh, God!"

She lurched toward Tom. She had to get him up. They had to get out before . . .

Scott Benson appeared before the altar. "You must finish. You must destroy her!"

"She's dying. I ripped the pact."

He shook his head violently. "Burn it! Now! Before he comes!"

He? Who? The devil himself? Oh, God!

Her eyes searched the ground for the silver lighter. Her ears heard Eliza's screeching. She tried to remain steady on the rolling earth, but she lost her balance and dropped to her knees. She crawled to the lighter and rolled her thumb over the wheel. The flame shot up and blew in the wind. When she touched it to the torn pieces of the pact, they caught. Slowly, the flames devoured them.

Eliza screamed in agony.

Kristen stared in disbelief as the woman burst into flames. The wind lessened, and the ground became still. Behind her she heard a rumble and turned and watched the fissure seal. She looked back at Eliza and shielded her eyes against the bright flames, then watched as Eliza turned to a pile of gray ash.

When Tom moaned, she struggled to her feet, ran to him and leaned over him. "Tom?"

"What?" he whispered and opened his eyes. They appeared glazed and distant.

She pressed her forehead against his shoulder, then sighed. "Let's go home." She reached behind his shoulders, then helped him sit up.

He cried out in pain as his hands flew to the wound in his chest where Eliza had dug in her claws. "I'm bleeding," he said as if drunk.

"I know." She helped him down from the altar, then tried to steady him. Her eyes scanned the ground for his clothes. She spotted his jeans and sneakers on the grass near the edge of the clearing and helped him into them, then draped his shirt over his shoulders. Using her body as a crutch, she helped him toward the path.

"Kristen," a voice whispered from behind.

She turned.

Scott Benson stood beside the ashes of Eliza Noman, smiling his tinseled smile. He nodded, then slowly faded.

Tears rolled down her cheeks as she tightened her grip around Tom's waist and headed home.

It lurked beneath the tribal burial ground — an ancient evil yearning to unleash unholy terror on an unsuspecting world!

TOTEM

By Ehren M. Ehly
Author of *Obelisk*

A golden hawk fell from the sky, ushering in a storm of terror, as the sleeping dead began to stir beneath the earth. Deaf to the hawk's strangled cry of warning, the workmen continued to uncover the ancient evil that lay hidden within the Indian burial ground; they unwittingly unleashed an unholy force on an unsuspecting world. For they had angered the Ancient One, and his appetite for revenge could only be satisfied with the souls of those who had disturbed him from his eternal rest. Only one woman could stop him, one woman rich in the knowledge of the old ways, one woman prepared to make the ultimate sacrifice at the bloodied base of the totem....

__2746-1 $4.50US/$5.50 CAN

BLACK DEATH
by R. Karl Largent

THE PLAGUE
It rose from the grave of a long-forgotten cemetery—virulent, malignant, brutally infectious.

THE VICTIMS
The people of Half Moon Bay began to die, their bodies twisted in agonizing pain, their skin ruptured and torn, their blood turned to a thick, viscous ooze. Once they contracted the disease, death was near—but it could not come quickly enough to ease their exquisite suffering. There was no antidote, no cure, for the . . .

BLACK DEATH
What God created in six days, the plague could destroy in seven. And time was running out . . .

____2591-4 $3.95US/$4.95CAN